Praise for Maeve Binchy

'Oh, the bliss . . . Maeve's back, on top form . . . The heart is the theme, literally and metaphorically, and this is heartwarming stuff – sweet but never cloying' *The Times*

'The book rattles along from one gripping story to another, leaving the reader with a satisfying glow' *Daily Mail*

'Warm, witty and with a deep understanding of what makes us tick, it's little wonder that Maeve Binchy's bewitching stories have become world-beaters' *OK Magazine*

'To read it is like being wrapped up in a pink blanket with a hot-water bottle – but, make no mistake, there is magic at work' *Sunday Times*

'Binchy is degrees better than most other novelists, and her storytelling ability is second to none' *Sunday Express*

'A Maeve classic, it'll leave a warm, fuzzy feeling in your tummy' *Company*

'It's always a treat to read one of Maeve Binchy's novels, and this is no exception . . . [she] leaves us caring about [her characters] as if they are our friends' *Bella*

'One of the world's best-loved writers'
Woman's Weekly

Maeve Binchy was born in County Dublin and educated at the Holy Child Convent in Killiney and at University College Dublin. After a spell as a teacher in various girls' schools, she joined the *Irish Times*. Her first novel, *Light a Penny Candle*, was published in 1982, and since then she has written more than a dozen novels and short-story collections, each one of them bestsellers. Several have been adapted for cinema and television, most notably *Circle of Friends* and *Tara Road*. Maeve Binchy was awarded the Lifetime Achievement award at the British Book Awards in 1999 and the Irish/PEN A.T. Cross award in 2007. In 2010 she was also presented with a Lifetime Achievement award by the Romantic Novelists' Association. She is married to the writer and broadcaster Gordon Snell. Visit her website at www.maevebinchy.com.

The Return Journey

Maeve Binchy

An Orion paperback

First published in Great Britain in 2009
by Orion
This paperback edition published in 2010
by Orion Books Ltd,
Orion House, 5 Upper St Martin's Lane,
London WC2H 9EA

An Hachette UK company

1 3 5 7 9 10 8 6 4 2

ISBN: 978-1-4091-0346-2

Typeset by Deltatype Ltd, Birkenhead, Merseyside
Printed and bound in Great Britain by
Clays Ltd, St Ives plc

The Orion Publishing Group's policy is to use papers
that are natural, renewable and recyclable products and
made from wood grown in sustainable forests. The logging
and manufacturing processes are expected to conform to
the environmental regulations of the country of origin.

www.orionbooks.co.uk

To dearest Gordon with all my love and thanks

Contents

The Return
Journey

Mother Darling,
It's as beautiful as you said. Having a really wonderful time. Will write soon. Keep well and happy.

Gina

Freda,
The card I sent the other day was for the neighbours. Or rather for you and your paranoia about the neighbours. Anyway, its purpose was that it could be left around and looked at, spied on and inspected by them. The truth is that the place is a shambles, it's cold and it's raining so hard I can't see whether it's green or yellow. The truth is that I still feel hurt and unhappy and not at all like writing letters. The truth is that I must care about you a great deal, otherwise why am I letting that call from the airport get to me so badly? I

believed you when you said you'd watch for a letter or an email. I will write but just now there's nothing to say.

Try not to worry about what people think and say. Honestly, they aren't thinking and saying much about us at all. They have their own problems.

Gina

Darling Gina,
You called me Freda instead of Mom. I wondered about that for a long while. I suppose it means you're growing up, growing away. I told myself it meant you liked me more, thought of me as an equal, a friend. Then I told myself that it meant you liked me less, that you were distancing yourself.

For someone who claims there is nothing to say, you sure have a lot to say. You say I am paranoid about the neighbours. Well, let me tell you that Mrs Franks came in to say she couldn't help reading your nice postcard and wasn't it wonderful that Gina was having such a good time. So! Do they look or do they not? You say that you are upset by the call from the airport. It was you who called me, Gina. I just said write to me often. You are the one who was crying, I was the one who says what any normal mother says to a daughter travelling abroad wherever they're going. I said, I'd like it if you wrote to me, is that so emotionally draining? Does it deserve the lecture, the sermon . . . the order not to live my life by other people's dictates? But I only say all this so that you'll know I'm still me, still the same prickly jumpy thin-skinned mother I always was. I like you to call me Freda. Don't stop now because you think I've taken it and run with it, that I've read into it more than there is. And don't stop writing to me, Gina. You know I didn't want you to go to Ireland this winter. But I did say . . . I always said it was an unreasonable feeling on my part. There are so many things I want to hear about Ireland, and so many I don't.

I think I want you to tell me that it's beautiful and sad and that I did the only possible thing by leaving it. And leaving it so finally. I think that's what I want you to say in your letters. And when you come home. I love you Gina, if that's not too draining.

Freda

I'm calling you nothing in this letter in case we get another long analysis. I had an odd day today. I left the B&B which is fine, small

room, small house, nice woman, kept telling
me about her son in Boston who's an Illegal. I
thought she meant the IRA but she meant
working in a bar without a proper visa or a
green card. Anyway I was walking down the
street, small houses, hundreds of kids roaming
round when school's out, the country is like a
big school playground in many ways. And I
saw a bus. It said 'Dunglass'. It was half full. I
put out my hand. And it stopped. I asked the
driver 'Where is Dunglass?' and he told me . . .
But I said isn't Dunglass not a house, a big
house. He said no it was a town. Mom, why
didn't you tell me it was a town? What else
did you not tell me? I got off the bus. I told
him I had changed my mind. Back at the B&B
the woman was happy. She had heard from
her son the Illegal. It was cold in Boston, lots
of ice and snow – is it snowing at home? I
asked her about Dunglass. She said it was a
village. She said it was a nice kind of a place,
quiet, peaceful but not a place to go in the
middle of winter. It would scald your heart she
said. Why didn't you say it was a village that
would scald your heart? Why did you let me
think for years that it was a big old house
with Dunglass on the gate? You even told me
what it meant. Dun, a fort and Glass, meaning

green. That much is true, I checked. But what else is?

Gina

Gina my love,
I wish you'd call. It's five days since you wrote. It might well be another five days before you get this, ten days could have changed everything. You may have been there by now for all I know.

I never told you it was a house. Never. Our house didn't have a name that's all, it was a big house, it did have gates, it was the biggest house in Dunglass which wasn't saying anything great. I just didn't talk about any of it. There are things in your life we don't go over and over. Go see Dunglass, go on a day when there is light and even watery winter sunshine. Go on a day when you might be able to walk down by the lake. Go see the house. Your grandmother is dead and in the churchyard on the hill. There is no one who will know you. But tell people if you want to. Tell them your mother came from Dunglass and left it. I don't think you will tell them. You are always saying that most people are not remotely interested in the lives and doings of others.

The snow has been falling for days now and I wish you were here with me. It never snows in Ireland the way it does here. It's one of the things I had to get used to. I love you and I will tell you anything you want to know.

Your mother Freda, in case you have
forgotten my name

Freda,
Stop playing silly games. And let us stop having an argument by mail. Yes I will go to Dunglass. When I'm ready.

And don't talk to me about my grandmother. She was never allowed to be a grandmother to me. Her name was not spoken to me, I got no letters, no presents . . . there were no pictures of me in a Granny's Brag Book on this side of the Atlantic. The woman who lies in the churchyard on the hill is your mother. That's the relationship. You might as well face it. Her name was Mrs Hayes. That's all I know. You were Freda Hayes, so my Granny was Mrs Hayes. Don't lecture me, Freda, about forgetting your name, you never even told me hers.

Gina

Dear Gina,

I have begun this twelve times, this is the thirteenth attempt and I will send it no matter what. Her name was Annabel. She was tall and straight. She walked as if she owned Dunglass. And in a way she did. It was her family who had the big house. My father married in as they say. I never knew why they sent me away to boarding school, why they made me leave such a lovely home. Peggy, who looked after me, used to whisper about rows, and ornaments being broken, but I couldn't believe that my dad could be like Peggy said he was, two men, one man sober and another man drunk. Everyone admired my mother, because she ran the place. Even after my father went away she never asked for sympathy. She was cold, Gina, she made herself cold and hard as ice. She used to say to me that we didn't need their sympathy, their pity. We needed only their admiration. Perhaps some of that has rubbed off on me, perhaps I care too much about people thinking well of me, rather than being natural. She had only one daughter, as I have. We could have been more alike than I ever realised. I can't write any more. I love you. I wish you were here. Or I were there.

No, I don't wish I were there, I can never go to Dunglass. But I want you to go and to get some peace and some of your history from it.

Freda

Dear Freda,
Thanks for yours. I think I'll cool it a bit on all the emotion. Don't forget I have Italian blood as well. The mix is too heady. I could explode. The days are getting brighter, I've been to Wicklow a lot, it's so beautiful . . . and I went further south, Wexford . . . the river bank is like something from a movie . . . and Waterford. The Illegal is home from Boston, his name is Shay. He is very funny about Boston, but I think he wasn't happy there, he says his dream is to have a little cottage in Wicklow, and write songs. It's not a bad dream.
I have no dreams really.

I'm doing an extra-mural course in the University about Irish history. It was full of dreams.

I'll give you my Irish number in case you're lonely and sad. But don't call just for talking. It's very artificial. Shay says that when he and his mother used to talk, they both put the phone down feeling like hell. We don't want *that Freda. Now that we're rubbing along OK. Yes of course I love you.*

Gina

Gina,
It was so different then. You can't imagine. I remember the year I met your father. All right. All right. The year I met Gianni ... the man I married. Does that satisfy you? When I met Gianni I tried to explain all about Ireland to him. We sat in a café, it was a cold wet day. He was an Italian American. He talked to me about America. It seems like a hundred years ago. And Gianni wanted to know where I was from, so I took him home to Dunglass. And Mother laughed at him because he told her how poor his parents had been when they got the boat from Italy.

And I didn't want to sleep with him, Gina, I was twenty-three like you are now, but in those days we were so different. Not just me ... everyone, I promise you. But I hated Mother so much for scorning him. And I despised her for saying that she hadn't gone through so much just for me to throw myself away on the son of a chambermaid and a hall porter. Gianni had told with pride how his parents, your grandparents, had got these jobs.

And Mother said it in front of Peggy. Just letting Peggy know how little she thought of Peggy's role in life.

I was glad Gina, I was glad when I was pregnant even though I was frightened at the thought of living with Gianni for ever. I felt it wouldn't last, that we didn't know each other, and that when we did we might be sorry. But we were never sorry, we had you. And you will admit, that difficult as I have been, and stubborn, I have never said anything bad about your father. He thought he could live in Dunglass and marry in like my father had. But my mother hunted him, and she hunted me too because I wouldn't stay one minute to listen to her harsh words.

I left my room as it was, my books and letters and papers. I don't know what happened to them. Ever. I closed that door and never opened it.

When Gianni left me I didn't feel as sad as people thought. I knew it would happen. I had my home in America, my daughter, my job in the bookshop, my friends. I may marry again.

I won't of course, but I say to myself cheerfully like Peggy used to say, it may be a sunny day after all, little Freda. My heart is heavy when I think of Peggy. I didn't write to

her because I didn't write to the big house, it
would have been twisting a knife too harshly
into Mother.

  Her name was Peggy O'Brien, Gina, they
lived in a cottage by the lake. I tried to write
after Mother died. But there weren't any
words. You were always good with words
Gina.

Love Freda

This is a postcard of Dunglass village. I bought
it in a Dublin shop. Has it changed much,
Mother? I'm going there tomorrow. I'll write
and tell you everything. I miss you.

Gina

The time gap is too long. I called you at the
B&B but Shay's mother told me you were still
away. You didn't say you were taking Shay
with you. It's nearly a quarter of a century
since I took Gianni there. Are we going to
repeat history all over again? Dunglass hasn't
changed very much. I had forgotten it was so
small.

  I wait to hear anything you may write.

Freda

13

Dearest Freda,

Your letter was cold, there were no dears or darlings or loves anywhere. Are you afraid that like my mother and my grandmother, I will marry hastily the wrong man who will leave me as happened to you and to Annabel? I went to her grave and I laid a big bunch of spring flowers on it. The countryside is glorious. There were little ducklings on the lake, and moorhens and two big swans. You never told me any of that. You never told me that you had a pony and that you fell off and broke your arm. You never told me about Peggy's big soft bosom where I cried like you cried. She bought a lot of your things at the auction. She said she didn't want strangers picking up your books and your treasures. She called them treasures, Freda, and she has them in a room. Waiting for you to come home and collect them.

She was left nothing in the will. It all went to charity. She bought them from her wages because she knew one day you'd come back.

I told her it would probably be in June. When the sun shines long hours over the lake and the roses are all out on her cottage. Not far from the one that Shay and I are looking at with our hearts full of hope.

*Send me an open postcard to Shay's house
so that his mother will know how much you
and I love each other. See I am like you after
all. I want them to think well of us. In many
ways I'm glad you kept it from me, it came as
such a rainbow of happiness. But don't keep it
from yourself any more. There are no ghosts in
Dunglass. Only hedges and flowers and your
great friends Peggy, Shay and*

Gina

The Wrong Suitcase

Annie checked in early. She had come out to the airport in plenty of time. None of this was going to be a hassle. Once she had taken her boarding card and seen the smart new case trundle off with its little tag telling it to go to London Heathrow, she sighed with relief; it was all happening now, nothing could stop it. She was going to have the luxury of really looking at the things in the duty-free shop for once, and maybe trying out a few of the perfumes on her wrist. She might even look at cameras and watches – not buy, but look.

Alan was late; he was always late checking in. But he had such a nice smile and looked so genuinely apologetic, nobody seemed to mind. They told him to go straight to the departure gate, and he did – well, more or less. They couldn't expect him to go through that duty-free without buying a bottle of vodka, could they? He showed no sign of fuss or confusion; he slipped onto the plane last, but somebody had to come in last. He settled himself easily into his seat in executive class. With the ease of the frequent traveller, he had stowed his briefcase and vodka neatly above, fastened his safety belt in a way that the air hostess could see it was fastened, and he had opened his copy of *Time*. Another business trip begun.

Annie smiled with relief when she saw her case on the carousel at Heathrow Airport; she always half expected it to be left behind, like she expected the Special Branch men to call her in and ask her business in England and the Customs men to rip the case apart looking for concealed heroin. She was of a fearful nature, but she knew that and said it wasn't a bad way to be because it led to so many nice surprises when these things didn't happen. She took her case and went unscathed through Customs. She followed the signs for the Underground and got onto a train that she thought must be like a lift in the United Nations building: there were people of every nationality under the sun, and all of their suitcases had different little tags. She closed her eyes happily as the train rushed into London.

Alan reached out easily and took his case as it was about to pass by. He helped a family who couldn't cope with all their cases arriving at once. One by one he swung them off the conveyor belt, and when he took one that wasn't theirs he just swung it easily back again with no fuss. The woman gave him a very grateful smile. Alan had a way of looking better than other people's husbands. He bought an *Evening Standard* in the paper shop and settled himself into a taxi. He had already asked the taxi driver if he could have a receipt at the end of the journey; some of them could be grumpy, always better to say what you want at the start and say it pleasantly. Alan's motto. Alan's secret of success. It was sunset; he looked out briefly at the motorways and the houses with their neat gardens away in the distance. It was nice to be back in London where you didn't know everyone and everyone didn't know you.

The train took Annie to Gloucester Road, and she walked with a quick and happy step to the hotel, where she had stayed many times. The new suitcase was light to carry; it had been expensive, but what the hell – it would last for ever. It was so nice, she had bought two of those little suitcase initials and stuck them on: A.G. At first she wondered if this was a dead giveaway, wouldn't people know that they weren't married if they had different initials? But he had laughed at her and patted her nose, telling her that she was a funny little thing and had a fearful nature. And Annie Grant had agreed and remembered that most people didn't give a damn about that sort of thing nowadays. Most people.

The taxi took Alan to Knightsbridge and the hotel, where they remembered him or pretended to. He always said his name first, just in case. 'Of course, Mr Green,' the porter said with a smile. 'Good to have you with us again.' Alan folded the receipt from the taxi driver into his wallet and followed the porter to the desk; his room reservation was in order. He made an elegant and flattering remark to the receptionist, which left her patting her hair with pleasure and wondering why the nice ones like Mr Green didn't ask you out and the yucky ones slobbered all over you. Alan went up to his room and took a bottle of tonic from the minibar. He noticed it wasn't slimline, so he put it back and took soda. Alan was careful about everything.

Annie opened her case in the small hotel bedroom where she would spend one night. She would hang up her dresses to make sure the creases fell out. She would have a bath and use all those nice lotions and bath oils so that they didn't look brand new tomorrow. The key turned and she lifted the lid. There were no dresses and no shoes. Neither the two new nighties nor the very smart toilet bag with its unfamiliar Guerlain products were in the case. There were files and boxes and men's shirts and men's underpants and socks, and more files. Her heart gave several sharp sideways jumps, each one hurting her breastbone. It had happened as she always knew it would happen one day. She had got the wrong case. She looked in terror and there were her initials; somebody else called A.G. had taken her case. 'Oh my God,' wept Annie Grant, 'oh God, why did you let this happen to me? Why? I'm not *that* bad, God. I'm not hurting anyone else.' Her tears fell into the suitcase.

Alan opened his case automatically. He would set his papers out on the large table and hang up his suits. Marie always packed perfectly; he had shown her how at an early stage. Poor Marie had once thought you just bundled things in any old how, but, he had explained reasonably, what was the point of her ironing all those shirts so beautifully if they weren't to come out looking as immaculate as they went in? He looked at the top layer of the case in disbelief. Dresses, underwear – female underwear neatly folded. Shoes in plastic bags, a flashy-looking sponge bag with some goo from a chemist in it. God almighty, he had taken the wrong case. But he couldn't have. It had his initials: A.G. He had been thinking that he must get better ones, these were a bit ordinary. God damn and blast it, why hadn't he got them at the time? For a wild moment he wondered if this was some kind of joke of Marie's; she had been very brooding recently and wanting to come on business trips with him. Could she have packed a case for herself? But that was nonsense; these weren't Marie's things, these belonged to a stranger. Shit, Alan Green said aloud to himself over and over again. What timing. What perfectly bloody timing to lose his case on this of all trips.

It took Annie a tearful seventy minutes on the telephone and many efforts on the part of the airline and of the hotel to prevent her from going out to the airport before she realised that she would have to wait until the next morning. Soothing people in the hotel and at the airline said that it would certainly be returned the following day. She had only discovered an office address for Mr Bloody Green, typed neatly and taped inside the lid of the case. An office long closed by now.

Tomorrow, the voices said, as if that was any help. Tomorrow he would have arrived expecting her to be in fine form and to have her things with her. They were going to go for a week's motoring holiday, the first time she was going to have him totally to herself. He was flying in from New York and would hire a car at Heathrow; he had told his boss the negotiations would take longer, he had told his wife . . . Who knew or cared what he had told his wife? But he would not be best pleased to spend the first day of their holiday in endless negotiations at the airport looking for her things. Was there no way she could find out where this idiot lived? If she phoned his home even, maybe his wife could tell her where he was staying. That was if his wife knew. If wives ever knew.

It took Alan five minutes to find the right person, the person who told them that there was no right person at this time of night, but to explain the machinery of the morrow. Yes, fine for those who hadn't arranged a breakfast meeting at seven-thirty a.m., before the shops were open, before he could get a clean shirt. And what was the point of a breakfast meeting without his papers? God rot this stupid woman with her cellophane bags and her tissue paper and her never-worn clothes. Her photograph album, for heaven's sake, and pages and pages of notes, a play of some sort. Hard-to-decipher writing, page after bloody page of it. But there was one page where it revealed the address of Miss Prissy A. Grant, whoever she was, and he was sure she *was* a Miss, not a Mrs. A letter addressed to her had 'Ms' on it, but Alan had always noted that this was what single, not married, women called themselves. Unfortunately it had no address, or he could have sent for an Irish telephone directory and found her mother and father and got the hotel that their daughter was staying at. That's if she had told them. Nutty kinds of girls who carry photograph albums, unworn clothes, and plays written in small cramped writing probably told their families nothing.

The man who ran the small hotel near Gloucester Road was upset for nice Miss Grant, who often came to spend a night before she went on her long trips to the Continent; she was a teacher, a very polite person always. He took her a pot of tea and some tomato sandwiches in her room. She cried and thanked him as if he had pulled her onto a life raft.

'Look through his things. You might discover where he is staying,' he advised. Annie was doubtful. Still, as she ate the tomato sandwiches and drained the pot of tea she spread all the papers out on the small bed and read. She read of the plans that Mr A. Green had been building up over the last two years. Plans which meant that by tomorrow he should be able to take over an agency for himself. If things went the way he hoped.

Mr A. Green would return to Dublin at the head of his own company. The arguments were so persuasive that the overseas client would be very foolish not to accept A. Green's offer. There were photocopies of letters marked 'For your eyes only' . . . There were files with heavy underlining in thick felt pen, 'Do not take to office'. A great deal of the correspondence was organised so that it showed A. Green's present employers, the people who were paying for this trip to London, in a very poor light. Annie sighed; she supposed that this was the world of business. At school you didn't go plotting against the geography mistress or getting the headmaster to lose confidence in the art teacher. But it seemed a bit sneaky.

Sometimes there were copies of letters his boss *was* shown pinned to those he had *not* been shown. It was masterly filing, and if you read the whole anthology, which up to now had presumably been for A. Green's eyes only, it made a convincing case. Annie decided that A. Green was a bastard and he deserved to have lost his case and his deal. She hoped he would never find either. But then how would she get back what was hers? And God almighty, suppose he had read her diary.

Alan Green decided to hell with it, he couldn't bear the flat taste of the soda. He opened a calorie-packed tonic water from his minibar and decided that he would do this thing methodically. Look on it as a business problem. Right. He had left his name with the airline, if she called. Of course she would call. Stupid girl, why had she not called already? Stupid A. Grant. She was probably in a wine bar with an equally stupid teacher talking about plays and how to write them in longhand at great length and maximum stupidity. What kind of play was it, anyway? He began to read it. He read of her romance . . . It wasn't a play, it was the real thing. This was a diary. It was more than a diary, it was a plan of campaign. It was dozens of different scenarios that could take place on this holiday.

There was the scene where he said he couldn't see her any more, that his wife had given him an ultimatum. This creepy A. Grant had written out her lines for that one, several times over. Sometimes they were casual and see-if-I-care. Sometimes they were filled with passion, or threats: she would kill herself, let him wait. She had written the whole thing out as if it were a play, even with stage directions.

Alan decided that A. Grant was a raving lunatic and that whoever the poor guy she was going to meet was, he deserved to be warned about her.

He felt glad that she had lost this insane checklist of emotional dramas and how to play them; he was glad that all her finery had gone astray and that she would have to meet the guy as she was. He realised that she had probably done some kind of repair job and washed her tights and whatever just as he had washed the collar and cuffs of his shirt and the soles of his socks. Then he remembered with a lurch that she might have read his dossier on the company.

Annie suddenly remembered she hadn't told the man in the airport where she was staying. She had been too upset. Suppose Mr Conniving Green had rung in with his whereabouts; they wouldn't have been able to contact her. She telephoned them again. Had Mr Green called? He had. This was his number. He answered on the second ring. He would come right around with her case. No, please, gentleman's privilege. Very simple mistake, must be a million A.G.s in the world. He'd come right away.

*

29

He held the taxi. She was quite pretty, he saw to his surprise, soft and fluffy. He sort of remembered seeing her at Heathrow Airport and thinking that if she was in the taxi queue he might suggest they share. Remembering the revelations of her diary, he shuddered with relief at his escape. She was surprised to see that he looked so pleasant; she had expected him to look like a fox: sharp-featured, mean pointed little face. He looked normal and nice. She thought she remembered him on the plane up in executive class laughing with the air hostess.

'I have your case here,' she said. 'It's a bit disarrayed, for want of a better word. I was hunting in it to see if I could find out where you were staying.'

'Yours is a little disarrayed too.' He grinned. 'But none of those nice garments you have fitted me, so they're all safe and sound.'

They grinned at each other almost affectionately.

He looked at her for a moment. It was only eleven o'clock at night; in London that meant the evening was only starting. She was quite lovely in a round soft sort of way . . .

She wished he didn't have to go. Maybe if she said something about why not go and let's have a bottle of wine to celebrate the found suitcases . . .

She remembered how he had described his boss as bordering on senility and how he had given chapter and verse to prove that the boss was a heavy drinker.

He remembered how she had proposed threatened suicide with attendant letters to some guy's wife, his children and his colleagues.

They shook hands, and at exactly the same moment they said to each other that they hadn't read each other's papers or anything, and at that moment they both knew that they had.

Miss Vogel's
Vacation

Miss Vogel was surprised that she had never married. Not so much upset as surprised. When she was young everyone thought Victoria Vogel would surely be one of the first in the neighbourhood to walk down an aisle.

Fair-haired, soft and pretty, a great homemaker, she even made dresses for herself and her sisters and their friends, as well as baking delicious desserts for any event where good cooking was needed.

The young Miss Vogel had an agreeable manner with everyone; no future mother-in-law would stand in her way, no family would object to the girl who worked pleasantly in her father's bakery. She was much in demand to dance at the weddings of her many friends, and although she caught the bride's bouquet on many occasions, it never led to a wedding of her own.

Miss Vogel didn't look back on her girlhood in

New York as a lonely time; she hadn't yearned always for a beau of her own. She always thought there was one around the next corner. She lived happily over the bakery and didn't really notice the years go by.

There were so many other things to think about. Like her mother's illness. The others were all married by the time Miss Vogel's mother took to her bed, so she did the nursing, which made sense because she lived at home.

And when her mother died and her father became gloomy and lost interest in his work, she had to work all that much harder in the bakery to keep it going. There was a manager, of course, Tony Bari. They spent long hours together trying to see how the bills could be paid, the overheads reduced, and the whole enterprise made sound.

Everyone thought one day they might marry.

Miss Vogel didn't really think they would, even though she would have been happy had their quick embraces led to a proposal.

But she was a practical woman and realised that Tony Bari was very interested in money and had told her several times that any sensible man in business was looking for a rich wife. Miss Vogel knew she wasn't in this category, and even though she did like his company, his big broad smile and the way his moustache tickled her cheek, she didn't weep when he told her he had finally met a lady of property and invited her to his wedding.

Not long after, Miss Vogel's father went to the hospital, and it was known that he would not come out. Tony Bari bought the business. His new wife did not think it appropriate that Miss Vogel continue to work and live there, so, at the age of thirty, she was unemployed.

People said Tony Bari had not paid enough, and indeed, after it had been divided between her sisters and brothers there was very little left.

Miss Vogel had nowhere to live, she had no real qualifications to get a good job anywhere, but with her customary good humour she decided to wait until something turned up. Then she saw a position as a type of janitor or superintendent in a small, new apartment building. A lot of the residents were female, and they had specifically sought a woman super. Miss Vogel, with her calm, pleasant manner, seemed ideal, and she now had a two-room apartment, with an address in a fine part of town.

Her friends were pleased for her.

'You'll meet very classy folk now,' they said.

Miss Vogel didn't mind whether they were classy or not, just as long as they were nice. And mainly they were.

She became involved in all their lives. She walked the little yapping dog, unsuitably called Beauty, for Janet, the discontented widow in Number One.

She babysat for the teenage daughter of Heather, who was a workaholic advertising supremo in Number Two. She took in the flowers and arranged them for Number Three, where Francesca, the attractive mistress of two business-men, lived. Tactfully, Miss Vogel made sure these two gentlemen never coincided on a visit.

She spent a lot of time in Number Four, where Marion sat and looked out the window, sad because her husband came home so rarely.

There were many others in the building whose lives were familiar to Miss Vogel. Her sisters sometimes said these must be rich, spoiled people who lacked nothing in their lives, but Miss Vogel didn't agree. As she sat in beautifully decorated apartments and drank coffee from a fine china cup or soda from cut-crystal glassware, Miss Vogel knew that unease and unhappiness didn't fly out the window just because you had money. A lot of the people had even more worries than the Vogel family ever had. Sometimes she went past the old bakery where Tony Bari had built a big business with his wife's money. It was now a delicacies shop, and people faxed in their orders for sandwiches, which were delivered to their offices. Imagine!

There were three children. Miss Vogel watched them grow up. She would have liked to have met them properly and known them, to have been invited into the store where she, too, had lived as a child.

But Tony Bari's wife never seemed to want her around.

Miss Vogel thought this was sad. She had always been welcoming and kind to the woman who had come to live there only because of her father's dollars. But then, you couldn't make people like you if they didn't.

Her days and nights were never empty or lonely, because of all the people in the apartments. Miss Vogel did not have what anyone would call a great life of her own, but she went through all theirs, their hopes and dreams for Thanksgiving and Christmas, who would come home, where they would be invited, what they would cook. Their diets for the new year, how many days a week working out at the gym, low-fat foods to be stocked in the freezer. Then she went through their new wardrobes for spring. None seemed to notice Miss Vogel didn't buy spring clothes, plan to lose ten pounds every

January, or discuss where she went for Thanksgiving or Christmas.

She was a listening person, not a talking person.

She was interested in their lives.

Now it was time to talk about vacations.

Janet was going to Arizona with her sister, so naturally there was the matter of Beauty, the bad-tempered little dog. Beauty didn't like kennels, so perhaps Miss Vogel . . .

Heather could take only a week and not one day more away from work, so she would fly to Los Angeles. This way, she could fit in one or two meetings on the West Coast as well as take fourteen-year-old Heidi to Disneyland and Universal Studios, so it would be a fantastic holiday for the child. But there was simply no time to get her any vacation clothes. Could Miss Vogel manage . . . one Saturday morning possibly? Just a quick trip to the department store?

Francesca was going to spend one week with one man and the other with the second man, but she had told each she was going to a health spa for the week she would not be with him. Would Miss Vogel mind very much taking the bus to this town two miles away, where the spa actually was, and mailing two postcards for her? You see, men were so possessive and so suspicious these days, and one didn't want to do anything silly.

Marion in Number Four was uncharacteristically cheerful because she and her husband were going to a quiet inn – he said he would like time to talk properly. That had to be good, Marion said, vacations were a time when people found new relationships if they had none or cemented an existing one that needed to be patched up.

That was the wonderful thing about vacations, wasn't it, Marion had said over and over.

Miss Vogel didn't know. She had never had a vacation. There had never been the opportunity, the money, or the time. And now, at fifty-three, there seemed little point in hoping she would find a new relationship, and there wasn't an old one to cement.

Tony Bari and his wife and children were going to Italy. Her sisters, brothers, and their families were going to a lake where they rented chalets every year. Nice for the cousins to get to know each other and keep in touch, they said.

None of them ever thought it might be nice for Miss Vogel to get to know them all and keep in touch, too. But then, she would be out of place. An elderly aunt on her own.

All the holidays seemed to come together. Miss Vogel would have a very empty building to look after. But she enthused about their trips, as she had enthused for so many years about everything they did.

She did all she was asked to do. She studied the feeding schedules of the small, aggressive Beauty to reassure Janet. She took Heidi on an outing to Bloomingdale's and with Heather's dollars bought her bright-coloured clothes to wear in the California sun. She planned the two bus trips so she could send the deceiving postcards for Francesca. She helped Marion pack romantic negligees for her week in the country inn.

And, of course, she would do all the other things that made them think Miss Vogel was an angel. She would turn out their lights, pull their drapes at different times each evening, sort their mail, so, when they came back, it would be in a neat pile on their hall table. She would see their garments were returned from the dry cleaner and hung in their closets; she would admit a television repairman here and an interior decorator there and listen to their holiday tales and look at their holiday photos with great interest on their return.

Often there was fuss and near hysteria at the actual time of departure; limousines had not been ordered in advance, for example, or taxis could not be hailed on the New York streets.

This year, Miss Vogel decided to cut through

all the drama and found a neighbourhood car service. She spoke to Frank, a man with a tired, kind face, who was at the desk, telling him she had four trips over two days, to La Guardia Airport for Heather and Heidi, to Grand Central for Janet, to Penn Station for Marion and her husband, and some secret pick-up place in New Jersey for Francesca.

'What commission are you looking for?' Frank asked wearily.

'Oh no,' Miss Vogel said. 'I was only trying to arrange something for the people in my building. They'll all pay you the rate. I don't want anything . . . I don't want anything for myself.'

'You must be the only person in the world who doesn't, then,' said Frank.

'It's just their vacations. They get very fussed, you know the way people do?'

'I don't know the way people do,' Frank said. 'I've never had a vacation.'

Miss Vogel gave him a big smile. 'Do you know neither have I? We must be the only people in the world who haven't.'

A bond was established between them, and they worked out the times he would be there to pick up the holidaymakers.

He was courteous and punctual, but more than that he was kind. He waited while Janet kissed

Beauty goodbye; he told Heidi she'd love Disneyland – everyone came back from it a new person;
he explained to Francesca that he was a genius at
finding out-of-the-way spots in New Jersey; he
told Marion and her husband that an inn in the
countryside was the very best vacation anyone
could choose.

Miss Vogel was sorry when the last had gone.
She enjoyed Frank's company. She would miss
regular visits when she always found time to
make him a coffee and give him some of her own
home-baked shortbread.

To her surprise, he turned up again.

'I was wondering, Miss Vogel, if you and I
should have a vacation in New York,' he began
tentatively. 'We could pretend we were tourists
here and see it through their eyes.' He looked at
her, hoping that she would not laugh at this or
dismiss it as a ridiculous idea.

'A vacation in New York City?' she said
thoughtfully.

'Well, a lot of people do, you know.' Frank was
defensive. 'I drive them to places. I should know.'

'That will be great,' said Miss Vogel. 'But first I
have to do a bit of fussing. That's essential.'

'Yes, I'll come around tomorrow morning.
Does that give you time enough to fuss?' he
asked.

44

Miss Vogel worked out that she could take a five-hour vacation each day. Then she ironed her clothes carefully and laid out a different outfit for each outing. She went to a beauty parlour on the corner and got her hair and her nails done.

She prepared several picnic lunches they could have and left them ready in the freezer. She got new heels on her comfortable shoes. She checked the weather forecast. She was ready for her vacation.

They went to Ellis Island and spent the day looking at where their grandparents had come into the United States from Italy and Germany, Ireland and Sweden.

'I bet they were four young people who never had time for a vacation once they got here,' Miss Vogel said.

'But they must have been adventurous young people,' Frank replied, 'not the kind of folk who would like to believe their descendants would be stay-at-homes.'

The next day they went to the Empire State Building to see the view and then back uptown to the zoo. Afterwards, they walked in Central Park in the sunshine.

They drove together companionably to the town where they had to mail Francesca's postcards and talked about how odd life was with so many people living a lie – Francesca herself and the two married men who were each taking her off for a week. They went to Chinatown and on a tour of the stock exchange on Wall Street.

They went back to where Miss Vogel grew up and looked at the big delicacies shop, so much changed in appearance since her youth. They went to see where Frank was raised, changed so very much from when he was a boy. He pointed out where he had lived with his wife for three years a long time ago, and also the hospital where she had died.

Neither had ever been to Carnegie Hall, so they booked a concert.

And as she had seen a ball game only on television, never in reality, they went to Yankee Stadium.

And the week flew by.

Frank helped Miss Vogel to sort the mail, arrange the curtains, and arrange deliveries for the tenants. Miss Vogel went to the car-service office and brightened it up by washing the curtains and putting some colourful ornaments around.

The next week, they could no longer afford five hours a day for vacation. Like everyone else in New York, they would now know that feeling which said the holiday was over.

But for Frank and Miss Vogel, there was something new and wonderful. No longer did they keep their thoughts to themselves, there was someone with whom to talk over the events of the day. Not only holiday memories, but what was happening in the real world as well.

So when Frank drove Heather and Heidi back from the airport, he could report that mother and daughter were hardly speaking and that the girl had been left alone in her hotel room looking at television, since Heather was tied up in meetings all day.

Miss Vogel could tell him that something very odd had happened in Francesca's life – perhaps both men had proposed marriage to her, both would leave their wives, but she wanted neither. Francesca was lying down with a cold compress on her eyes, trying to get the courage to tell them.

Janet told Frank in the car her holiday with her sister had been a huge mistake – there would be no more family get-togethers. What did people want family for, anyway? A good dog was worth twenty sisters.

Marion told Miss Vogel that her rat of a husband had taken her to the inn only to tell her he was leaving her. And amazingly, Marion didn't really mind all that much. Once it was out in the open, she enjoyed the walking and peace of the countryside, and her husband had been startled and annoyed at how well she adapted to the new situation.

But nobody asked Miss Vogel if she had enjoyed her time when they were away. And if they saw Frank around the place a lot, it was because, they assumed, he was driving people. Sometimes Miss Vogel wasn't quite as available to babysit, walk dogs, listen to problems, arrange flowers. Nothing you could put your finger on. And if she looked happier and walked with a spring in her step and smiled with brighter eyes . . . they thought she might have lost a few pounds or something.

Tony Bari's wife noticed, however. She had returned from a tedious vacation in Italy with a lot of possessive in-laws and was glad to be back in New York. Her eyes narrowed when Miss Vogel came into the shop. She always suspected Tony Bari harboured feelings for the daughter of the house, and if she had had any money, he would very probably have asked Miss Vogel to marry him.

'Did you have a good vacation, Miss Vogel?' she asked politely, her sharp glance taking in Miss Vogel's improved posture, hairstyle, and general manner.

'Very pleasant, Mrs Bari. I stayed in New York, got to know my own city. It was delightful.'

Tony Bari's wife, who would love to have done the same, was envious.

'Well, at our age, Miss Vogel, we don't expect very much from vacations, do we?' She was trying to remove the pleased smile from Miss Vogel's face. But she was not succeeding.

Miss Vogel paused in her choosing of expensive mushrooms, speciality cheese, and exotic olive oils and smiled confidently at the woman who had taken away her only hope of marriage and a home, merely because that woman's father had money.

'Oh, Mrs Bari, how sad, how very sad to hear you say that,' she said, as deeply sympathetic as if she were offering condolences at a funeral.

Tony Bari was at the other side of the shop. He was fat now and balding, his face set in lines of disappointment and greed. Life had not turned out as he might have wished. How could she ever have thought he would have made her a good husband? Had it all worked out at the time, then she would have just returned from a weary journey to Italy with this bad-tempered man. She would have known no other world but this one; she would never have gone in and out of the lives of the existing people who lived in her building.

She might have looked wistfully at the kind face of Frank, a limousine driver, if she had ever met him, and wondered what it would be like to live in easy companionship with someone who saw beauty everywhere and gain and opportunity nowhere. Tonight, for his birthday, she would cook him a great feast. They had plans for the future, plans young people were making all over the world, but were no less loving and hopeful just because Miss Vogel and Frank were no longer young.

'Oh, Mrs Bari,' she repeated, her voice full of genuine sorrow. She had been about to ask, 'What *is* the point of living at all if we don't expect something from every vacation and every day?' but it sounded a bit preachy, and Miss Vogel had learned firsthand from her apartment complex that happiness does not always go hand in hand with having a lot of possessions, so instead she said that to have unrealistic dreams should not be part of the ageing process.

And head high, her shopping basket full of exotic ingredients, Miss Vogel left the delicacies shop that had once been her father's bakery and, without a backward glance, walked into the sun-filled streets of New York.

By the Time We Get to Clifden

They went on a week's holiday every year.

Not abroad since Harry didn't like foreign food and Nessa was afraid to fly.

But there were plenty of places in Ireland if you looked around you. One year they had been to Lisdoonvarna and another to Youghal. They had found nice bed and breakfast places and always kept the card in case they went back again. But they never did.

In twenty-four years of summer vacations they never once went back to anywhere, no matter how wonderful they said it was at the time.

This year the research had come up with Clifden. They would drive there from Dublin on a Tuesday, starting early, leaving plenty of time. They would pack sandwiches and a flask of coffee because you never knew. They began to pack their suitcases on the Friday before they left. Better to pack early, Nessa said, because you never knew what you might forget. Harry liked to pack from a list. Wiser to write it out and tick each item off as it went into the case, he said, otherwise you could easily think that things were packed when they weren't.

Nessa brought their five pieces of silver to the bank, each one wrapped in a piece of cotton and then all zipped into a little yellow bag. For the rest of the year they lived in the bottom of a cupboard. No point at all in tempting burglars by displaying them on shelves or anything.

Harry went round all the window locks and tested the alarm system several times. Better be sure than sorry, he always said. They wished they had a reliable neighbour who might water their little garden but sadly it was only a wild unkempt girl with red hair and a boyfriend who stayed over nights. No point in asking *her* to do anything for you.

They nodded at her courteously, always better to make friends of these kind of people rather than enemies. She used to shout, 'Howaya, Nessa? Harry?' which was very forward of her since she must have been less than half their age.

The evening before they set out for Clifden they had everything ready for the off. Sandwiches in the fridge, two eggs to boil and just enough bread to toast for breakfast. The house would be left neat and tidy to welcome them back a week later. Then Harry would have five full days to recover before he went back to work. It was a long, *long* journey, they knew that. They would both be very tired.

There was a ring at the door. They looked at each other in alarm. Eight o'clock at night! Nobody would call at that hour.

'Who is it?' Harry asked fearfully.

'Melly,' the voice said. 'Can I come in, please, Harry?'

They didn't know anyone called Melly.

'From next door,' the voice said. 'It's urgent!'

They let her in. Her red hair was spiky, she wore a horrid purple top that exposed her middle bits and jeans with patches on them. Her face was very pale.

'I just don't want to be alone right now. Could I stay for an hour, please? I won't be any trouble. Please, Nessa? Harry?'

She looked from one to the other.

'Are you unwell?' Nessa asked. 'Should you go to a doctor? The hospital?'

'No, I'm frightened. Mike, my fellow, he's been smoking bad stuff, God knows what he might do to me. I don't want him to find me at home.'

'Won't he come looking for you here?' Harry

was very alarmed at inviting such trouble under his roof.

'No, he'd never think I'd come here,' she said.

'Well . . .'

They were doubtful.

'Oh, go on, Harry, Nessa, you can keep your eye on me. I'm not going to go off with your silver or anything. Just an hour or two or whatever.'

'I don't know,' Harry said.

'Harry, you're a decent man. How would you feel if I were beaten to death and you could have saved me?'

They found themselves nodding.

'But we can't stay up late because we're going to the West tomorrow, and by the time we get to Clifden we could be very tired.'

'I'll just get my bag,' Melly said and hopped back home, returning with a giant lime-green sack. 'I've everything here,' she said, as an explanation.

'But . . . um . . . Melly, we told you we're going to Clifden tomorrow!'

'I'll come with you!' Melly said, overjoyed. 'He'll *never* think of looking for me in Clifden, it's perfect.' She smiled from one to the other.

She slept on the sofa with her things strewn over the floor. During the night they heard him shouting and looking for her.

'Do you think we should *do* anything?' Harry whispered to Nessa in bed.

'We *are* doing something – we're driving her to the other side of the country,' Nessa said, trying to put the man's raised voice out of her mind.

Next morning Melly took all the hot water for her shower and used the nice new towels they had prepared ready for their return. She made them breakfast, however, saying that since there were only two eggs she had made an omelette and divided it into three.

Harry and Nessa looked at each other, aghast. Their whole plans had been thrown totally out of order by this ridiculous girl whom they hardly knew. By now they should have been in their car and beyond Lucan. Instead they were still at home, plotting how to get Melly into the car.

'He could be looking out the window so we'd better take no risks,' Melly warned. 'You could lay a rug over me and I could crawl very slowly into the back seat.'

Then there was her lime-green sack, he would certainly recognise that. So Harry had to hide it in a black plastic bag.

'By the time we get to Clifden we'll be ready to go to a mental hospital,' Nessa said into Harry's ear.

'If we ever get there,' Harry whispered back. 'She's talking of doing things en route.'

That was something Harry and Nessa never did, visit anything en route. They just got their heads down and drove there, wherever there was. It didn't look as if it was going to be like that this time.

When they finally got away and Melly emerged from the rug, it was nearly time to put on their audio cassette and listen to an improving book. By the time they got to Clifden this year they would have heard the three-and-a-half-hour version of Thackeray's *Vanity Fair*. But they had reckoned without Melly. She didn't like it at all. She did, on the other hand, like the scenery and the places they passed. She chattered non-stop about the housing estates, the road signs, the huge walled demesnes, the factories and the traffic, so that Harry and Nessa lost completely the story of Becky Sharp and were forced to turn it off.

'That's better,' Melly said. 'Now we can chat properly.'

She phoned ahead on her mobile to friends in Mullingar and said she wanted them to prepare lunch, that she was bringing two pals called Harry and Nessa.

They protested vigorously. By the time they got

to Clifden it would be very late. And they did have sandwiches.

But Melly would have none of it. And in Mullingar the two hippies who lived in a squat had made a magnificent lentil and tomato dish with lots of crusty bread. The hippies were perfectly at ease with Harry and Nessa and asked them to deliver some honey to Shay in Athlone because he had a bad throat.

'But we might not stop in Athlone,' poor Harry began.

'Normally you wouldn't,' they agreed with him. 'But because of Shay's sore throat you will this time, won't you?'

Shay was very welcoming, and he made tea and toasted scones for them. He said that Harry and Nessa were Everyday Angels, that was the only phrase for it, rescuing Melly from that monster.

'If she hadn't met two Everyday Angels like you he'd have trashed her, you know. He'll probably have trashed her house and yours as well when you get back,' Shay said cheerfully.

Nessa and Harry looked at each other. Their glance asked the question. Should they go home? Now, this minute? There was no time. Melly was on the mobile phone to Athenry. And then they were waving goodbye to Shay and back in the car heading west.

They were expected in this pub in Athenry, you see, there would be chicken in a basket for them when they got there and a great gig.

'By the time we get to Clifden they'll have given away our room,' said Harry in a voice that sounded like a great wail.

'Nonsense, Harry, we can give them a ring,' Melly said.

Nessa took out her little sheet called 'Emergency Numbers and Contacts for the Journey' and found the number of the B&B.

'Could you ring them, Melly?' Nessa asked. 'You seem to know our plans better.'

Melly saw nothing wrong with that.

'Hiya, you've got a couple called Nessa and Harry coming to stay with you . . . Yeah, Mr and Mrs Kelly, that's it, it's just that we keep getting held up on the way, you know the way it is.'

The voice seemed to know the way it was and sounded sympathetic.

'Oh, no idea at all when, could you leave out a key and a note, you see we're not even in Galway, only on the way to Athenry as it happens . . . Thank you, yes, thank you for being so understanding, see you when we see you then. Oh, and could I sleep in a chair or something for one night just till I get myself settled?'

That seemed to be agreed too.

'Who am I? I'm Melly, I'm their great friend and neighbour, and they sort of rescued me. No, not fussy people at all, dead easygoing, you must be thinking of other people. No, real cool. We're going to a gig in Athenry, maybe have a drink in Galway just to be sociable, and then we're going to get out of the car in Maam Cross and look at the goats and the sheep and smell the Atlantic, we wouldn't be with you before one or two in the morning anyway, but haven't they the week to get over it?'

She leaned in between them from the back seat of the car.

'There, now that's sorted,' she said proudly.

Nessa and Harry smiled at each other, absurdly flattered to have been called dead easygoing and real cool.

Melly genuinely didn't think they were fussy people.

And by the time they got to Clifden perhaps they wouldn't be fussy people any more.

The Home Sitter

It would be a new start. Not everyone got such a chance, Maura told herself. Three months in a warm climate, and the people were supposed to be very friendly over there. Already she had got letters from faculty wives welcoming her. James would be visiting lecturer in this small university in the Midwest of America. Both fares were paid and they would have a house on campus.

The only problem was their house. James and Maura lived in a part of Dublin where people suspected burglars of lurking in the well-kept shrubbery, waiting till the owners had left each day. If they were gone for three months, the place would be ransacked.

But it was quite impossible to let the place. First there was the fear that you might never get the people out. You heard such terrible stories. Then it would mean locking everything away – no, it would be intolerable. How could they enjoy three months in a faraway place terrified that everything they had was being smashed and they might have to go to the High Court to evict the tenants.

There were no possibilities, either, in their families. Ruefully they agreed that James's mother would be an unlikely starter. She was forgetful to the point where nobody could leave her in charge. The burglar alarm would be ringing night and day, making the neighbours crazy. She did love their dog Jessie, but she would forget to feed her, or else give her all the wrong things. She would allow Jessie out and there would be litters of highly unsatisfactory puppies on the way when they got back.

They couldn't ask Maura's sister Geraldine, either, because she hated dogs. She would leap in terror when Jessie gave a perfectly normal greeting. And Maura feared that Geraldine would poke around, look in drawers and things. There would be so much hiding involved, and having to send Jessie to a kennel, that it literally wouldn't be worth it.

Their neighbours weren't the kind of people you could give a key to. These were big houses with sizeable gardens. Not estates, or back-to-back terraces like Coronation Street, where everyone knew everyone's business. On one side there were the Greens, elderly, mad about gardening, hardly ever out of their greenhouse. Very pleasant to greet, of course. But that was all. And then, on the other side, there was that high-flying couple, the Hurleys, who were always being written about in the papers. They had started their own company. They had three children of their own and had adopted others. They had his mother and her father living in a kind of mews. They always seemed to have at least three students of different nationalities living with them and minding the children. You couldn't ask the Hurleys to take on any more. They'd sicken you with how much they were doing already.

'I don't know *what* we're going to do,' Maura heard herself say for the tenth time to James, and saw with alarm that familiar look of irritation cross his face.

'Everything is a problem these days,' he said. 'Most people would jump at this opportunity. All it does for us is create more and more difficulties.'

She knew that this was true. Other people would see it as an excitement, a challenge, an adventure. She was being middle-aged beyond her years to see the summer as another Bad Thing. She must pull herself together. This trip to America was probably the last chance she would have to make her marriage work. They would be together in a new place, sharing everything as they had ten years before. There would be freedom, there would be time. James wouldn't work late at the college there, as he did at home. He wouldn't stop for drinks at the club rather than coming back to her. He wouldn't invent things to do on weekends to escape the house and the prospect of yet more time mending, fixing, and titivating their home.

Maura reminded herself that she was resourceful, that that was how she had found James in the beginning, her lecturer in college whom everyone had fancied and yet Maura had won. That was how she had found the house. It was good to be hardworking and practical. That was what had saved them both when little Jamie had died, a cot death at three months. Maura had planted the garden and bought a young collie dog. James had always said that she was a tower of strength in those months.

But that had been six years ago, and things had changed a lot since then. It wasn't just the lack of a child. They both knew that. There seemed to be a gulf between them that no amount of shared interest would bridge. There were so many things that they did share already – the house, the garden, the walks with Jessie – and yet there were so many silences. Another child, even if it had come along, would not have cemented them together. James lived more and more in the college, Maura more and more in her office, which she didn't really enjoy, but since the work was routine and simple it gave her plenty of time to think about her home and its constant improvement.

There was something about the frown of impatience on James's face that made Maura realise the urgency of sorting out the house matter without any more fuss.

'Leave it to me,' she said reassuringly. 'I'll think of something. You have enough to do to prepare your lectures.'

The frown went, and there was something of the old James. 'That's more like it,' he said. He was very handsome when he smiled. Maura realised with a sudden lurch of feeling that at least three marriages had ended in the college. It had been shock and horror and scandal at the time, but now all those men had settled down happily with their second choice. The furore had died down except in the hearts of the three women who had been left alone. It could happen with James very, very easily. If someone wanted him desperately enough. If Maura was foolish enough to drive him out of the home with her fussing and creating problems where none existed.

She spent the next day on the phone. Did

anyone know anyone? And eventually someone did. An old school friend Maura hadn't seen for years knew someone called Allie.

'Is she an Arab?' Maura asked. The Hurleys had a boy called Ali staying one year.

'No, it's short for Alice, I think. She's a kind of a home sitter.'

'Is she in an organisation? Does she get paid?'

The friend, a colourless woman called Patsy, said no, Allie was a law unto herself. 'She's our age, but you'd think she was years younger. She hasn't anywhere to live, no real job, she just moves on from place to place minding people's houses.'

'Sounds a bit unreliable,' Maura said disapprovingly.

'No, she was very good here, actually.' Patsy sounded grudging.

'And what did she do all day?'

'I wish I knew, but she had the place in fine shape when we came back from Brussels. Everyone around spoke highly of her.' There was still something ungiving about Patsy. Maura wondered if she was being told the full story about this Allie.

'You didn't like her, did you?' she asked.

Patsy sounded aggrieved. 'Lord almighty, Maura, you asked for someone to mind your house, I found you someone. Did I like her? I hardly met her. I only saw her twice before we left, and once when we came back. She did everything she said she would, and what more can anyone ask?'

Maura thanked her hastily and took Allie's present phone number. She was minding an art gallery for someone. It would be lovely to go to a home with a dog and a garden, she said.

'And two budgies?' Maura added.

'Super,' said Allie.

She sounded eighteen, not thirty-five-ish. When they met her, she looked much nearer to eighteen also.

Allie had long, dark, curly hair, the kind you knew she shampooed every morning and just shook it dry. She had a great smile that lit up her whole face, she had long golden legs and arms, and she wore what Maura thought was an overshort denim dress.

Allie sat on the grass as she talked to them in the garden. She smiled up at James, and Maura felt a resentment that she had not known possible. Not just at the fact that Allie *could* sit on the ground without falling over. But at the way she looked at James. It wasn't flirtatious or coy, it was just a look that was full of interest. Everything he said seemed worthy of consideration;

Allie would nod eagerly or shake her head. She was reacting on a very high level. Not for Allie the nods and grunts and half-attention that James must have been used to from Maura.

To be fair, and Maura struggled to be fair, Allie seemed very interested in her too. She asked Maura about her job, and even James seemed surprised at some of the things he heard about Maura's daily routine.

'I didn't know that,' he said, interested, and Maura realised with a pang that she hardly ever told James anything about work nowadays except to complain about the manager or the difficulty in parking a car or getting any shopping done at lunch hour.

Allie had a big red notebook, and she wrote their names down neatly, and all contact addresses that she would need. She was practical, too, asking about plumbers and electricians, and the number to phone if she smelled gas. She asked them to be sure to put any silver in the bank and to spend a couple of hours assembling all their private papers and documents and to lock them up somewhere.

'We don't need to do that.' James was smiling that slightly besotted smile men in their late thirties smile, Maura noticed.

'Oh, but you do, James.' Allie was firm. 'You

see, I come from having minded dozens of homes; you haven't. When you are over in America you'll suddenly remember that you left something out you'd prefer that nobody else saw. This way you'll know you didn't. Also, you can't ask me to pay your dentist's bill or find your income tax for you if it's all locked away, so I'm protecting myself, too.'

Allie had a marvellous laugh; she threw her head back and laughed like a child. She had perfect teeth, and her neck was long and suntanned.

Maura felt herself patting her hair. She was middle-aged, frumpish and settled, in her tights and shoes beside this lovely, leggy thing, all canvas shoes and golden limbs. And if Maura noticed it, then you could be sure that James did.

Allie asked about relations and friends, noted their names and numbers. She wrote down that Maura's sister didn't like dogs, and that James's mother didn't lock doors behind her. She seemed to understand everything in an instant.

Allie told them that she would write every week and give them an update on everything. She took instructions about phone messages and redirection of mail.

'Well, wasn't that the direct intervention of God,' James said when Allie had finally left.

Maura felt that this was both going too far and also ignoring her own part in finding the home sitter.

'Yes, well, and my friend Patsy!' she said mulishly.

'Of course.' He didn't care about niceties like this. 'Isn't she a treasure? She's exactly what we want,' he said happily. 'I didn't dream that anyone like that existed.'

A cold, hard knot formed in Maura's stomach. She felt a physical shock, like the feeling you get if you think you've swallowed a piece of glass. She realised she must not show her anxiety.

'Yes, she seems terrific, all right.'

'Aren't you clever?' James said.

Maura could feel the back of her neck get cold and clammy. As she sat in her garden, she knew in a disembodied way that she would remember this moment for ever. She knew the time and the date, and the way she sat on the garden seat with her hand stroking the head of Jessie the collie dog. Maura knew, with a certainty that she had never felt before about anything, that Allie was going to bring danger into her life. Real danger, threatening everything she had hoped for.

She had often wondered how women behaved once they knew for certain. But then she supposed few women were possessed of the foresight that she had. Other women had to wait for evidence and proof, or a friend whispering that perhaps she ought to know. Or worse still, the husband saying there was something he had to tell her.

Maura wondered if it was better to know so far in advance. Did it give her any advantage over the others? Were there any points to be gained in the game of trying to keep James for herself, and resist the siren call of Allie, who had already captured his heart?

It wasn't a question of competing. Maura had fine, fair hair; she couldn't grow a mop of dark curls to shake around. Her mouth was small, almost pursed; this had once been thought an advantage, but she couldn't laugh showing all those pearly teeth as Allie did. Maura's legs and arms were white, not long and golden. If it were a straight fight, Allie would have the sceptre and the crown. It couldn't be a straight fight.

They saw her once more before they left – the very morning of the departure. She had brought her own sheets, she told them, and they saw them peeping from a huge straw basket.

'Is that the only luggage you have?' Maura tried hard to stop her voice from sounding like Allie's mother or her schoolteacher.

Allie dimpled back at her. 'I'm a gypsy, you see. I don't need possessions. I use everybody else's.

I'll watch your television, look at your clocks, listen to your radio, boil your kettle . . . I don't need to clutter myself up with a lot of things.'

James was listening to this as if it were words from the Book of Revelations. He was also looking at the corner of Allie's sheets. Pretty blue and pink flowers with frilly edges on them. Maura knew that her own dull fitted sheets in white and pink were uninviting by comparison.

It had never been difficult to work out James's thought processes. They were very simple and direct; they went relentlessly from point A to point B.

'We never asked you, Allie, if there is anyone . . . any friend . . . boy . . . man . . .' He broke off in confusion.

'Allie knows she can invite any friend here.' Maura was crisp.

'No, I meant . . . you know.' James looked pathetic; he was dying to know if there was anyone. Maura held her breath, but not with any hope. What she had felt as she sat on that garden seat had not been a suspicion, it had been a foresight. It wasn't a matter of fearing that this golden girl would destroy Maura's life. She didn't just fear it, she knew it.

Allie laughed lightly. 'Oh, don't worry about

that, James,' she said. 'I'm between lovers at the moment.'

'I'm sure that state won't last very long.' He was being gallant, arch. Idiotic.

'You'd be surprised.' The smile was easy. 'I have to wait for the right man.'

Maura knew that Allie would wait three months. The right man, James, was being taken out of the country temporarily, but she would wait and plot and plan for his return.

She wrote every week, addressing the letters to Maura, but this was only a ploy. She talked of long walks on the beach in Killiney throwing the sticks for Jessie, chatting with James's mother. A remarkable woman for her age, and so interesting about the year she had spent in Africa.

'Poor Mum, delighted with a new audience,' James said.

Allie had contacted Maura's sister Geraldine; they had, it seemed, been visiting each other a lot. Maura hoped this didn't mean that Geraldine would be dropping in at all hours when they got back.

Geraldine had been frightened by a dog when she was young; this was where her fear stemmed from.

'I didn't know that,' James said.

'Neither did I.' Maura was grim.

The visit to the Midwestern campus was a sort of success. Only a 'sort of', Maura thought.

There was indeed a chance to get closer. Evenings on their own. Walks together. None of the pressures of home, no traffic to cope with or talk about, since they lived in the centre of everything. No duty calls to people, no telephone ringing except from kind neighbours asking them to drop by for a barbecue or a drink.

But the week seemed to be spent waiting for Allie's next letter and analysing the last one.

'Imagine, the Hurleys asked her to dinner,' James said.

Maura had noted that too. 'Very kind of them. They're wonderful at looking after strays,' she said. It had been a mistake. James frowned.

'I don't think you'll find that they classified our Allie as a stray,' he said.

Maura hated her being called 'our Allie'. She also hated hearing in a letter that old Mrs Green was much better now and would be coming home from the hospital soon with a new hip.

'I didn't know . . .' James began.

'I didn't know she had a hip replacement either,' Maura said. 'They keep themselves very much to themselves.'

'Not any more they don't,' James said tersely.

'Will we send them a card?' Maura sounded tentative.

'You were always the one afraid of drawing them on ourselves.'

'Well, since they've *been* drawn . . .' She knew her voice sounded sharp.

'Up to you.' He sounded a million miles away. Or a few thousand miles away. Back in that house and garden, in those flowery sheets, on warm terms with the neighbours. Maura felt that cold knot return. Like a flashback in a film, she saw herself sitting with a hand on Jessie's soft velvet fur.

There was a chill in the warm American evening, and she gave a little shiver.

'Are you all right?' he asked, concerned. He would always be kind to her, see that she managed as well as possible in the circumstances. She could see into the future, when he would call around once a year to discuss investments, and whether the roof needed to be redone.

But where would he call? She would *not* give him the house, she would not walk out and let Allie take over that place she had loved and lavished her heart on for ten years.

She would live there alone if need be. Her eyes filled with tears.

'You seem very tense here,' he said kindly. 'If

you like, we can get away a little earlier. I mean, I can cram the lectures together a bit towards the end. Be back sooner.'

'What about Allie? She thinks she is staying three months.'

'Oh, she can stay on with us surely? Until she goes to her next place. She's not a fusser, our Allie.'

Maura said she didn't feel a bit tense, she simply loved it here, there was no question of going home early. She knew her smile was small and pinched. Without surgery she would never have a broad, open smile like Allie's.

It was a perfect September day when they got home. Maura rang Allie from the airport.

'How did she sound?' James was eager.

Maura wanted to say that she sounded like an overgrown schoolgirl, laughing and welcoming them back and words tumbling over each other. Instead she said that Allie sounded fine, and that she had arranged a few people to come in. 'That was lovely of her.' James smiled happily. 'Friends of hers, is it?'

'No, friends of ours, I think,' Maura said.

'We don't have that many friends,' James said absently.

'Of course we do,' Maura snapped.

Around them in Dublin Airport passengers

were being met, embraced, and ferried out to cars. Maura and James pushed their trolley of luggage to a taxi ungreeted.

'We *could* have been met if we had wanted it,' Maura said in answer to no question.

On their lawn, Allie had set up a table. She had vases of flowers, and jugs of sangria. James's mother was there, helping and feeling as if she were in charge. Geraldine was there with her mute husband Maurice, chatting animatedly to the elderly Mr and Mrs Green, and discussing the success of the operation. The Hurleys were there with their extended family. The children all seemed to know Allie well. Maura had to struggle to remember their names, there were so many of them. A couple from across the road whom Maura and James had never met were among the crowd milling around.

'I do hope we aren't intruding,' the woman said. 'But Allie was so insistent, she said you'd love everyone here.'

'She was utterly right.' Maura strove to put the warmth and enthusiasm into her voice that she knew were called for.

'Have a shower, you must be exhausted.' Allie had thought of everything.

Maura stood under the water while James shaved at the washbasin nearby.

'What a girl,' he said at least three times. He was anxious to be back down there joining in the fun. 'Wasn't this a smashing idea of hers?'

Maura's voice was shaky. 'Great,' she said, hoping the running water covered the sound of a sob. 'Simply great. You go on down. I'll be out in a minute.'

She stood in her bedroom and tried to find something that might look festive and happy to wear. She seemed to see only blouses and skirts or matronly dresses that would make her fit into the generation of James's mother or the Greens.

Allie was leaving that afternoon; she would not stay and destroy Maura's life by taking her husband. Her next job was abroad. Minding a farmhouse in the Dordogne.

But Maura had been right that day on the garden seat. Allie had ruined her life; she had opened up golden doors and shown everyone else how wonderful things could be, but would never be again. James's mother would never again be asked to tell long stories about Africa, Geraldine wouldn't be invited to tell rambling tales of self-pity about barking dogs in her youth. The old Greens would go back into their greenhouse, and the high-flying Hurleys behind their hedge.

The people who lived across the road would

never intrude again. James would frown without knowing why, and only Maura would know that nothing would ever be the same.

Package
Tour

They met at a Christmas party, and suddenly everything looked bright and full of glitter instead of commercial and tawdry, as it had looked some minutes before.

They got on like a house on fire and afterwards when they talked about it they wondered about the silly expression. 'A house on fire'. It really didn't mean anything, like two people getting to know each other and discovering more and more things in common. They were the same age, each of them one quarter of a century old. Shane worked in a bank, Moya worked in an insurance office. Shane was from Galway and went home every month. Moya was from Clare and went home every three weeks. Shane's mother was difficult and wanted him to be a priest. Moya's father was difficult and had to be told that she was staying in a hostel in Dublin rather than a bedsitter.

Shane played a lot of squash because he was afraid of getting a heart attack or, worse, of getting fat and being passed over when aggressive, lean fellows were promoted. Moya went to a gym twice a week because she wanted to look like Jane Fonda when she grew old and because she wanted to have great stamina for her holidays.

They both loved foreign holidays, and on their first evening out together Shane told her all about his trips to Tunisia and Yugoslavia and Sicily. In turn, Moya told her tales of Tangiers, Turkey, and of Cyprus. Alone among their friends they seemed to think that a good foreign holiday was the high spot of the year.

Moya said that most people she knew spent the money on clothes, and Shane complained that in his group it went on cars or drink. They were soul mates who had met over warm sparkling wine at a Christmas party where neither of them knew anyone else. It had been written for them in the stars.

When the January brochures came out, Moya and Shane were the first to collect them; they had plastic bags full of them before anyone else had got around to thinking of a holiday. They noted which were the bargains, where were early-season or late-season three-for-the-price-of-two-week holidays. They worked out the jargon.

Attractive flowers cascading down from galleries could mean the place was alive with mosquitoes. Panoramic views of the harbour might mean the hotel was up an unmerciful hill. *Simple* might mean no plumbing, and *sophisticated* could suggest all-night discos.

The thing they felt most bitter about was the single-room supplement. It was outrageous to penalise people for being individuals. Why should travel companies expect that people go off on their holidays two by two like the animals into the Ark? And how was it that the general public obeyed them so slavishly? Moya could tell you of people who went on trips with others simply on the basis that they all got their holidays in the first fortnight in June.

Shane said that he knew fellows who went to Spain as friends and came home as enemies because their outing had been on the very same basis. Timing.

But as the months went on and the meetings became more frequent and the choice of holiday that each of them would settle for was gradually narrowed down, they began to realise that this summer they would probably travel together. That it was silly to put off this realisation. They had better admit it.

They admitted it easily one evening over a plate of spaghetti.

It had been down to two choices now. The Italian lakes or the island of Crete. And somehow it came to both of them at the same time: this would be the year they would go to Crete. The only knotty problem was the matter of the single room.

They were not as yet lovers. They didn't want to be rushed into it by the expediency of a double booking. They didn't want it to be put off-limits by the fact of having booked two separate rooms. Shane said that perhaps the most sensible thing would be to book a room with two beds. This had to be stipulated on the booking form. A twin-bedded room. Not a double bed.

Shane and Moya assured each other they were grown-ups.

They could sleep easily in two separate beds, and suppose, just suppose in the fullness of time after mature consideration and based on an equal decision with no one party forcing the other . . . they wanted to sleep in the same bed . . . then the facility, however narrow, would be there for them.

They congratulated each other on their maturity and paid the booking deposit. They had agreed on a middle-of-the-road kind of hotel, in one of the resorts that had not yet been totally discovered and destroyed. They had picked June, which they thought would avoid the worst crowds. They each had a savings plan. They knew that this year was going to be the best year in their lives and the holiday would be the first of many taken together all over the world.

The cloud didn't come over the horizon until March when they were sitting companionably reading a glossy magazine. Shane pointed out a huge suitcase on wheels with a matching smaller suitcase. Weren't they smashing, he said; a bit pricey, but maybe it would be worth it.

Moya thought she must be looking at the wrong page. Those were the kind of suitcases that Americans bought for going around the world.

Shane thought that Moya couldn't be looking at the right page; they were just two normal suitcases, but smart and easy to identify on the carousel. Just right for a two-week holiday. But for how many people? Moya wondered wildly; surely the two of them wouldn't have enough to fill even the smaller suitcase. Well for one person, me, Shane said with a puzzled look.

Between the two happy young people there was a sudden grey area. Up to now their relationship had been so open and free, but suddenly there were unspoken things hovering in the air. They had told each other that their friends' romances had failed and even their marriages had rocked because they had never been able to clear the air. Shane and Moya would not be like that. But still, neither one of them seemed able to bring up the subject of the suitcases. The gulf between them was huge.

Yet in other ways they seemed just as happy as before. They went for walks along the pier, they played their squash and went to the gym, they enjoyed each other's friends, and both of them managed to put the disturbing black cloud about the luggage into the background of their minds. Until April, when another storm came and settled on them.

It was Moya's birthday, and she unwrapped her gift from Shane, which was a travelling iron. She turned it around and around and examined it in case it was something else disguised as a travelling iron. In the *hope* that it was something disguised as a travelling iron. But no, that's what it was.

It was lovely, she said faintly.

Shane said he knew ladies loved to have something to take the creases out on holidays, and perhaps Moya shouldn't throw away the tissue paper; it was terrific for folding into clothes when you were packing, it took out all that crumpled look, didn't she find?

Moya sat down very suddenly. Absolutely on a different subject, she said she wondered how many shirts Shane took on holiday. Well, fifteen obviously, and the one he was wearing and sports shirts and a couple of beach shirts.

'Twenty shirts?' Moya said faintly.

That was about it.

And would there be twenty socks and knickers, too? Well, give or take. Give or take how many? A pair or two. There seemed to be a selection of shoes and belts, and the odd sun hat.

Moya felt all the time that Shane would smile his lovely, familiar, heart-turning smile and say, 'I had you fooled, hadn't I?' and they would fall happily into each other's arms. But Shane said nothing.

Shane was hoping that Moya would tell him soon where all this list of faintly haranguing questions was leading. Why she was asking him in such a robotic voice about perfectly normal things. It was as if she asked him did he brush his teeth or did he put on his clothes before leaving the house. He stared at her anxiously. Perhaps he wasn't showing enough interest in her wardrobe? Maybe he should ask about her gear.

That did not seem to be a happy solution.

Moya, it turned out, was a person who had never checked in a suitcase in her life; she had a soft squelchy bag of the exact proportions that would fit under an airline seat and would pass as carry-on baggage. She brought three knickers, three bras, three shirts, three skirts, and three bathing suits. She brought a sponge bag, a pair of flip-flop sandals, and a small tube of travel detergent.

She thought that a holiday should never involve waiting for your bags at any airport, and never take in dressing for dinner, and the idea of carrying home laundry bags of dirty clothes was as foreign to her as it was to Shane – that anyone would spend holiday time washing things and drying them.

'But it only takes a minute,' pleaded Moya.

'But it takes no time at all if you bring spares,' pleaded Shane. 'The arms would come out of your sockets carrying that lot,' said Moya. 'We wouldn't get into the bathroom with all your clothes draped around it,' said Shane.

They talked about it very reasonably, as they had always promised each other they would do. But the rainbows had gone, and the glitter had dimmed.

It would have been better if they had actually met on holidays, they said, with Moya carrying the shabby holdall and Shane the handsome and excessive luggage. Then they would have known from the start that they weren't people who had the same views about a package tour and how you packed for it. It was a hurdle they might have crossed before they fell in love. Not a horrible shock at the height of romance.

They were practical, Moya and Shane; they wondered if it would iron itself out if they paid the single-room supplement. That way Moya wouldn't see the offending Sultan's Wardrobe, as she kept calling it, and Shane wouldn't be blinded by wet underwear, as he kept fearing. But no, it went deeper than that. It seemed to show the kind of people they were: too vastly different ever to spend two weeks, let alone a lifetime, together.

As the good practical friends they were, they went back to the travel agency and transferred their bookings to separate holidays with separate hopes and dreams.

The Sporting
Decision

Martin had wondered recently whether he was now totally past the possibility of falling in love. He used to consider himself quite a dashing lover when he was young. Well, not technically speaking, of course, not like Casanova or anything, but Martin was never without a girl on his arm, or in his sports car. And as time went on they became ladies.

He had never married.

'No one would have me,' he'd laugh.

But everyone knew this wasn't true. Martin Grey was quite a catch. A very successful lawyer in mainly high-profile cases. If you got Martin Grey to defend you, it meant that you or someone close to you had money and that your case was tricky.

He had spoken in the courts for religious communities, for bankers, for politicians, alleged murderers, gangland bosses and, increasingly in post-divorce-referendum Ireland, for disturbed first wives. His name was rarely out of the papers, he was often seen on the evening television news, his handsome animated face talking to clients.

He lived in a Georgian town house within walking distance of his work and the many dinner parties to which he was invited.

People had almost given up hoping that he would form a permanent relationship with anyone he met over an elegant dinner in their homes. But he was always witty and good company. He sang for his supper and was universally charming, apparently indiscreet, but in fact giving nothing away.

People put his ongoing bachelor status down to his having been very busy in the marrying years and now, as he was in his late fifties, to having become too set in his ways to change them to accommodate anyone else.

His little weakness, as he was often heard to say, was an over-concern for the horses. He was always to be seen at Punchestown, Leopardstown, the Curragh and down the country, too. He never seemed to be *with* anyone, but since he knew everyone all he had to do was to say to the people he met that they should all meet up in this bar or that, or in some of the hospitality tents, and he had a ready-made circle of friends for the day.

He was also interested in antique furniture, items that would suit his tall, narrow Georgian home. He never boasted about his Chippendale chairs, but he *did* arrange for them to be very well lit so that people could admire them, and only then would he tell a little of their origin, always slightly self-deprecating, as if he knew nothing about it really.

Once or twice a year he took time off from the racecourses of Europe to go to some of the major antiques markets. Which was why he found himself going into the Grosvenor House Hotel.

He was in London anyway, for a case conference on a very sticky extradition matter. Martin Grey's client was running out of time and excuses, but not money. A huge refresher fee had been handed over.

Martin decided to look at some mirrors. He knew exactly what he wanted, something with an Adamesque urn and trailing foliage on it. A mirror that he could laugh at lightly and say how strange it was to think that people were examining themselves in it as long ago as 1770.

And that was when he saw her.

He saw the most striking woman he had ever

seen. She looked about thirty, a good twenty-five years younger than he was. Tall and slim and wearing an oddly old-fashioned, full, black silk skirt with a crisp white shirt.

She had no jewellery, he noticed, and that included no wedding ring. Her hair was short and slightly damp-looking, as if she had just got out of a shower. She had a soft black leather shoulder bag, and pointed-toe, low, black shoes.

He took all this in in seconds.

She was examining different mirrors from his choice. Slightly over-ornate, he thought. They were Georgian, certainly, but they had candle-sticks attached, a little fussy for today's world, yet they had been hugely popular for a long time.

Martin pretended to look at his own choice, but all the time he watched her.

She wasn't what you would call languid, but her movements were slow, almost rippling. Yes, that was it, rippling. She reminded him of a beautiful filly stretching and arching her neck.

For the first time in his whole life he felt an uncontrollable urge to go straight over and put his hand on the arm of someone he did not know.

He wanted to talk to her, tell her how her particular simple style of beauty had touched him, suggest they have dinner.

He pulled himself together sharply. That kind of thing would be pure sleaze, completely vulgar. A mature man reaching out to stroke a beautiful young woman, a stranger. This wasn't what an eminent counsel did while browsing at one of the smartest antiques fairs of the season.

She would be frightened by him, repulsed. He must not even think of doing it. But he could *not* let her disappear from him. Not now that he had seen her.

Twice in his life he had thought he might be in love. Once with Francesca, a hopelessly unsuitable but beautiful Italian woman who eventually married one of Martin's colleagues and made the man unspeakably miserable. Once with Shona, an intense law lecturer who might certainly have been a suitable wife in that she could hold her own at a dinner party, and they would have had plenty in common. But Shona lacked glamour and style.

And for all that he admired her mind, Martin found it hard to overlook the fact that she wore shabby cardigans and didn't look after her hair and her nails.

Unlike this goddess who stood examining the mirrors.

How he wanted to sit opposite her at a dinner.

He knew exactly the restaurant to suggest to her. Once they got talking . . .

Why was there no way to let her know that he was a really respectable person? That, if they were in Ireland, everyone would know his face and, to be honest, everyone would be pleased, almost honoured to be addressed by him?

It never mattered to Martin that he was well known, it sat lightly on him. But now, on the one occasion he needed to be recognised, he had to be in London, a city of ten million people for God's sake! How very unfair!

She had one of those long, swan-like necks that you sometimes saw on models, but yet she didn't look haughty or aloof. Not unlike a taller Audrey Hepburn, but not as pixie-like.

He ached to talk to her, to say something pleasant so that she would reply and he would hear her voice.

What would his friends say in such circumstances? The lawyers would make arch legalistic remarks. 'Would my learned friend care to inform the court what conclusion she has reached . . . on the sculptural girandole with scrolled acanthus leaves?'

The people he knew from racing would offer odds on it being a genuine Robert Adam piece or not. Nothing seemed right.

And soon she would move away and he would never see her again. The thought terrified him.

'Are you interested in horses?' he blurted out suddenly.

Her eyes widened in surprise. He wished he were twelve feet under the ground. She looked him up and down.

'Fairly interested,' she said eventually. She had a slight Australian accent.

'I've always wanted to go to the Melbourne Cup,' Martin said foolishly.

'Well, why don't you go then?' she asked reasonably.

'Oh, I will one day,' he reassured her.

She was just about to move on, thinking presumably that she had met a madman. Martin just couldn't let her go.

'I have a wonderful tip for you for next Sunday,' he stuttered, completely unrecognisable as the silver-tongued lawyer who could silence a court with his opening sentence.

'You have?' She had such a lovely voice, not strident, not affected. Warm, interested.

She didn't seem to think it at all odd that a stranger should come up and offer her a tip. Maybe people were doing that all the time.

'Yes. She'll be placed. No question.' Martin's voice was still slightly shaking.

He was having a real conversation with her and she wasn't walking away in disgust or anything.

'She? It's a filly then?'

'Indeed. Called Alexander Goldrun. Great animal altogether, full of heart, runner-up in last month's Irish Guineas. On Sunday, she's in Chantilly . . . the four-thirty race. It's called Diane Hermes. Back her for a place now, won't you?'

'Only runner-up in the Irish Guineas?' she asked, frowning doubtfully.

'But you should have seen that race!' Martin had a light in his eye now. 'She was runner-up to Attraction, a horse never beaten, undefeated, before and after.'

'I see.' She was thoughtful.

'I wasn't suggesting you put the deeds of the house on her or anything,' he said with his famous Martin smile.

'No, indeed,' she agreed.

There was a silence between them.

'What *were* you suggesting, actually?' she asked.

'Well, I would *like* to have asked you out, but people don't do that to strangers, so I thought I'd do it differently. I am sort of giving you my credentials in a way by giving you this tip. And I thought that I'd also give you my name and phone number and if . . . when . . . Alexander

Goldrun comes in, then you might give me a ring and we could go out to dinner?'

He managed to look hopeful but laid-back at the same time. He had sent out the message that his life would continue even if she did *not* call him.

She looked at him for a moment.

'Fair enough,' she said.

He wrote down his name and his mobile phone number on a piece of paper and handed it to her.

'And are you a breeder, a trainer, an owner?' she asked.

'None of these things, I'm afraid, just an enthusiastic guy who hands my money over to the bookies,' he laughed.

'They must have handed some of it back.' She looked at his expensive clothes.

'A bit, from time to time, but I have a day job, too, I'm a lawyer.'

'Ah, cautious to the end,' she said.

'Normally yes, this time no.'

'I'm Megan,' she said.

'I'll hear from you Sunday night then, Megan,' he said, and moved away.

He felt light-headed with excitement. She wasn't a girl who would play games. She would call when the horse romped home in the first three.

*

Megan wondered what it was about her that attracted lawyers.

She had just finished a four-year relationship with a sharp Sydney barrister, who really should have been with a brainless bimbo, not a business-woman.

And when she had eventually found him with such a bimbo, she had left him without a backward glance and returned his letters un-opened.

She had come to Europe to decide what kind of a fresh start she would make. For one thing, she would create a different place to live, not a minimalist, near-empty space looking out on Sydney Harbour. She wanted furnishings and items of beauty around her, like those she had seen at the antiques fair.

She'd never expected such a handsome, attract-ive man to approach her. Why hadn't he asked her out directly, instead of all this waiting around until some horse won some race? But that was lawyers for you, always playing games.

Megan knew a fair bit about horses. Her father had been taking her to the races since she was a child. He would be *very* pleased she had met up with another gambling man. The Sydney lawyer wasn't ever a man for the racecourse.

Four days now until the damn race. And

suppose the horse fell? She could ring him to sympathise. Or would that be pathetic? Megan didn't do pathetic.

Martin stayed on in London. In theory he should have gone back to Dublin, but what was the point? He would be seeing Megan on Sunday night, so why waste the time going back and forth?

The next few days hung very heavy on Martin's hands.

Megan asked the porter in her hotel how she would get the results of a race in France that was not televised in Britain.

He said he'd find out.

'Oh, the Prix Diane,' he said knowledgeably. 'I have a tenner on Grey Lilas myself. For a place, of course.'

'Of course,' she said.

Why on earth was time going so slowly? Why had she agreed to risk her whole future with a really attractive man on the results of some horse race in France?

She paced the foyer, watching the porter, willing him to make the phone call and give her the good news.

Martin sat in his club, clenching his fists and

unclenching them, and trying to keep his eyes away from the clock. In fourteen minutes he would ring his bookmaker.

In thirteen-and-a-half . . .

He must have been mad to let it all depend on this. Stone mad.

'You must have a lot on that filly,' the porter said to Megan. 'I never saw anyone so anxious.'

'More than you'd believe,' Megan said.

Only three minutes.

'Go on, Kevin, go on, Kevin Manning, ride the race of your life,' Martin Grey cried out to the walls.

Under the French skies, Latice came first, Millionaia second and Grey Lilas third. A very good fourth came Alexander Goldrun.

Martin put down the phone from his bookmaker. His heart was heavy. It was a place, of course, but *fourth* place.

He had a very strange feeling that he was going to cry. But he knew that once he started he might never stop. The mobile phone was on his table beside him.

Megan had not telephoned.

Megan sat shell-shocked. The porter was trying not to look too pleased about Grey Lilas.

'Do they pay out on fourth?' she croaked to him.

'In handicaps they do, if there are sixteen or more runners,' he began.

'So it *is* a place then, is it?' Her face was full of hope.

'It's France, you see, they don't have bookies over there, it's all the Tote, pari-mutuel they call it, and they don't pay on fourth, no matter how many runners.'

'Would *any* bookie pay out on it, do you think?'

The porter was puzzled.

'Well, you *could* have made an individual arrangement with a bookie and agreed with him that he pay on fourth.'

'Could I?' She had hope again.

'But you didn't,' he said.

'No, I didn't,' she said.

'Did you lose much?' The porter was sympathetic.

'Almost everything,' she said.

Martin waited in his club until Tuesday, then he left for Dublin. She wasn't going to ring. She might have thought that a fourth paid out. Or that it counted. But she didn't care enough.

Back to work.

*

Megan went to the airport on Tuesday. She was going back home.

She would put it behind her. It was a foolish thing to have agreed to. She should have spoken at the time. If she had called him and said that fourth counted, he would always have despised her. She had never run after a man. She wouldn't start running after one now.

'Which terminal?' the taxi driver asked.

Megan couldn't remember. It was three weeks since she had come into London, how could she recall the terminal where she arrived? It didn't matter anyway, there was surely transport from one to the other. And she had plenty of time to spare.

'Terminal One,' she said, uncaring.

Martin was in the bookstore. He would get something that would take his mind off this woman. A thriller. A good, creepy, bloodthirsty thriller.

When he got home, he would have a shower, change and sit on the terrace of his elegant Georgian house and read.

He realised with a sense of pain how very lonely his life seemed. There were long, empty years ahead.

He shook himself. It was nonsense to think like

this. She might have been entirely unsuitable for him, he might have been far too old for her. He *must* get rid of this ridiculous sense of loss.

Megan realised that she should be in Terminal Four. She decided to have a coffee before she made the trek. A lot of the life had gone out of her.

She had enjoyed her long trip over from Australia. Now she felt tired and weary. There was a sense that she had missed something. She must get rid of such a negative feeling.

And then she saw him. His face looked grim. He was unhappy today. Not at all the boyish, eager man she had seen at the antiques fair. But still very handsome, a face of character, a warm expression. A man you could trust.

She took out her mobile phone and dialled his number.

'Hello?' His voice was as she remembered it.

'It's Megan,' she said.

'It *is*?' There was joy in his face, she could see it.

'Megan, where are you?' he cried. She saw how pleased he was she had called.

'At Tie Rack,' she said.

'*Where?*'

'A shop that sells ties and scarves about twenty metres away from you.'

He looked over, saw her, dropped his briefcase and started running towards her. She left her luggage and ran to meet him.

In an airport, it's not unusual to see people embracing. Welcoming someone home or saying goodbye.

There's usually a lot of embracing going on. But never as ardent as the way Megan and Martin held each other with tears of relief and the joy of discovery in their eyes.

The
Apprenticeship

It was to be one of the most stylish weddings of the year. Florrie thought that if anyone had been giving odds a quarter of a century ago when she was born whether this child would ever be a guest at something like this, those odds would have been enormous. A child born in a small house in a small street in Wigan didn't seem likely to end up as the bride's best friend at what the newspapers were calling the wedding of the decade. If only her mother had lived, Florrie thought, if only her father had cared. They might have been able to get some mileage out of it, some reward for the long hours of work, the high hopes.

There would be pictures of Florrie in tomorrow's papers, probably a glimpse of her on tonight's television news. She would figure certainly in the glossy magazines, her hat alone would ensure she was well snapped. She would be seen laughing and sharing a joke, probably with some youngish and handsome member of the aristocracy. This would not be hard, because unusually for a society wedding there might not be many young women friends of the bride around. And the groom's friends, being horsey, would not be as photogenic. No, Florrie knew that she would figure in the *Tatler* and *Harper's*. And she knew how to smile without showing a mouthful of teeth and how to raise her chin in a way that made her neck look long and upper class.

She knew that it looked much more classy not to be seen with a glass in her hand, but to appear fascinated by the particular braying chap that she was meant to be talking to.

Florrie knew all of this because she had worked at it, and learned it. Like she had never worked at anything when she was at school. Long ago in a different place and at a different time, with Camilla, except of course that Camilla had not been Camilla then, she had been Ruby. And Ruby and Florrie had been best friends. As in many ways they were still best friends today. The society columns might well describe Florrie tomorrow as a very close friend of the bride. But it would not say that they had grown up together, that they had shared great doorstep sandwiches in their lunch hour, that they had collected old newspapers just so that they could read the society pages and see how people lived in a different and better world.

They had read their subject carefully, young Ruby and young Florrie. No hint of social climbing or being a hanger-on. Not even the most suspicious could fault Camilla or catch her out in a lie today. Camilla had always said she was from way up north, that her parents were dead, that she had hardly any family. Better to stick as close to the truth as possible, she had advised Florrie, less for them to unearth, and you can never be caught out in a lie. Even if they found out she had once been Ruby, Camilla was prepared to say it had been a pet name. She thought it was terribly brave and funny of Florrie to hold on to her name. But then, Florrie was such a character! Florrie had held on to her name because she remembered her mother holding her as a little girl.

'I had a doll once called Florrie,' her mother had said. 'I never thought I'd have a little baby of my own, a beautiful baby to look after.' Florrie was three when she heard this first, hardly a baby, and still further from babyhood when her mother dressed her for school and held her face gently between red rough hands. 'Florrie,' she had breathed in a voice full of admiration and love.

'Such a beautiful name for a beautiful little girl. They wanted me to call you Caroline ... but I wanted a beautiful name for you, one you'd love ... Florence. It means a flower, little Florrie, beautiful little flower.'

Ruby's mother might have thought she was a little jewel. She might even have said so, but Camilla never said it. Camilla said nothing about her parents. Except that they were dead. Which was true.

They had died together in a coach crash, on the very first holiday of their married life. Florrie's father had said that's what you got for grand ideas, coach tours to the Continent, no less. Florrie's mother had said maybe they should take in the child. Ruby was eleven, and she had nobody else. Everyone had said it was a great idea. After all, it was unusual to be an only child in their street. Now Ruby and Florrie were like twins. And apart from reading all those 'silly books', as people called the magazines they read, they were sensible girls, too. Not silly like some, not getting into trouble with boys. Hardworking. On Saturdays they worked in the beauty salon, and they learned how it was all done. The proprietor never had two such willing assistants. As well as sweeping floors and folding towels, they stood entranced watching the facials and manicures.

The customers liked them, two bright youngsters full of unqualified admiration. The customers didn't know they had come to learn – as they went to the fashion stores to learn, and as they worked in the good hotel to watch. And they did secretarial courses at night. By the time they had their O levels they were ready for anything. Ruby was ready to leave, to go south to start Stage Two. Florrie could go nowhere, her mother was failing fast.

She sat by her mother's bed and listened to the homespun wisdom, with a heart that was filled with impatience as well as love. She heard her mother beg her to believe that Dad was a good man really. It was just that he was a bit mulish, and drank a little too much. Dad had said no kind word in the seventeen years that Florrie had lived in his house. She nodded and pretended that she agreed with her mother, who would not be leaving hospital and coming home. Her mother said that Ruby was right to have gone to London, she was impatient, she would have been silly to stay around. The woman found nothing odd that the child she had taken in had abandoned her. Ruby has great unhappiness in her soul, she said. Florrie sat by the bed and gritted her teeth.

Patience and forgiveness like this were unrealistic. Surely they couldn't be considered virtues. The nurses liked her, the handsome tall girl, a blonde with well-cut hair and long pink fingernails, unlike her stooped and work-weary mother. The daughter had character, the nurses told each other. She wouldn't stay long with the bad-tempered father once the poor woman passed away.

Florrie stayed a week. Her father's farewell was grudging, as every other gesture had been. He had always known she would go, he said, too high and mighty by far for them. No, she needn't keep coming back up, there wasn't all that much more to say.

Florrie was astonished at the change in her friend in ten short months. Vowel sounds had altered, and that wasn't all. Ruby was no longer Ruby. It's only a name, she had explained, it could have been anything.

'I know,' Florrie had said. 'I should have been Caroline.'

'Then *be* Caroline,' Camilla had begged.

'Never.' Florrie's eyes had flashed at the thought.

They looked at each other then, a long look.

'It's only the name,' Florrie had said eventually. 'I'm on for everything else.'

And it was like the old days. They laughed as they heard each other's phrases; you never said you had been to the WC or the toilet, it was the lavatory. You didn't say serviette, you said napkin, and it wasn't posh to have paper ones that you could throw away when they got crumpled. They had plenty of time: it was an apprenticeship, they told each other. They had until they were twenty, then they would be ready. To move among the smart and the beautiful, to be at ease among them, to marry them and live in comfort for the rest of their lives.

It would only be hard if they were unprepared. They had heard too many tales of people being trapped by their humble origins. Camilla and Florrie would be different. They would invent no pedigree that could be checked and found faulty. They would shrug and ask did such things matter any more. They would look so much the part and seem to care so little about proving themselves that soon they would be accepted. They would try hard but would never be seen to try at all; that was the secret.

And soon they were indeed ready. And it wasn't nearly as difficult as they thought. There was a career structure. Chalet girls in ski resorts, a few weeks working in smart jewellers and in art houses so that they met the right type of girl.

They were slow to take up with the right type of men at the beginning. They wanted other girls to be their allies at the start. And anyway they wanted to be ready when they found the really right men. They had noticed that it wasn't only the Royals who liked their girlfriends not to have played the field; a lot of the Uppers thought that girls who had been around a lot might not be good wife material, and after all, one wouldn't like to think that lots of chaps had been with one's wife. What?

And in the meantime, because they *were* so bright and met so many people, they actually got good jobs. Camilla was high up in an estate agency and Florrie was now a partner in a firm of interior decorators. Years of watching for quality and trying to define it had paid off for both of them.

And then Camilla showed a couple of town houses to a chap who thought she was quite super and asked her to his place in the country for the weekend. She went, but she was slower than he thought to begin with a teeny affair, as he called it. In fact, she was adamant about not beginning it. He complained about her bitterly over a bottle of Bollinger to his friend Albert. Albert said that it was very rum, the girl must be mad. He'd like to meet her; he always liked meeting mad people.

Albert was of blood so blue that it almost frightened Camilla off. But she decided to take him on. This was the challenge she had spent years rehearsing for. This was the prize she had hardly dared to hope for.

Albert was intrigued by her. The girl who hadn't been to bed with his friend, who wouldn't go to bed with him either. Who wasn't frightened of his mother, who was casual to the point of indifference about her own background. She was not a gold digger, she had a position of importance in her firm. Nobody could see the potential like Camilla, they said. She dressed well, she seemed to have lots of girlfriends who all spoke glowingly of her. She had no past.

Camilla played it beautifully. She waited until Albert was truly besotted and at that precise moment she told him she was thinking of moving to Washington, DC. There had been interest and offers; she was vague lest he ask her what interest and which offers. But she had timed it right. Albert couldn't let her leave. Albert's father predictably said she was a fine-looking filly but had she any breeding? His mother unpredictably said she was about the only kind of woman who might make a success of Albert and the rolling acres, and the complicated property investments and the tied cottages. The wedding of the decade was on.

It was decided between them that Florrie should not be the bridesmaid; the press would be too inquisitive, would ask about their origins. Papers nowadays did horrible things. They might send a photographer up to that small street and, perish the thought, find Florrie's father, surly in his braces. And he might tell that Camilla was Ruby and that her parents had been killed on their first coach tour abroad.

Better to have six flower girls and Albert's horsey-looking sister. Wiser to have the lovely Florrie stand out among the guests. A young woman of elegance, successful in her field. Further proof, if any were needed, that the bride was the right stuff or as right as you can get in these days of social change and upheaval.

Florrie stood in the old church and looked up at the flags of the regiment that Albert's family had fought in. The stained-glass windows remembered various ancestors, and the pews had brass plates recalling the family. The bishop was old and genial. He spoke of duty and of hope. Florrie listened as she looked at Camilla's beautiful face; she knew that her friend was listening, too.

Then the bishop spoke of love. He told how it conquered everything and that it cast out envy and ambition and greed. His eyes became misty when he talked of love.

The night before, Florrie and Camilla had talked for a long time. They had talked as they had never been able to talk since that day when Florrie had come to London and said she would change everything, everything but her name. They laughed as they hadn't laughed for years, they drank champagne instead of the lemon tea they had learned to like when they were fourteen because they had read it was lower class to take milk.

They had said that the battle had been half won, and now that Camilla was in, she could have the right kind of dinner parties and house parties to launch her friend. Her talented friend with the wonderfully funny name. They had embraced and congratulated each other on their magical apprenticeship.

But they hadn't talked about love. And in the church where Albert's bones would lie one day, very probably beside the bones of her friend Ruby, Florrie shivered. She knew that as far as she was concerned the apprenticeship was over. She had got far enough. Perhaps she had got much farther than her friend who would appear in tomorrow's papers as the bride of the decade, who would be called Lady Camilla, who would live a life without love. They said that young girls' heads were meant to be filled with stories of love, but that had never happened to Ruby or Florrie. There had been no room in their heads, the space was too filled with rule books on how to behave and how to say 'glad to know you' rather than 'pleased to meet you'. It had been too busy an apprenticeship to allow for thoughts of love.

Florrie would make time for it, she thought. She would not list the likely dinner guests that she might trap at her friend's long table, smiling at them confidently through Albert's family silver. When a bishop or vicar or a registrar came to say the word for Florrie, the word *love* wouldn't have an alien ring to it.

She felt somehow that the mother who had thought of her as a flower would have been pleased with her, and she was aware of tears beginning to well up in her eyes. But she willed them back, because the upper classes do not cry at christenings, weddings, or funerals. It is, after all, what sets them apart. Her apprenticeship had not been wasted.

The Business
Trip

Lena had loved him for four long years. Not that he knew, of course. Men like Shay wouldn't even consider that they could be loved silently and unselfishly like that. It didn't make sense.

He probably assumed that Lena was fond of him, admired him, and might under the right circumstances be attracted to him. But if he thought of her at all, he might have assumed that she had a private life of her own. He would never have thought that this quiet, efficient assistant of his spent her entire life, both in and out of the office, thinking about him, trying to make his life easier and better, and in her dreams trying to share that life with him.

According to Maggie, Lena was not in love. She was suffering from an obsession, an infatuation. It wasn't healthy for someone who was twenty-six to develop this kind of crush on a man who didn't return it and wasn't even aware of it.

And however unwise it might have been to have allowed a temporary fascination to take over, it was positively dangerous to let it continue the way Lena had. She stopped being twenty-six and became twenty-seven, and twenty-eight and twenty-nine. Soon she would be thirty years of age, and what had she to show for it?

Lena said spiritedly that she had as much to show for it as anyone had to show for anything. She had been happy, she had made his life better. She hadn't made a public fool of herself, as so many women had. She hadn't settled for second best, as so many others had done. She loved every second of her working day, which was more than you could say for a lot of people. She was appreciated if not loved in her office, and only Maggie knew her secret. She was not an object of pity. Maggie wouldn't tut-tut and shake her head over coffee with the girls about Lena's foolishness. Maggie was an ally, even if she didn't understand.

Maggie was Lena's aunt. But they had always been much more like cousins or sisters. Only ten years divided them in age, and the teenage Maggie had loved the toddler, Lena, and treated her as a friend. Now Maggie, almost forty, with huge dark eyes and a great mane of black curly hair, looked and acted younger than her niece.

Her life was fuller by far. Maggie's problem had never been making men love her. It had been trying to stop them from loving her unwisely. And sometimes trying to stop herself from loving them in return – equally unwisely.

She had been married twice, widowed the first time, separated the second time, but these were only small milestones in the list of Maggie's love: sensible married men, fathers of large and settled families, wanted to throw up everything and move in with Maggie. She often had great trouble persuading them to do nothing of the sort. It wasn't that she gave them unmentionable sexual favours, she told Lena with her big dark eyes full of honesty, it was just that they saw, however foolishly, a kind of life with her where they wouldn't be hassled and troubled. They saw a strange and unrealistic freedom in living with Maggie, something they didn't have at home. Maggie would never ask them to come to the supermarket and push the trolley; Maggie wasn't a one for wanting the grass cut or the house painted, the car cleaned or the patio built up to impress the neighbours. Maggie would be happy to eat a meal of wild mushrooms and brown bread followed by strawberries. Very far from real life. Maggie would agree with them fervently that she was indeed far from real life and they must see her only now and then. The more she protested, the more they wanted her. Lena said she was outraged at the way Maggie got every man she wanted, and yet she, Lena, who kept all the rules, couldn't get just the one.

Lena did keep the rules as written in the women's magazines. She had shiny, well-cut hair, she was tall and slim, she had been to make-up lessons to make the most of her good complexion, her fair skin, and blue eyes. She dressed well and kept her clothes immaculately. Well, why wouldn't she, Maggie grumbled, if she stayed at home every evening dreaming of lover boy Shay. There was all the time in the world to iron her blouses and sponge her skirts and polish her shoes, handbags, and belts till they shone. But had it done one bit of good in the department where she wanted it to succeed? No. None at all.

Lena's friends and colleagues all said she looked very smart, but their praise and admiration was of no interest to her. Sometimes they wondered why she didn't have a man in her life. She put them off with a laugh. And apart from Maggie, nobody had an inkling.

Maggie's grumbling had always been good-natured. But now it was different. Two things were coming up: Lena's thirtieth birthday, and a business trip with the famous Shay. Yes, he had asked the loyal Lena to London with him. Driving in his car, for a whole week.

Maggie felt it was time to play the heavy aunt for the first time in her life. She sat Lena down and told her to get ready for a serious lecture.

'Oh, not now,' Lena had cried. 'Not now. There's so much to be done, so many preparations. I have to decide what to wear, what to say, what social plans to set up, as well as all his business meetings. Can't the lecture wait till I get home?'

'No, it can't.' Maggie was adamant. 'It's about the trip; this has to be the make-or-break time. When you come back on the ferry and drive off the ramp, Shay must either be involved with you properly or else you will have given up all notion of him.'

Lena's blue eyes filled with tears. 'I don't want anything as definite, as black-and-white, as that. Why does it all have to hinge on this trip?' She looked appalled at having to abandon what was after all the central part of her life.

'Because you are leaving your twenties and for the first time you are leaving the country with this beauty, and you have the rest of your life ahead of you.'

'It's too frightening. I don't want to try and

seduce him or something like that.' Lena was trembling at the thought.

'Well, what's all the fuss about what you're going to wear and how you're going to look? If you don't want him to fancy you, why don't you just go in an old sweater and a pair of jeans?' Maggie was ruthless.

'It's different for you, you can make anyone fancy you.'

'So could you if you bothered. It's got nothing to do with well-cut jackets and applying your blusher properly,' Maggie said.

'How, then?' Lena was eager.

'I'll tell you, but only if you promise me that you will decide one way or another at the end of the week. When you come back off that car ferry, you'll either be involved with him properly as two normal people who love each other, or you will leave that job, and put him out of your mind and heart.'

'It's like doing a deal with the Devil,' Lena complained.

'Much more like a guardian angel,' Maggie said.

They sat for three hours, Maggie with her notebook. At no stage were outfits or perfumes mentioned. There was no strategy about booking one room by mistake instead of two. There was to be no research into romantic restaurants in London where the lights would be low and there might even be violins in the background. No, if Lena was to get her man these kinds of cheap tricks were only Mickey Mouse efforts, according to Maggie. And since almost every man who moved in Dublin seemed to fancy Maggie in some way or other, she was worth listening to.

Maggie seemed shocked that Lena had worked for this man for four years, not to mention thinking that she had loved him for this length of time, and still knew so little about him. Maggie asked a string of questions. Lena knew nothing about his schooldays, whether he had liked it there or not, and how he had got into the business world in the first place. She didn't know who his first employers had been, whether he had found it easy or frightening. She didn't know what television programmes he watched, and when he went to a match if it was because he knew all about the game or because he liked the sociability of it. Lena didn't know how he got on with his two brothers and sisters, how often he went to see his mother. She didn't know if he liked being with his nephews and nieces. If he felt lonely on weekends, as so many people did in Dublin. How he decided what to eat and whether he had a washing machine or went to the launderette.

'What *do* you know about him, for heaven's sake?' Maggie asked with some impatience.

Lena knew all about his current and past girlfriends, and she knew the restaurants he went to, and the nightclubs, and the bills for bouquets of flowers. She knew that and she knew about him at work, where he was tough and not afraid to go into a meeting and fight.

'Well-briefed by you, of course, with reports you have been working on all weekend when you weren't putting more henna in your hair, hoping he'd notice.'

'I love him,' protested Lena.

'No, you don't love him at all. You don't know the first thing about him apart from these empty social things. You might love him when you get to know him, and he might love you. But you might find him empty.'

Lena refused to accept this but agreed meekly to follow Maggie's advice. In the ship's dining room over a meal she would begin, and in the long drive across Britain she would not veer between business talk and gossip-column chat about nightclubs she didn't even know. She would talk to him about himself.

'Suppose he asks me about myself?' Lena asked fearfully.

Maggie didn't much think he would, but if he

did, then she was to tell him the truth. Say she was perfectly happy, she had no wish to change from her life the way it was, assure him it was satisfactory. There was nothing that drove men as mad as that – the thought that women were actually contented the way they were, not scheming and conniving.

'But that's not strictly true. I'm not totally contented the way I am,' Lena complained.

Maggie shrugged. 'You always tell me you are when I try to change you.'

It was unanswerable.

The day before the trip Maggie rang her to wish her luck. 'One thing, Lena, and remember this: he will notice you, he will fancy you. Truthfully, but you may not fancy him.'

'I probably gave you much too shallow a view of him,' Lena whispered in case anyone in the office would hear.

'If that was your view of him after four years of loving him, then I'm sure what you told me was very accurate,' Maggie said.

Lena learned a lot that night at dinner on board ship. She learned that his mother was demanding and never satisfied, that his brothers were discontented and jealous of his success. She heard that Shay's sisters didn't know how to bring up their children properly and gave in to them in everything. She heard that his school was full of sadistic teachers and moronic pupils, that they had ripped him off in his first job and cheated him in his second, and he had seen them coming in his third. He liked to cook but not to wash up; he thought these service apartments he lived in were a bit cramped, but he didn't want to take on the whole palaver of gardens and roofs and drains in a house. He was probably looking for something like a town house.

In the old days, like every day up to this, Lena would have immediately said she would make enquiries about town houses, and go to endless trouble ringing up auctioneers and estate agents. This time she made no offers.

'What about your house or flat, is it what you want?' he asked, almost cursorily, as if he had felt that he might have been talking just a little too much about himself.

'Oh, it's fine. I'm very happy there,' she said. She told him it was a garden flat and had plenty of light as well as nice shrubs and bushes outside big windows. He nodded briskly but seemed to look at her with slightly more interest.

On the long drive to London, they talked about friends. Shay said that he ran with a very lively crowd. No, they weren't around on weekends much, but then, he often came into the office on Saturday afternoons to do a little catching up. Lena knew this only too well. She had to cope with the results of it on Mondays: confused notes, complicated questions. She had begun every week for as long as she could remember by sorting out his thoughts for a secretary to type up. He had got all the credit. Somehow it was disappointing to know he came in only because he was bored on Saturday afternoons. She had thought it was ambition.

He took his washing to his mother, it turned out. She could not believe it, but it was true. He had to go and see the woman once a week anyway, and she had a machine, so it made sense to leave her one load and collect another. And she liked it; what else had she to do?

By the time the signposts saying Central London came up, Lena had opened more doors than she might have wished to in Shay's life.

He suggested they grab something to eat, and she said thank you but no. She had friends to see in London, so unless there was anything they wanted to discuss about work for the conference tomorrow, she would leave him to his own devices.

He seemed quite put out by this. Lena looked

at his handsome face scowling with almost childlike disappointment.

'Don't tell me you're going to do the clubland circuit in London?' he asked, not very kindly.

'Lord no, that's not my world at all. Just dinner with friends.'

It was true. Dinner with two old school friends – one a nun, one a nurse. They laughed and talked over old times. Something was lighter in Lena's laugh; she felt it wasn't an effort.

Next day they worked companionably at the conference, but she excused herself at lunchtime to sneak in a little shopping and said that she had a theatre date in the evening. He was thoroughly bad-tempered on the second day of the conference.

'Are you going to keep running away all the time, or will we see each other at all?' he grumbled.

Big blue eyes wide, she said that honestly she was sorry ... but since they never went out socially at home, she assumed it would be the same here. But, of course, she would be delighted to have dinner with him if he had anywhere in mind.

'I thought you might arrange somewhere,' he said.

'Oh no, I wouldn't dream of it. If you are

asking me to dinner, then you must, of course, choose where.'

It would once have been her wildest dream. Not only was the place expensive and romantic, but as he told her tale after tale of being misunderstood, betrayed, cheated, having got even, he took her hand.

'You're very easy to talk to, Lena, and you look very lovely. I hadn't realised.' She had smiled. It was a smile of someone who had known that this was predictable, not of someone who thought it was perfect.

When the evening ended and he suggested a brandy in his room, she said no. Perhaps she would prefer to have the nightcap in her room, he suggested, probably thinking that this was the height of sensitivity. No nightcap at all, Lena said. She who had planned this night for so long, and all it would lead to.

At one stage she began to wonder if Maggie had set her up. Every single harmless question she had asked had brought such a negative response that she had managed to strip Shay, the man she had loved for years, of any lovable quality. It was as if Maggie had known the answers in advance.

Maggie hadn't suggested that Lena talk to Shay of love.

But that night she did. They were in a restaurant looking out on the river, and he told her that he thought he loved her – yes, strange as it might seem, and having worked together for so long – but he did think he loved her.

She looked at him for a long time.

'Well, say something,' he said petulantly.

'I don't have any words,' she said truthfully.

He reached for her hands, but she pulled them away.

'What are you thinking about?' she asked him.

'How nice it is to love you, how there you were under my nose all the time.'

At least, she thought, at least he is honest in a childish sort of way. It must be nice for him to think he's found a ready-made love under his nose, as he put it.

For years she had seen how suitable she would be for him, how right as a companion, a friend, a wife. How much she would help his career and cope with his weaknesses.

Until tonight she had never seen what it would be like for her. A lifetime of putting up with his moods, building him up when he was low, lying for him, pretending for him. And turning a blind eye when he wanted to run with a lively crowd and do the clubs and go after the blondes.

She smiled at him affectionately. It was the way

she had seen her aunt Maggie smile at a multitude of men.

'What are *you* thinking about?' he asked. He was sulking now; his declaration of love had not only not been returned, it had been smiled at, patted down, soothed away.

'I was thinking about going home, about driving out of the ferry and going home,' she said.

This was a very puzzling response. 'Why, what will you do then?' he was anxious to know.

Lena wondered what would she do. She wouldn't leave her job just because he had said he loved her and she wouldn't love him back. She liked her work, she would stay there and overtake him if necessary. She would not fight with him or explain or apologise – Maggie never did that. She was happy in her garden flat, and now she was free as well. If some man came along – as men came along for Maggie – that she really did like, then she was free to love him.

'What will I do?' she answered him almost dreamily. The world was so full of possibilities now that the question was hard to answer. 'What will I do when I get home? I think I'll telephone my aunt.'

The
Crossing

'It's like a real cruise, isn't it?' Mary said, then wished she hadn't said it. What did she know about a real cruise except reading the brochures?

'I was just thinking that too,' said Lavender, the older woman. 'Not that I was ever on a cruise, mind, but it feels like we should have two weeks, and visit exotic places every day instead of just getting out at Liverpool.' They laughed, united in never having been on a luxury cruise liner, united in admiring the seagulls, and valuing a few minutes away from the family.

'Are you going or coming back?' Lavender asked. She had a kind face and bright, interested eyes. Mary felt you could talk and she really might care what you said.

'Going over. The children have never seen their grandparents. It's a bit of an ordeal really.'

Why had she told that to a stranger? She hadn't told any of her neighbours, nor her best friend

Kath, nor her sister Betty. Why did she blurt it out to a woman with a North of England accent on the B & I boat?

'Oh, I know,' Lavender consoled her. 'It's always an ordeal, isn't it? Maybe we should have to live with our in-laws all the time in the same tribe and never move, or else we should never see them at all. It's the in-between bit that causes all the guilt.'

This was so exactly true that Mary almost jumped to hear her own feelings echoed . . .

'Did you have that kind of . . . well, that kind of thing, you know, with your husband's parents? Wanting to make it all closer and then getting it a bit wrong?'

'Tell me,' Lavender said.

And Mary did. Every bit of it. Slowly, hesitating sometimes, going back over bits in case they hadn't been fair. How she met John when he was on a cycling holiday in Ireland. John was unhappy at college, he found it was hurting him inside his head, the stress and the worry. It wasn't only exams and study. He didn't think he would ever be happy as a teacher. He was too anxious in the classroom practice, he wouldn't be able to keep control, and he could not look forward to a life that would be a constant battle and a series of confrontations in the classroom every day.

'Why don't you do something else with your life, then?' Mary had asked him. 'We only get to come onto the earth once. Wouldn't it be a pity to spend it all doing something that makes you unsettled?'

It was like a revelation to John. There and then he decided to abandon the idea of being a teacher. He wrote to the college, he wrote to his parents and to his girlfriend in London. He said he had been feeling a bit lost; now he was going to find himself in Ireland. He was going to work on a farm while he was finding out what to do with the rest of his life.

Nobody was pleased – not the college, which worried about his grant, not his girlfriend in London, who worried for four weeks and then sent a card telling him it couldn't matter less whether he found himself or didn't, since she had found somebody more normal. And his parents worried most of all. He was an only child; they had their hopes set on his being a teacher, and now he was a farmhand in Ireland, for heaven's sake. They were very disapproving. They were not people who wrote letters much or made cross-Channel phone calls. But they disapproved none-theless. Heavily.

And when John and Mary got engaged, they

assumed that it was a shotgun marriage, which it wasn't, and that it would be in a Roman Catholic church full of images of saints and the Virgin, which it was. And they said they couldn't come to the wedding.

Mary sent pictures of the children, Jacinta, now eight, and John Paul, who was born the day the Pope came to Ireland and was seven. Looking back on it, Mary wondered if she should have chosen different names for the children. But surely that wasn't important. John's parents could hardly disapprove of a child's name as being from a different tribe. And Mary had been careful to send pictures of the children at Christmas rather than the First Communion snapshot that she felt the instinct to send each time.

Lavender was full of praise. Mary had done more than her share. And where was the problem?

It wasn't exactly a problem; there was no out-and-out war, just a distance in every sense of the word. And a dread of meeting these people, who wouldn't come to Ireland, who had never shown any greater interest than a dutiful card at Christmas. Mary was not looking forward to hearing what a brilliant career had been cut short when John had met her in Ireland ten long years ago.

She didn't want to make excuses for the life

they led in a small country town where John worked happily on a farm and Mary was a dressmaker.

And they were going now because John's father was unemployed, had been for a year, and the word had trickled back from a woman neighbour that John's dad was taking it hard. Mary had suggested they visit Ireland and as usual it had been turned down, so, gritting her teeth, she had then suggested that they take the children to visit their grandparents, and this had been agreed to. Ungraciously, of course. 'You'll have to take us as you find us.' But still agreed.

It was a two-week visit. Too long, Mary thought, but it was a huge undertaking, four of them to go to London; it would be a great waste to go for less time.

Lavender said that Mary was a positive gem among women. She said she was sure that the parents-in-law would be so pleased that in a few days they would all wonder whether the distance could possibly have been in their imaginations.

'Would you like a little advice?' she asked, almost shyly.

'Oh, I'd love anything you could tell me, you being English and a bit older, not that you'd be as old as them or anything, but you know . . .'

Lavender leaned her back against the rail,

squinted into the sun, and talked not directly to Mary but as if she was speaking to herself. She looked very much like a woman who should be on a luxury cruise liner waiting for an executive husband to come back from a game of deck tennis with the captain.

'I wouldn't apologise or explain too much. Maybe let them think they were part of your lives, even though they weren't. The children should know a bit about them, like their birthdays and their names, and where they grew up themselves. And perhaps you might ask, all of you, about your husband as a little boy, you know, when he was seven or eight, what he read and what toys he played with. They probably have them still. And it could be assumed rather than said that one day, soon, but not a fixed day, the grandparents would come to Ireland.'

Lavender seemed apologetic. She felt she had talked too much, had seemed to be laying down the law.

'I wish you wouldn't say you were laying down the law. I'm just overjoyed to get some ideas. That's a very good thought, you know. I don't know their birthdays and the children don't know anything at all about them.'

'There'll be plenty of time on the train to London.'

'You have children yourself?' Mary was diffi-dent.

'One, a daughter.' There seemed to be a full stop.

'That's nice,' Mary said. 'Or isn't it?'

'Not much at the moment, it isn't.'

They had started to walk around the deck. People sat in chairs lathering themselves with Nivea. Duty-free bags were being tucked under the sunbathers, children ran round excited, passengers had all started to talk to each other in the relaxed way of holidaymakers. There might be long drives, or train journeys, or even family ordeals ahead, but on the ship they were suspended. It was time out of time. People spoke, as they often had no time to speak when on land.

'I'm sorry,' Mary said to Lavender. 'You're so easy, you should have a good time with a daughter.'

'I did until she was fourteen. Then she met this lad. Oh, I think a hundred times a day how different life would have been if she hadn't met him.

'She never opened a schoolbook from that day to this. We were before the courts for her every month of the year. If it wasn't truancy it was shoplifting, then it was glue sniffing, then it was a stolen car.'

It had certainly not been the life they had hoped for their Emma.

'And did she get over the lad?' Mary sighed, thinking that all this might easily lie ahead for her with Jacinta in a troubled world.

'No, she'll never get over him. She's eighteen now and she misses him so much that she just sits and cries. She's sitting down in the restaurant now with her dad, crying. I couldn't take it any more; she cried all through this holiday in Ireland we took specially to give her a treat. I couldn't see it for one second more. That's why I came up on deck.'

'I'm glad you did,' Mary said.

'So am I,' said Lavender. 'But you can see I'm not one to be handing out advice. You see how poor my own situation is. I can't even sit and talk to my own daughter.'

'Wasn't it nice of you to bring her to Ireland on a holiday, though?' Mary said admiringly. 'A lot of mothers would not have done, with a girl who got into all that sort of trouble. She's lucky.'

'She doesn't think so, she thinks she's cursed with middle-aged, old-fashioned parents. She'd like to be left alone with that yobbo.'

'Still, she came with you. She's eighteen, grown up, she needn't have come unless she wanted to.'

'True.' Lavender's face was sad.

'What would be the best that could happen? The very best?'

Lavender was thoughtful. 'I used to think if he disappeared off the face of the earth that would be the best. But in their mad white-faced Mohican-hair way with chains dangling and safety pins all over their ears . . . they love each other. So I suppose the best that could happen is for them to love each other without breaking the law and for him to be a bit civil to us. We are part of Emma's life too; for years we held her by the hand and dreamed of what she would do. If he took that into consideration a bit . . .'

'That's why you told me to ask John's parents about the toys, wasn't it?' Mary said.

'Love, it's a different world to yours. You're a lovely warm woman trying to build bridges; he's just a yobbo with a face like the devil trying to break up everything he comes across.'

'They must have thought that about me too,' Mary said. 'I only realise it now. I was so alien and so determined. All the time I was annoyed they couldn't be a bit warmer. But I never thought what it was like to *be* them, having held John's hand for years and listened to his baby talk and watched him starting out to school.'

They walked companionably on their tour. They would never meet again, nor write to each other. Mary would never know if the yobbo reformed, or if Emma dried her tears over him. She wouldn't even know what Emma looked like, or her father, who was sitting patiently handing her more and more paper table napkins to wipe the sad, pale, punky face.

And Lavender would never know if the visit went well, and if John's parents took out his old train for John Paul to play with and if Mary became friendly with his mum and helped in the kitchen. She would never hear if the invitation to Ireland, which would be just assumed rather than stated, would in fact be taken up.

Their lives would never cross again.

But while they did cross on a sunny day on a blue sea they talked as all shipboard passengers do in a way that would sound to the seagulls above that these people were friends for life.

And Lavender told Mary that all her sisters had been called after flowers and Mary told Lavender that in her class at school there were eleven girls called Mary and it had been very confusing.

They never knew that their husbands were having a drink at the bar.

Emma's tears had dried, John Paul and Jacinta had found a new friend, and it happened that Lavender's John and Mary's John were standing having a pint. They talked about golf, they talked about the shambles the World Cup had been, and they talked about prices and politics and trade unions.

And Lavender's John and Mary's John had a second pint and that was it. They were getting near Liverpool now, and so they found their families and their luggage, and one family went north and one went south.

Gerald and Rose

They met by chance at the little newspaper shop in the hotel. The tiny blonde behind the counter with the impossibly long eyelashes was sorting out newspapers from what seemed like every nation on earth.

'Do you have any Irish papers?'

Gerald and Rose spoke almost in unison, then they turned to each other and laughed.

'Isn't it ridiculous?' said Rose. 'I feel lost unless I know what's going on at home.'

'No wonder we don't assimilate as well as other races,' Gerald said, full of shame at having been caught looking for a link with home.

The blonde said they didn't sell any.

'You've got things from outlandish places here,' Rose complained. Gerald didn't want to be a paddy seen demanding his rights.

'I imagine we'll have to survive,' he said loftily.

The tiny blonde, whose bosom was even more

improbable than her eyelashes, dimpled up at him and wiggled around as she directed him to a news-stand that did deal in such things. She made it sound racy as if he had been asking for some very specialised pornography. She ignored Rose completely.

They walked companionably to the news-stand. Back in Dublin, it turned out, they lived not far from each other at all.

He saw a tall handsome woman of about thirty-five, expensively dressed, possibly difficult, the kind of wife that made a scene at parties, he felt, attractive but too independent. Too free a spirit for his liking. She saw a businessman, forty maybe, cautious, ungiving, for example he would not part with his name unless it was beaten out of him. She had already made two elegant efforts and failed.

'How are you going to spend the day?' she asked, knowing that he wouldn't ask her.

'Read the paper, now that I've got it, and then . . . well, there *was* a meeting but it was cancelled so I have a little . . . er . . . a little unexpected free time.'

Gerald spoke cautiously as if he were stepping dangerously like Indiana Jones into the Temple of Doom rather than just admitting in broad daylight to a harmless and respectable fellow

Dubliner that he had some time on his hands. His face showed that he greatly regretted having been so frank and open. It was as if he knew it would all end badly. Rose nodded as she absorbed this reckless throwing around of information, and her great mane of golden-brown hair with its careful highlights bobbed at him tigerishly.

'What a coincidence!' she said. 'I have a little unexpected free time too. I was going to the Wimbledon Tennis Museum, but the silly place isn't open on a Monday so I'm at rather a loose end too.'

She looked helpless and beguiling and slightly roguish. Gerald knew it was up to him to say something, anything. He was never a man to speak before he had decided what he was going to say, which was why he felt so ill at ease at having blurted out that his meeting was cancelled. It left him at a disadvantage.

'Well, heavens,' he said inadequately.

'Yes, heavenly, isn't it?' Rose deliberately mis-understood him. 'Imagine a couple of hours away from everything, there's nothing we couldn't do.' She registered the alarm in his face and decided to temper it. 'That is, until lunchtime. I'll have to fly off and leave you then.'

She saw the relief start to flood into his face and after it a tiny touch of bravado. Gerald was thinking, slowly and creakily. A couple of hours. Until lunchtime, so no question of getting tied up for a boozy session ending in real ambiguity. After two Armagnacs at 3 p.m. – no, no, nothing like that. He straightened his tie and put on a slightly jaunty look.

'Let's have a coffee and see what we could do,' he suggested. And so Rose and Gerald went into a place with lovely fresh coffee and Danish pastries.

They discovered that they both loved the flavour of cinnamon, they adored watching tennis on television but neither was very good on the court, they thought Japanese food was very bland, they found most things much cheaper in London than at home, but were appalled at the price of property.

In the last year they had each been to London three times, and they had seen the same musicals. Three of them. In fact, it turned out that they had travelled over from Dublin on the same plane the previous day. At that point they risked introducing themselves but not fully.

'I'm Rose,' she said, and shook hands formally across the table.

'Oh ... well ... how do you do ... I'm Gerald,' he admitted grudgingly and shook her hand firmly.

The young Italian waitress looked at them and

shook her head. She had thought they were long married. Life was very odd in London.

'So ... um ... Rose,' he said. 'We'd better make plans for this morning off. What were you thinking of?'

'We could go to the Old Bailey,' she said eagerly. 'We might catch a murder trial and see the murderer being dragged off screaming and saying he didn't do it.'

'Oh,' said Gerald. 'Yes, I suppose they do let people in.'

'What do *you* suggest?' she asked.

'We could go to the National Portrait Gallery,' he offered. 'You know – start on the top floor and sort of work our way down, it's chronological, you see.'

'Is it?' she said dully. 'Yes, yes, we could do that, of course.'

The magic was beginning to go out of the morning. The sun wasn't as bright, the second Danish pastry, the one they had agreed to halve, wasn't as crisp or as cinnamon-flavoured as the first. But Rose and Gerald were determined to rescue things.

'What would you *really* like?' they both said at exactly the same time, as they had asked for their Irish newspapers at the same moment. Then they burst out laughing and a lot of the magic came back.

'I didn't really want to go to the Old Bailey. We'd have to queue for hours, and it wouldn't be like at home, we wouldn't know anyone.'

'No, and I didn't really want to go to the Portrait Gallery. It's just that I've been to London so often and always meant to and never got round to it.'

They were conspirators now. They were going to do as they liked till lunchtime.

'Let's count to three and then each say what he wants, we might come up with the same thing,' Rose said.

Her eyes were amazing. He had thought they were brown but in fact there were spots of gold in them, if you could have gold eyes. He smiled at her across the table of cakes and coffee cups.

Rose thought he wasn't bad at all when he smiled. Really, he was quite dishy. There was a little-boy look that didn't go at all with his briefcase and his civil servant sort of edginess.

They linked little fingers with each other as children do and then they counted one-two-three and shouted out, '*Shopping!*'

Again their laughter filled the café and again the young Italian wondered were they mad or drugged and hastened to give them their bill.

Exclaiming over the chance that two people with such similar tastes and such fortuitous free time could be thrown together like this, they walked companionably in the morning sunshine towards Oxford Street. Anyone who saw them would have thought, as the Italian girl had thought, that they were a couple who had left two young children at home with the au pair and were having a short break in London.

Rose wondered about Mrs Gerald and decided that, whatever she was like, she was certainly not the kind of woman who would pick a man up at 9 a.m. and stride purposefully off to the shops with him.

Gerald wondered about Mr Rose and thought that he might well be a man who was too busy with his work or, indeed, dark suspicion, too busy with a little dalliance of his own to notice that his tall, attractive wife was bored and that it was unwise to allow a bored beautiful woman to prowl in London's morning sun.

But neither of them mentioned the other's spouse. To mention Mrs Gerald or Mr Rose was to bring some reality into this unreal time.

They decided to take it in strict rotation. First a belt for Gerald because they would be passing some men's shops, then a clock radio for Rose, after that they would look for casual pull-on shoes in soft leather for Gerald who had always worn tie-up shoes and this was to be his first venture out of them. They would then find a handbag that was big enough to carry guidebooks and sunglasses and a camera but didn't look like a rucksack. That was what Rose had said she needed.

The time just flashed by. Rose said that she felt somebody must have been moving the hands of the clock like a speeded-up film. Gerald said that he had never enjoyed shopping before. Rose had steered him away from a gold-buckled belt on the grounds that he had a silver watch strap. Gerald had advised her against a clock radio that was so small it would need tweezers to set the various functions.

He was going to suggest she get a little earphone so that she could listen to it when Mr Rose was asleep and she didn't want to wake him. But he decided against anything that might bring up the matter of bed. Or, indeed, of Mr Rose.

When it came to the shoe shop, Rose sat and discussed the pull-ons with interest. She was most helpful about the little tassels and about beating away all the persuasive attempts to get him to buy shoe trees and special waterproof wax to clean them with. She was about to say that Mrs Gerald probably had a press full of shoe-cleaning waxes herself. But she didn't. She didn't want to think of Mrs Gerald somehow.

Gerald talked her into a smaller bag. She honestly didn't need to carry guidebooks and cameras everywhere, now did she? He got halfway through a sentence that was going to be about married couples sharing the responsibility of carrying the guidebooks but he didn't want to appear critical of Mr Rose or even to acknowledge him.

Then it was lunchtime and they stood regretfully. Gerald had no appointment for lunch but Rose had said she did. She had said ages ago that she would have to fly at lunchtime. What a pity because they both liked French food and he knew of a place not too far and his afternoon meeting wasn't until four o'clock.

Rose thought she saw him look a little longingly but she remembered that she had only managed to ensnare him for that happy morning by assuring him she wouldn't hang around and be a nuisance. She would have loved to sit and sip cold French wine and eat something very light with a humdinger of a sauce.

Gerald shook her hand formally and, as he thanked her for all her help, he thought that Mr Rose should be taken out and shot.

Rose said that she hadn't enjoyed herself so much for years and thought viciously that it was always the same – Mrs Gerald was probably a small dull mouse who thought foreign food gave her an upset tummy and would tell him that his new shoes were a bit sissy.

They turned and waved exactly at the same time. And they both laughed again and their smiles were real and warm. They had a great deal of telepathy, Rose and Gerald. But not enough for Rose to know that Gerald, who had been too busy to find a wife until he had become secure in his career, had decided that now he was going to look around, seriously. Or that Rose, who had been the other woman for so long, had recently told her married man that she was going to wait no longer, and he had found a younger and more patient lady friend.

They stood on a warm summer day in this city with its red buses, full of thousands of people they didn't know, and waved goodbye, good-naturedly and wistfully, to what they each thought would have been a handful of trouble.

And as the traffic lights changed for them to cross in their different directions, they turned one last time and waved again.

Part of
it All

He had given up bread in May. Brian, who used to eat it in doorsteps. And in June he had said that he'd have a Campari and soda rather than a pint. He had little pellets of sweetener to dissolve in his coffee, and she had been very alarmed the first time she heard the groans from the bathroom but they were only exercises. He had rung up a shop to know how much a folding bike would cost, but his brother told Brian that these bikes were useless in the city because you got more dirt and dust down your lungs than if you were down a mine and you arrived everywhere in a muck sweat. Brian had forgotten about the bike, but he hadn't forgotten about his stomach, he was flattening it for the holiday.

'But who will we know there, who'll be looking at your stomach?' Maura had cried. It wasn't as if they were going to run into a soul who would say approvingly that they'd been looking smart on the Riviera. Now if it had been for Kinsale, where they'd have known everybody, or for their son Sean's wedding, where half the country were looking at them, that she could have understood. But the South of France? It was impossible to know what he was at.

Still, it was all to the good. Men of his age were always getting what were called little shocks. Look at Harry. Not a real heart attack, naturally. But a fright. A spell in intensive care, a change in lifestyle. Look at her own brother, not able to go upstairs, moved to that desperate bungalow miles from anywhere. Look at the death notices you read all the time, young men, men in their fifties who didn't take care of themselves. She should be delighted. She patted her own stomach, it was hard and small as it had always been. Her friends had always resented it. But it was worry, of course. She burned it off in worrying. You couldn't tell that to people nowadays. Worry was more unacceptable than bad breath. Everyone was meant to be very relaxed.

She had been surprised that Brian said they should have a holiday. Surprised and delighted. He had come home from work with brochures one day and spent a couple of hours adding and subtracting figures on a sheet of paper.

'Ahem, I have a proposition to make,' he said,

his face as proud as a child who has a bunch of flowers behind his back as a surprise.

'What's that?' Maura had looked up from her magazine. Upside down she had read the names of French resorts and had seen the rings he had put around package deals to Nice. She thought that there must be a conference and he was going to see if he could wangle her out there for the weekend. She had said nothing so as not to spoil it.

'You are going to be taken for a fortnight to the French Riviera,' he had said, bursting with pride at the words. 'Yes, two weeks in the South of France, we'll hire a car. We'll go to St Tropez and let Brigitte Bardot have a look at us. We'll go to Monte and have a flutter with the Rainiers down in the casino. Well, what do you think of that?'

'Brian, *how* can we afford it?' She wished she hadn't said that. His face clouded a little.

'Of course we can afford it, aren't I twenty-five years in the firm next month, aren't I fifty-four years of age? Haven't we everything we want? Why do you think we couldn't afford it?'

'I don't know ... It sounds so ... well, extravagant ... you know ... not like Majorca where everyone else goes.'

'I want the best. I want to see it once. I want to take you to the best place,' he said.

She had stood up and gone over to hug him, she had sat on the arm of his chair while he pointed out hotels, and pictures of cafés. They would drive to Cannes, and to Menton, and to this place and that . . . They would have lunches in shaded restaurants like that . . . They would see a bit of life . . .

'Yes, imagine us sitting there watching the world walk by,' Maura said enthusiastically.

'And better still, imagine the world watching Brian and Maura O'Neill walk by,' Brian had said.

She had laughed. He had said, 'Why not, aren't we as good as any of them?'

They talked long into the night, and when Maura went out to the kitchen to make the flask of tea that they took to bed every night in case one of them woke up with a dry throat, she looked back and saw him smiling into the brochures still.

'Aren't you marvellous to think up something like that, aren't you really great?' she called in affectionately.

'Oh, there's still life in me,' Brian said happily.

Their friends were pleased for them, and surprised.

'What will you do all day?' Frances had asked her. 'It won't be like going to Spain like we did before poor Harry . . . It was organised there, you came down to the swimming pool, and then in to lunch and then back to the swimming pool. But you'll be moving on from place to place.'

'Brian's not going to have hotels booked, he says what they do down there is to drive on and when they see somewhere they like they settle,' Maura said doubtfully. It sounded very much what jet-set people did.

Even young Sean's in-laws were impressed. Maura had felt very put down several times by Orla's people who managed to be lofty while pretending to be very friendly, but they were definitely impressed about the holiday.

'We never thought of you as Riviera people,' said Orla's mother.

'Well, well, well, you'll be buying your own yacht next,' said Orla's father.

Maura wondered to herself once or twice during the summer, were they mad to be going to such a place. She kept coming across articles in magazines describing the parties and the jewels, the film festivals and famous people. What were she and Brian thinking of, hiring a car, driving on the wrong side of the road and spending a fortune in a fortnight? But she never said a word because the very mention of the place and the holiday brought more life to Brian's face than she had seen for years.

'Will you be getting your hair changed, you know, more like they wear it out there?' he had asked once. She thought it was fine up in a curly swoop on top of her head, and good for the heat too. But he had seemed to hesitate.

'They seem to wear it loose down there,' he had mumbled.

Loose? A middle-aged woman with a head of grey hair down her back? Still, something in the way he said it made her hold her laughter back.

She talked to Mrs Moore, the hairdresser, who still saw people in cubicles for nice confessional chats rather than in all that open-plan noise and frenzy. Mrs Moore said they could try a bit of colour in it. Highlights rather than full tint and that she could wear it tied back with a ribbon if that was what Mr O'Neill liked. Mrs Moore implied that all men were missing their marbles but that it was easier for a quiet life to go along with what they wanted.

Maura had thought that the outfit she had bought for Sean and Orla's wedding would be the mainstay of her holiday. She took it out of its plastic covers and admired it. Brian said that he didn't think she understood about the Riviera, it was very casual there, people wore jeans and T-shirts.

'No, it's not, it's smart, it's very smart,' cried Maura, her eyes stinging with the upset of it all.

'It's smart casual, that's what it is. The people who go down there go to get away from it all, they wear bare feet, and simple clothes, that's the beauty of it,' said Brian.

'Well, let them wear their bare feet and their raggedy jeans, aren't we only going to be looking at them?' she said, a lot of the joy going out of the expensive silk coat and dress she thought she would be wearing in French society.

'There's no point at all in going out there and deliberately dressing ourselves up like sore thumbs, is there?' Brian had asked.

For a man who had never taken a blind bit of notice of what he wore or anyone wore, this was a new departure. Maura watched with alarm the buying of jeans and four white T-shirts, she watched the packing of three pairs of espadrilles, Brian had no intention of taking his sandals. Irish sandals in the South of France, he had roared with laughter.

Maura had packed her own summer clothes, she had taken the sleeves out of two dresses, she had got lots of Nivea crème in case her skin dried up, and conditioner for her hair in case the burning sun did unspeakable things to the new blonde bits in it. She felt she was prepared.

When they arrived, of course, it was beautiful. With all the goodbyes and the instructions about watering the garden and feeding the cat, and the envy of friends and the polishing up of the few French phrases, Maura had not had time to think what it would actually be like. She hoped in her heart secretly that Brian would not be disappointed. She had felt very over-protective about him, like when Sean was a five-year-old and she had seen him off with his new satchel to school.

She hadn't expected all the flowers and palm trees and the lovely blue sea and the big white buildings. She clasped her hands together and exclaimed with pleasure at it all. Brian was delighted, he patted her knee happily as he drove confidently on the wrong side of the road and coped with all the French drivers hooting their horns aggressively.

'Didn't we do the right thing?' he said.

'Brian, imagine us here looking at all this!' she cried happily.

'Part of all this,' Brian said, equally sunnily.

It hadn't been a bad summer at home so they had got a bit of a basis for their suntan. They weren't going to be milk white as they might have been in another year. They had a glass of duty-free whiskey in their bedroom. Brian had booked only the first night in Nice and the hotel was a big one with a balcony looking out on the Mediterranean. Together they stood and drank to each other's health as the sunlight dappled the bodies that lay shinily on the beach on wooden-slatted beds covered with rubber mattresses.

'This is the life ... Now we'll have another snifter and get out to join the action,' said Brian. He had his red open-necked shirt over his jeans, his red espadrilles, and a medallion, which Maura had never seen before.

'It's my Child of Mary medal!' she screamed in amazement.

'Is that what it is?' He looked shamefaced. 'I found it at home, I didn't know what it was, I thought it might look good on me.'

'At least it might save us from being drowned or getting sunstroke,' she said, and they laughed.

'Aren't you going to get changed?' he asked.

'Aren't I grand in this dress, it's nice and cool?' she said.

You paid to go on the beach, or rather you paid for a slatted bed and a parasol. Maura had heard that the women didn't wear tops to their bikinis in this part of the world, but she thought it would be on special beaches, not here, not within a few feet of the main road. Oh well. And didn't they look casual and carefree, these young girls with their beautiful figures, not an ounce of self-consciousness. They lay there almost unaware that they were naked or nearly naked. Nobody giggled, nobody whistled. Their boyfriends or husbands or fathers also seemed quite undisturbed by it. Wasn't it a great way of going on really, Maura thought to herself. No sense of shame and guilt, none of all this covering yourself up and looking furtive like when she had been a youngster.

Brian looked about him happily.

'Isn't this the life?' he said and he tucked up the edges of his swimming trunks a bit to make them look shorter and more like the indecent-looking briefs that all the Frenchmen wore, briefs that seemed to be only a bit of string, to Maura's averted eyes.

She didn't feel out of it, she didn't feel old. She didn't feel plain and she didn't feel provincial. She was happy to wander arm in arm with him that evening through the squares where the young and the pretty sat, where the older and more suave cruised slowly by in big, purring cars, where laughter tinkled through the hot evening and people discussed food with an intensity unknown at home.

They took out the map and planned the next

day's journey. They would go to St Tropez . . . or would they go to Juan les Pins? Such a richness of choice and thirteen whole days to do what they liked. Thirteen days before Brian went back to work on the 8.50 bus every morning and Maura went back to the shopping and cleaning and getting the garden ready for winter.

That night he said that her blue panties were just like a bikini bottom and she could wear those next time on the beach. He himself was going to buy a proper 'slip', he thought was the French word. His own were ridiculous like those old-fashioned ones that men used to wear with vests. She said firmly that she was not having her bosoms burned to a crisp. They were nice old bosoms, she said, she was fond of them. She had to keep light-hearted because she was so shocked that he expected her to lie naked on a beach at her age.

He said she needn't turn her bosoms up at the sun the whole time, she could lie on her front if she was afraid she was getting too burned.

'Why do we have to do everything they do here? We only came to watch,' she said.

'We didn't come to watch, we came to be a part of it,' Brian said, putting his arm around her. At home they slept in separate beds, but the French apparently hadn't heard of such a thing. 'If we wanted to watch it, we could have gone to the pictures and seen a film about it, couldn't we?'

He wore the jeans and the T-shirts, and her Child of Mary medal, and she wore the blue panties three times and lay uncomfortably in the sun with her face down, and wondered what the nun who had placed the ribbon and medal around her neck nearly forty years ago would have thought to see it ending up like this. Brian bought the grotesque-looking slip, which cost a ridiculous amount of money for the cheapest one in the shop. He said it felt wonderfully free, he was surprised people at home hadn't thought of them years ago. Maura was afraid to look at him when they went into the sea or when he sat up suddenly because she kept thinking he had fallen out of it.

She would have been quite happy to watch it all, as if it had been one great pageant put on for their benefit, which in a way it was. She liked looking at the old women, the brave old ones in turbans and high-arched eyebrows and long sari-type skirts, but still showing plenty of gnarled brown skin. She liked looking at the greying playboys and their antics with the young girls, and she loved the poutings and the head shakings of the girls themselves. It was better than watching a musical comedy.

At first she was embarrassed when Brian wanted to join in the parade from café to café, wanted to sit on the waterfront and throw the ball back if some little French dollies let their beach ball stray in his direction. Maura had thought he looked a little ridiculous, stomach still visible despite the noble efforts of the summer. It must be obvious to everyone that they were two middle-aged Dubliners who had no right to be taking part in the lovely silly games that people played on the Riviera.

But Brian didn't think like that. No, he was never happier than when someone asked him in French for a light, or if a pretty French girl tried to sell him a bunch of roses for Madame, or if somebody asked him had he a boat. His big broad face was full of smiles. She couldn't understand it, they had nobody to impress. Orla's mother and father would never hear that someone mistook Brian for a person who owned a yacht, nobody she knew would ever know that the hotelier could not believe they had a married son. These were just little private perks, so why was Brian feeling so much in the swim of everything, and acting out the fantasy as if his whole life depended on it?

That was it. He had actually stepped onto the set. Maura suddenly understood. It was as if he had thought all this was real life and he felt you had to play according to the rules. It was very sad and silly, and in a million years she could never tell Brian that this was what he was doing, but in the end what did it matter? As long as it only lasted for the holidays, as long as they went back to normal afterwards, then why not? And if it made him happy, well, she'd play along with him.

'Will I get a pair of jeans like yours, just for the holiday, the rest of it?' she asked one day.

He was delighted. In the shop he had stood just like a Frenchman while she had tried on several pairs and then decided she looked best in pink denim Bermudas. She had let her hair fall loose, she caught sight of herself in a mirror and decided that if she were at home, a Garda car would pick her up and bring her to St Brendan's. She looked wild and out of place. The shop assistant was pert and pleasant, she seemed to see nothing tragic and insane in Maura's appearance.

Maura examined her hair.

'*Avez-vous quelque chose?*' she asked timidly and pointed to her head. Brian beamed at her, there she was speaking the language, playing the part.

The little girl brought out a sun visor, the kind of thing people wore watching tennis matches. It was pink, like the shorts. She suggested pink shoes too, not the sensible sandals of three summers ago, which had never had a proper airing until this holiday.

They walked out of the shop and along the promenade. Never in her life had Maura felt so foolish. They looked ridiculous, the two of them . . . They were ridiculous. What did they think they were *doing* here? This holiday had cost so much that it meant that they would hardly be able to go to Kinsale again in their lives. They would never see the new curtains in the sitting room and a kitchen like Orla's mother's kitchen would for ever be a dream. People must be laughing at them, young people must look up from their tall glasses of cold white wine and cassis, and smile indulgently at this old couple dressed like hippies, wandering pathetically down the esplanades of a foreign land.

She raised her eyes nervously under the sunshade, but nobody seemed to be looking their way. Brian's arm tightened on hers.

'Isn't it grand?' he said.

She forced herself to smile. Why do all this unless some value was gained, unless one of them at least got something from it?

'Grand,' she said. 'Would you ever have thought it?'

'I wanted you to have this,' he said, looking at

her lovingly. 'You've never had enough fun in your life, Maura, not enough style and splash. I was determined that before we got old, we'd show ourselves that we could be as much part of anything as anyone else.'

And proudly he led her to a restaurant, where they were grilling fish out in the open air, and where lithe young girls in bikinis draped themselves over the railings at the entrance, but moved aside pleasantly as Maura and Brian O'Neill came up the steps.

The Women
in Hats

It was very exciting watching people come on board, said the purser. After a few journeys you could size them up pretty well. That woman would fight with her husband two days out, he would spend all his time with the bar people, she would find a younger man and a little shipboard romance. That woman over there, she would keep her husband by her side with a rod of iron; she was one of these so-called 'invalids' who had nothing wrong with them, except a very serious case of self-importance.

The purser was a beautiful dark-eyed gay Canadian who missed his boyfriend terribly, and rang him from every port and regarded his job as so much torture necessary in order to save enough money for a house on the Great Lakes.

He liked talking to Helen; she was forty and friendly and didn't show any dangerous tendencies of jumping at him some night and assuring him of her powers of being able to make the earth move for him. She played gin rummy with him, told him funny tales about the people at her table, and seemed very interested in his tales of Garry. Helen used to advise him not to call Garry so much. 'Telephone calls are very unsatisfactory and expensive,' she had said. Paul the nice agreeable purser was beginning to think she was right. He would miss her when she got off at Singapore. He'd have to find a new friend.

Leaning over the side at Piraeus, Paul saw a good-looking man squinting up into the sunshine. A pang of infidelity to Garry swept over Paul, but it was gone as soon as it arrived. Anyway the handsome man didn't look very available. A very beautiful woman with sunglasses in her hair rather than on her face with a golden suntan, and a blue flowing dress exactly the same colour as her eyes, seemed to have her hand possessively on his arm.

'What do you make of that pair?' he asked Helen.

'Honeymooners?' wondered Helen.

'No, they don't have that absorbed look,' Paul said. 'They seem to be talking about something, not just "Imagine, this is us getting on a ship". That's the way honeymooners go on.'

The tanned girl had a huge blue and white hat

tied by a ribbon around her neck. For no reason she annoyed Paul. People should put sunglasses on eyes, and hats on heads. What was she looking at anyway? He followed her gaze.

At the top of the gangway was the fattest woman Paul had ever seen. She wore a huge pink and white hat, on her head, he was relieved to notice. She had a flowing pink and white dress that could easily have been a tent for several people. She carried an enormous beach bag, white but with a name embroidered on it in pink. 'Bonnie', it said.

Paul couldn't see her face, but he got the feeling she was young. Immediately Paul felt protective towards her. Even if it wasn't his job, he would look after her. In fact, she might become his friend when Helen left.

'Let's ask the pink elephant lady to have a drink with us,' he said to Helen. 'I think she's on her own and she'd appreciate it.'

'No,' said Helen. 'She's not on her own, she's with the non-honeymoon couple – I saw them all get out of the same taxi. But I'm all for a drink with anyone any time.'

Paul looked at Helen with affection. She had talked him out of phoning Garry because of the time difference, the known unreliability of Greek phones, and all the unnecessary angst he would cause himself if there was no reply. Helen must have been through all this love business too, but unlike most women, she didn't seem to want to discuss it or recall it way into the night. Paul called her a purser's joy, someone who didn't complain and who helped other people to enjoy themselves; he said she should really be getting a fee, not paying a fare.

Paul thought Helen must be wrong about big Bonnie. She couldn't be with the golden couple; she wasn't old enough to be the mother, she wasn't young enough to be their child. But when he went to see how they were all settling in, he found the threesome was as Helen had said.

The good-looking boy sat in the middle and on either side of him huge hats bobbed, one blue over the slim tanned girl, one pink over the enormous smiling Bonnie.

'I'm Paul Preston, the purser . . . you are very welcome on board.' Bonnie looked up with a big welcoming smile and offered him a huge hand to shake.

'How nice and alliterative,' she said. 'I'm Bonnie and this is Charlie and this is Charlotte . . .' She waved delightedly at the golden couple. Paul still couldn't figure out what relation they were to her.

'That's pretty nice and alliterative too,' he said about their names.

'I'm always saying that about them,' said Bonnie. 'It's the most amazing coincidence, my two best friends in the world both called after some no-good Stuart king.'

Paul thought it was more of a coincidence that two people called Charlie and Charlotte should have met and married each other than to have turned out to be friends of Bonnie's, but he decided not to follow that line of chat.

They discovered he was from Ottawa originally, would like to live on the Lakes, had been a ship's purser for four years and was aged twenty-nine. He discovered they were from Australia originally, but had lived so long in Europe now they had almost forgotten the Outback. Bonnie was twenty-nine and Charlie and Charlotte were twenty-seven each. Another coincidence. They had been living in Greece for the summer, all three of them, and now they were going to Hong Kong on this ship to see if they could set up a little import-export company, and then they were all going to take a cheap flight back to Australia where they would stay until Christmas. None of them was very enthusiastic about going back home. Bonnie said her parents were dead and she had no ties. Charlie said his father thought people who left Australia were traitors. Charlotte said that her mother wanted her to marry a man who had a big share in a sheep station. They all seemed so easy and relaxed in each other's company that it looked as if they had been friends for years.

Had they been in business long together, he wondered? No, they had only met that spring. All of them had been working in London. Bonnie had advertised for fellow Australians to set up a venture, and that was how they had met.

'And that's how you got together?' said Paul, smiling at the two golden heads of Charlie and Charlotte as they sat together near Bonnie's knees on the deck. They looked like an advertisement for something, so healthy and happy did they seem.

'Yeah, that's how we all met,' said Charlie, sounding puzzled.

As the days went on Paul saw no way of making Bonnie into a special friend, since she was never alone. If Charlie and Charlotte, or one of them, weren't with her, she was surrounded by others. She had offered to embroider people's names on their towels or bags, and was doing a roaring trade. Paul was sure that some by-law said she couldn't charge fees, but he never looked it up.

In Ceylon he bought a beautiful shirt for Garry. Helen had said it was much wiser than spending money on a telephone call, everyone knew how unreliable the Sinhalese telephone service was.

He was admiring the shirt lovingly when a big shadow and a soft footfall came upon him. It was Bonnie.

'Shall I do your name on it?' she asked. 'In off-white on the pocket, so that you'd have to strain to see it, that would be nice.' In fact, that would be very nice. Paul admired her taste.

'Could you put "Garry" on it?' he asked shyly.

'Is that your boyfriend?' asked Bonnie.

'Well, yes,' Paul said. He didn't feel at all at ease with her like he did with nice, comfortable, undemanding Helen. In a funny way this enormous woman seemed to consider herself quite socially acceptable. Was there even a hint of a flirtation with him and a sense of regret that there was a Garry in the background?

Paul began to wonder was he losing his reason. He must be imagining it. He must.

They sat in the sunset for a bit, then he told her about the flying fish that sometimes came up on deck, and she told him how much she loved embroidery and sewing and she was going to make herself a huge patchwork cape someday with a hundred colours in it. It would shine out everywhere and nobody could ignore her.

This made Paul strangely uneasy again. With someone like Helen he could have said what came into his mind, which was that he didn't think it a good idea for a gigantic woman to call further attention to herself. He had told Helen several times that she would look nicer if she wore lipstick, and eventually she bought some and wore it just to please him and everyone admired her. He would love to say this to Bonnie, that she should be more restrained, there was no need to go around like a lighthouse. But he didn't dare. Nor did he dare to suggest that she should have white wine and soda instead of the great pint of beer she was drinking as the sun went down.

So Paul didn't become a friend of Bonnie, but he became, to his great amazement, a great observer of her. He noticed the way she settled herself by the swimming pool early with her embroidery, how Charlie and Charlotte would appear and consult her about how the day was to be spent. Bonnie had four sundresses, each one louder and more attention-getting than the one before. Some had sunflowers, some had huge roses, one even had multicoloured designs. And there was always a huge hat as well, usually matching the dress. The hat upset Paul most of all. It was like a flag saying 'Look at me'. It was especially tasteless, he thought, since Charlotte also wore huge hats. Hers looked lovely, they made her seem like a slim Mexican boy, while Bonnie looked like a giant toadstool.

And it wasn't a question of disliking her. She was one of the most easygoing, pleasant people he had met. He couldn't work out why he felt uneasy with her. He even discussed it with Helen.

'You've been obsessed with her since they came aboard,' said Helen grumpily. 'In a way I'm a bit jealous. I don't know why you are doing all this analysing. It's very simple to understand.'

'Well, I wish I understood it,' said Paul.

'You want to patronise her, pity her, bring her out of herself, get her to join in things . . . and it isn't necessary. She doesn't need pity, she's already out of herself, she does things without your having to organise it, in fact she's on a nice little number with all that sewing people's names on things. She's taken in a couple of hundred dollars.'

Paul thought about this. Well, there was a little truth in what Helen had said . . . just a little. He wasn't upset because Bonnie rejected his friendship . . . it was just that she seemed quite complete without it. That's what was the little pique, the slight wound.

But he was drawn to them all, like someone charmed. He watched them every day, Charlie with his lithe athletic body playing deck games, Charlotte looking like an advertisement for the glamour of cruising, and Bonnie more ridiculous looking, more calm and sure of herself every day. Paul's mother had been fat. Back in Canada she had hardly moved outside her house. But then his mother had been a lady, she had dignity. In a million years she would never have understood this Bonnie who behaved . . . well, like a normal woman.

The words pulled him up short when he felt himself thinking them. Of course, in many ways his mother and Bonnie were normal women, they actually were ordinary people, just fatter than the accepted shape. But Mother had known that it was dignified not to go out and about if you looked different from other people, and when Mother had to go out she wore dark concealing clothes, the most restrained garments she could find. Bonnie with her big mad hats, wide smile, and her red lipstick would have been like a creature from Mars.

He wondered, were Charlie and Charlotte attracted by her in the same mesmerised way as he was? Did they have this mongoose/snake thing with her that he did? One day he decided to discuss it with Charlotte. She was sitting alone for once, feet up on the ship's rail, hat hanging from its ribbon around her neck. She looked very gentle and beautiful.

He wondered, how did Charlie feel able to share her so much? Not that Paul was any authority on women, but he did feel that if you were married to such a dazzling woman as Charlotte you might want her for yourself rather than spend all your time in an odd trio.

'What are you thinking about?' he asked the still girl.

'Oh, I was thinking about how undemanding life is on board a ship. Somebody else decides where you're going, how long you'll stay. I love not having to make any decisions.'

'Do you have to make all that many in real life?' he asked.

'Constantly. How to earn money, who to live with, who to trust, where to be, when to leave . . . all the time.'

'But that's all over now, I mean can't you do it as a team?' asked Paul. He assumed that Charlie must make at least fifty per cent of the decisions for the couple.

'Yes, that's the great safety of being with Bonnie,' said Charlotte.

'Well, I meant Charlie really,' he said.

'Oh, Charlie feels the same, he's often said it to me. He said he felt such a wave of relief when he proposed to her and she said yes. He knew he'd be safe for the rest of his life . . .'

'When he proposed to Bonnie?' Paul stuttered, confused.

'Well, not proposed, asked her to marry him, whatever people do,' said Charlotte. Then suddenly, 'What's wrong?'

'I thought you and Charlie were married,' he said, 'to each other, I mean.'

'No, I'm not married to anyone. Charlie and Bonnie were married in spring. You must have known they were married, or together anyway. I mean, they have a cabin and everything . . .'

Paul was digesting this very slowly indeed.

'I didn't know,' he said. Even as he said it he didn't know why he was so shocked. He couldn't sit here and think about it any more. He got up quickly and made some mumbled excuse – so inadequate that the lovely Charlotte actually sat up in her deck chair to watch him disappearing off down the deck. She shrugged and went back to her book.

Paul found Helen.

'Did you know that he's married to Bonnie, not to Charlotte?' he said.

'Oh yes, I discovered that a couple of days ago. I heard someone call them Mr and Mrs.'

Paul was annoyed that she took it so calmly.

'It's ridiculous. They're so unsuited.'

'I think they get on particularly well,' said Helen, spiritedly. 'I mean, look at the other couples on the ship who are fighting or yawning or sulking. I think Bonnie and Charlie are a tonic.'

Paul felt affronted. He was astonished at the violence of his own reactions. He liked them all, he loved none of them. Why should it matter who was hitched to whom? But it did. It really did. He felt very adrift.

Helen looked at him sharply.

'You really have been building up some kind of fantasy about these three, haven't you?' she asked, not unkindly.

'I don't know what you mean,' he said defensively.

'You're obsessed by them, and Bonnie in particular. Now, you're the last person on board to realise that it's she who's married to the young blond Adonis. It may have caused a momentary flicker in the rest of us, it's nearly knocked you down.'

'I think she's gross,' he said suddenly. Helen looked shocked.

'No, of course you don't. She's not nearly as gross as that retiring German missionary who got on at Bombay, and she's not nearly as fat as the Greek woman who has to lift her stomach up in front of her. What can you mean, Paul? She's just a fat girl with a lovely face. You can't ever have looked at her properly if you don't realise that she's absolutely dazzling looking. Just too much fat.'

'My mother was very attractive until she let go,' said Paul in a mulish small-boy voice. 'But she never went around in such garish colours calling the full attention of the world to herself.'

'Did she go around much at all?' asked Helen with interest.

'No, she had respect for herself. She knew she didn't look well, so she hid herself away. She was very dignified.'

'And probably very depressed, too,' said Helen very sharply. 'How have you the slightest idea whether your mother was dignified or was going nutty as a fruitcake having to stay in the great Canadian indoors just because her pretty little son and her handsome husband might be a teeny bit embarrassed if she ventured out? You don't know anything about anyone.'

'You said I was getting upset. You're the one

who's shouting now,' said Paul, startled by this change in easygoing Helen.

'You make me shout, intolerant insensitive little pansy,' said Helen. 'Yes, pansy, pouf, queer, I can't remember the other words, but I'm sure they're there. Ten years ago, that's what people would have called you. Ten years ago your particular minority didn't go out very much, it was dignified and depressed and hid itself.

'Stop looking wounded and betrayed. I only say this because you annoy me so much with all your unliberated attitudes. You think it's modern to be able to tell me about Garry . . . I think it's just so much rubbish. You can't see that your own mother was a victim to your narrow-mindedness about physical appearance. You want a world of beautiful identical robots. You want a Nazi world, only the fittest and the finest shall be tolerated . . . You want to grow up, Paul.'

Paul was still for a while.

Then he said, 'Helen, I don't want to upset you, perhaps you're right, but why do you take it so badly? You're not fat, you can't have an axe to grind for Fat Rights. Tell me what it is that makes you feel so strongly.'

'I might have told you once. I might have given in to this seductive shipboard thing of confiding. I thought you were a gentle kind boy with a new open soul. But not now, I'll never tell you. You'll have to guess, and you can spend months guessing, and you'll never know.'

Helen laughed at him, not unaffectionately.

'No, little Paul, you'll never know whether I had a fat lover who died from slimming, or whether I was once fat, or whether someone I cared for was hurt by cruel insensitive attitudes such as yours. But that doesn't matter very much. It's just one shipboard story fewer to hear. What does matter is that you realise you are the one out of step, not big Bonnie. She's modern and liberated, she's no prisoner because of her flesh. I don't have an ounce of sympathy for that girl, she's a happy soul, she's got an adoring husband, she's got a good business sense. She's not gross, Paul – you could be. You and Garry could end up in some community where people don't like gays . . . and I'd hate to think where your courage and inner resources might be then.'

She gave him an awkward kind of matey hug as she left the room. She didn't want to close every door to him.

With a numbness a bit like the way you feel after having a tooth filled, Paul walked to the upper deck and looked down below. It was sunset, and at sunset every evening, the glorious

Charlie sat sipping a drink, flanked by the women in hats, and they were all laughing contentedly in the pinky-red light.

Excitement

Everyone said that Rose was immensely practical. She was attractive-looking, of course, and always very well groomed. A marvellous wife for Denis, and wonderful mother for Andrew and Celia. And a gifted teacher. People said that Rose was a shining example. Or if they were feeling less generous, they said that they had never known anyone to fall on her feet like Rose. Married at twenty-five to a successful young man, two children, a boy and a girl, a job to stop her going mad in the house all day, her own car, her own salary every month, no husband grousing about the cost of highlights. Why wouldn't she be a shining example?

It had been Rose who suggested the idea of Sunday brunches. They had all come from the tyranny of family lunches with great roasts and heavy midday meals. So they moved from house to house every Sunday, everyone bringing a bottle of wine and some kind of salad thing. They all dressed up. The children played together. If any couple wanted to bring along a friend, they could.

They congratulated themselves, it kept them young and exciting, they thought. Not dead and lumpen like their parents had been. And it had been Rose's idea in the first place.

Of course, another example of Rose's luck was that her mother lived way down in Cork. She wasn't constantly on the doorstep, criticising the way the grandchildren were being brought up. Twice a year Rose's mother came up to Dublin; twice a year Rose took the children to Cork. It was yet another example of how well she organised her life.

So they would have been very surprised if they had known how discontented Rose felt as half-term was approaching. She seemed to have been teaching for ever. The same things every year, and in the same words. Only the faces in front of her were different, the younger sisters of the children she had already taught.

Then, on the home front, there would be the same arguments with Andrew, six, and Celia, five, about which place to visit when they went to the zoo: Andrew wanted snakes and lions, Celia wanted birds and bunnies. And there would be the same discussions with the au pair. A different name every year, but always the same discussion – the time she came home at night, the long-distance phone calls. And Denis? Well, he was pretty much the same too. There would be the usual jokes about life being a holiday for teachers, about the workers of the world like himself having to toil on. In a million years he would never suggest the two of them went away together. It wouldn't matter what kind of a place. Even a simple guest house. But it wouldn't cross his mind. And if Rose were to suggest it, Denis would say he really shouldn't go away. Business was different from teaching – you had to stay in touch. And then what about Sunday? Surely Rose wouldn't want to miss their Sunday with all the gang? Rose began to wish she had never invented these Sundays. They were a lash for her back.

Always being bright and cheerful, always thinking up a different little dish to make them ooh and aah, blow-drying her hair, putting on make-up, reading the Sunday papers so as not to be out of the conversation, bribing Andrew and Celia to behave. It was always the same.

Rose was quiet as the time came up towards the half-term holiday. Nancy, her friend in the staff room, noticed.

'Where's all the zip and the get-up-and-go?' she

asked. Nancy was single and always saying in mock despair that she would never find a man.

'A bit of the magic seems to be going from it all,' Rose said more truthfully and seriously than she had intended to.

'Maybe he has the seven-year itch,' Nancy said. 'A lot of men get it just because they think it's expected of them. We poor spinsters keep reading about such things just so that we'll be ready for marriage, if it ever comes. It'll pass, though, it usually does.'

Rose looked at her in disbelief. Really, Nancy was as thick as the wall. It wasn't Denis who had a seven-year itch. It was Rose. She was thirty-two years of age and, for the foreseeable future, her life was going to be exactly the same as it was now. A lifetime of smiling and covering her emotions had made Rose very circumspect. She was, above all, practical. There was no point in having a silly row with her friend and colleague Nancy.

'Maybe you're right, let's hope that's all it is,' she said with her mind a million miles away from the mild expression on her face. Because Rose now realised the truth. She was restless and unsettled. She was looking for something, a little spark, a little dalliance. Possibly even a little affair. She felt a shiver of excitement and disbelief. She wasn't that kind of person. She had always thought wives who strayed were extraordinarily foolish. They deserved all they got, which was usually a very hard time.

Rose found that, in the days that followed, everything had become even more samey than it used to be. Denis said, 'Sorry, what was that?' to almost every single sentence she spoke to him, sometimes not waiting until she had finished. Every day Maria Pilar said, 'I mess the buzz, the buzz was late.' It was useless to tell the stupid girl that either she was late or the bus was early. Rose gave up trying. Andrew said every day that he hated cornflakes and Celia, to copy him, said the same thing. Rose's mother phoned from Cork regularly to say how good the life was down there, how dignified, gracious, and stylish compared to the brashness, vulgarity, and violence of Dublin. Rose listened and murmured, as she felt she had been doing for years. A meaningless murmur.

And then it was Sunday again. She prepared a rice salad with black olives and pine nuts for the gathering at Ted and Susie's. She knew before they even rang at the door what Susie would say. Susie, a colourless woman who would have looked very well if she had dyed her eyelashes and worn bright colours, in fact did say, exactly as Rose had known: 'How clever you are, Rose. You always think of marvellous things. I don't know how you do it.'

Rose had the urge to scream at her that occasionally she opened a bloody cookbook, but stifled it. It would not be practical to shout at a friend, a hostess. She smiled and said it was nothing. She went into the room – there they all were, each playing the role that could have been written for them.

Bill was talking about the match, Gerry about the cost of airfares, her Denis was nodding sagely about business expansion schemes, Nick was telling them about a horse he knew. And the women had roles, too. Annie talked about the litter in the streets, Nessa about the rudeness of the people in the supermarket . . . Susie, as she always did, apologising and hoping everything was all right.

Rose's mind was a million miles away when Ted, standing beside her and spooning some of the rice salad onto his plate, said into her ear: 'Very exotic.'

'Oh, it's quite simple, really,' she began mechanically.

'I didn't mean the rice, I meant you,' he said, looking straight at her.

Ted. Ted with the new car every year and the fairly vague job description, married to mousy Susie, who had the money.

'Me?' Rose said, looking at him with interest.

'Well, your perfume, it's very exotic indeed. I always fancy that if we were all in the dark I'd find you immediately.'

'Well, it's hard to prove seeing that it's broad daylight.' She laughed at him, her eyes dancing like his.

'But it won't be daylight on Tuesday,' he said. 'Not in the night-time, that is.'

'Now, *what* made you make a deduction like that?' She was still playful but didn't sound puzzled or outraged. It was as if she were giving him permission and encouragement to go on.

'I'm going to Cork on business . . . overnight . . . and I thought that perhaps we could test out this theory of the perfume, you know. See whether I knew what part of the room you were in. What do you think?'

It was the moment to ask did he mean to include anyone else. It didn't need to be asked. 'And have you thought out how this could be managed?' she asked. She spoke in her ordinary voice, as if they were talking about any of the same things they talked about in each other's houses for the last seven years.

'I gave it a load of thought,' said Ted, 'like it's your half-term and you could be staying with your mother, as it were.' He was leaning on a shelf and looking at her. Interested. That's what he looked. It was a lovely, almost forgotten feeling to have someone looking at her like that. Rose felt a tightening of her throat, and a small lurch in her stomach.

'You've thought of everything,' she said.

'I don't see any obstacles, do you?' Ted might have been talking about garden furniture.

'Only the messy one of upsetting people,' she said.

'Ah, but you and I wouldn't do anything like that. It's not as if we're falling in love or leaving anyone or breaking up any happy homes. It's just a bit of . . . well, how would I describe it . . . ?'

'A bit of excitement?' Rose suggested.

'Precisely,' he said.

She thought it was very sophisticated of them indeed not to make any plans and think up any cover stories. If it was going to happen, which she thought deep down it would, then these would all come later. They rejoined the group.

Rose let her glance fall over the others, Nessa and Susie and Annie, Grace. Did none of them ever ache for a little excitement in their lives? And if they did, whom would they have found it with?

Hardly her own Denis. He had barely time and energy for that kind of activity in his own house without thinking of arranging it with someone else's wife. The Sunday ended, as every Sunday did, with a visit to the pub. They had their traditions in this too. No big rounds, meaning that people stayed all night. Each family bought their own drink. It was very civilised, like everything they did. And very, very dull, Rose realised.

As they left the pub for the car, Andrew said he hated fizzy orange, and Celia, who had drunk very little other than fizzy orange in her life, said she hated it too.

Denis opened the door of the car for Rose. 'Don't we have marvellous friends?' he said unexpectedly. 'We're very, very lucky.'

She felt a hard knot of guilt form in her chest. But she swallowed it and agreed.

'But we work at it, of course,' Denis said. 'Having friends means a commitment of time and effort.'

Rose looked out the window. If working to achieve a Sunday exactly like this every single week was the result of time and commitment, then she was absolutely within her rights to want a day off, a night out.

The knot of guilt had quite disappeared.

Ted rang casually and told her there was a

great place to leave her car in for an overhaul, only a few miles beyond Newlands Cross. Rose took down the details and thanked him. If the call had been bugged by every private detective and secret service in the world, it would have seemed totally innocent. Rose went into town and bought herself a black lace night-dress, a bottle of full-strength perfume with matching talcum powder, and body lotion. If she was going to have a bit of excitement with Susie's handsome husband, he was going to remember it for a long time.

'I want to go to the zoo tomorrow,' Celia said at supper.

'That sounds nice,' said Denis, not looking up, 'Mummy's on half-term.'

Rose looked at her son, hoping he would speak on cue. He did. 'I hate the zoo,' Andrew said.

'I hate the zoo too,' said Celia.

'That's settled, then. Maria Pilar will take you out for a lovely walk and an ice cream.'

'I get tired when I go on a lovely walk,' said Andrew.

'So you can go on the buzz. Maria Pilar loves the buzz.'

'Eet is not the buzz, eet's the bussss,' said Maria Pilar, hissing across the table.

'So it is, I keep forgetting.' Rose got up briskly

from the supper table. 'Now, I've got lots to do, I'm off to see Grannie tomorrow.'

'I want to see Grannie,' Celia said.

'I hate Grannie,' Andrew said. Before Celia remembered that she hated Grannie also, Rose said no, this was a flying visit.

'Are you taking the plane?' Andrew asked with interest. His hatred of his grandmother might be tempered by a new experience like going in an aeroplane.

'Sorry, what was that, you're going to see the old bat?' Denis asked.

'Has Grannie got a bat?' Andrew was very interested now.

'I want to see the bat,' Celia said.

Rose glared at her husband. Now she would have to pretend that Grannie did have a bat. 'It's out a lot,' she said. 'Especially at night.'

'It's too much down and back in one day,' Denis said.

'I know, I'll stay the night.' Rose was surprised how easy it came when it had to, the lie, the cover-up. She always thought that women who weren't used to this would bluster or redden and give themselves away.

'You're doing your purgatory on earth, that's all I can say.' Denis left the supper table and went into what they called Denis's Den. He would be there until midnight. There were a lot of figures to be sorted out – coming up to sales conference time, he would tell her if she protested. Or Annual Report time or the AGM or the Visiting Firemen. There was always something.

Rose slept a guilt-free sleep. No woman was meant to sign on for such a dull life. That had been part of no bargain. Somewhere in the air there was a little clause allowing for a few excitements along the way.

Ted was waiting exactly where he had said at ten o'clock. He was relaxed and easy. They transferred Rose's little overnight bag into his boot.

'This is great fun,' he said.

'Isn't it just?' said Rose.

On the journey, they flirted with each other mildly. Rose said he drove the car in such a masterful way. Ted said she curled up like a kitten in a very seductive way. They played Chris de Burgh tapes. Ted had to do a few calls, but he had booked a table for lunch somewhere he thought Rose would like. Perhaps she'd like to settle into the hotel first and meet him at the restaurant. They didn't mention Denis or Susie. They told each other none of the cute little things said by Andrew and Celia or by Ted and Susie's children.

This was an Excitement, time out and away from all that.

Rose examined the bedroom with approval . . . She hung up her good dress, hid all the perfumed unguents in her case. She didn't want it to look as if everything had come out of a bottle. She looked at her own face in the mirror. She was exactly the same as she had been last Sunday morning, only two days ago, before Ted had come up with the offer of the Excitement. The same, but a little more carefully groomed. She had waxed her legs. Always a dead giveaway about affairs, people said, but Denis wouldn't have noticed. She strolled happily along to the restaurant, where she was greeted by a cry that froze her blood. 'Rose, Rose, over here.' It was her mother.

Sitting with Nora Ryan, the most horrible person in the South of Ireland or maybe in the whole of Ireland. A woman with beady eyes and a tongue that shot in and out like a snake's tongue. Delivering harsh, critical words every time. They were sitting at a table for three, and they pulled out the third chair for her. Rose felt a pounding in her head. It was as if they had expected her.

'How did you know I was . . . um . . . coming to see you . . .?' she stammered.

'Well, I rang. I rang and that not very bright girl said you were in zee Cork.'

'Europeans,' said Nora Ryan, casting her eyes up to heaven.

'We're all Europeans,' snapped Rose before she could stop herself.

'How observant of you, Rose dear,' said Nora Ryan with three flashes of her thin, serpentine tongue.

'And what did you say?' Rose spoke to her mother.

'I said that's great, and that Nora and I were having lunch here, but that stupid girl couldn't understand a word I said.'

'Spaniards!' said Nora, her eyes nearly reaching the brim of her hideous hat.

'So what did you do then?' Rose felt a sense of blind panic that she had never known before.

Now the unthinkable had happened. Her mother must have told her husband there had never been any question of a visit. Was there a hope in hell Rose could pretend it had been meant as a surprise?

'I had a very odd conversation with my grandson, who seemed to think the house was infested with bats and that you were coming down to deal with them.' Rose put her head in her hands. 'So then obviously I rang Denis at the office to find out what was happening.'

'And what did he say?'

'Questions, questions, really, Rose, you're like one of these interrogators on television,' said Nora Ryan.

Rose flashed her a look of pure loathing. 'Mother, what did Denis say?'

'He said he was well, he said he was busy coming up to the sales conference . . .'

'Before I have to take you by the throat and beat it out of you, Mother, what did he say about my coming to Cork? What did he say?'

'Really, Rose,' Nora Ryan began.

'Shut up, Mrs Ryan,' said Rose.

They stared at her. Rose tried to recover the lost ground. She spoke very slowly, as if talking to someone of a very low IQ. 'Can-I-ask-you-Mother-to-tell-me-what-did-Denis-say?'

Rose's mother was fingering her throat, the one that Rose had threatened to shake her by. She seemed almost afraid to speak. 'I don't see *why* you're talking like this, Rose, I really don't. I told Denis that if you called before you went out to the house this is where we'd be having lunch. To save you . . . to *save* you the journey out to the house . . . that's what I was doing and inviting you to lunch in a nice smart place like this . . .' Rose's mother had taken out a handkerchief and dabbed the corner of her eye. 'I most certainly didn't expect dogs' abuse and interrogation about it.' She was hurt and she didn't mind them knowing it.

Mrs Ryan was now in the totally unaccustomed role of being a consoler. 'Now now, now now now,' she said, patting the shaking shoulder awkwardly and flashing glances of hate at Rose.

'Did he know I was coming to stay with you?' Rose's voice was dangerously calm; the words came out with long spaces between them.

'Of course he knew,' her mother sniffled.

'How did he know?'

'I told him.'

'How did *you* know, Mother?'

Rose's mother and Nora Ryan looked at each other in alarm. Perhaps Rose was going mad . . . seriously mad.

'Because Maria Pilar had told me, my grandchildren had told me . . .'

The breath seemed to come out of Rose more easily now. 'Yes. Well, that's fine, that's all cleared up,' she said.

And at that moment Ted came into the room, carrying a single red rose wrapped in cellophane. The blood drained from her head yet again.

He saw her and came over. 'What a surprise. What a huge surprise,' he shouted like a very bad actor in an amateur play.

The two older women looked at each other; again their alarm increased.

'Good God . . . it's Ted,' cried Rose. 'Of *all* the people in the world!' She looked around the room as if she expected to see a few other equally unexpected people, like Napoleon.

'I'll tell you the most extraordinary thing,' Ted shouted, unaware that the entire dining room was now looking at them and could not avoid listening to them.

'This is my mother,' screamed Rose. 'My mother that I was coming down to Cork to visit.'

'How do you do?' Rose's mother began, but she might as well have been talking to the wall.

'The *most* extraordinary thing,' Ted repeated. 'I was back at the hotel before . . . um . . . before coming along here, and who did I meet but Susie's brother and his wife. Susie is my wife,' he said to the sixty or so people who were now part of his listenership. 'They are in Cork and staying in the same hotel.' He paused to let the words sink in with all the diners. 'The very same hotel.' He didn't get the reaction he wanted, whatever it might have been, so he said it in a different form. 'The *selfsame* hotel, I think you might say,' he said triumphantly.

Rose began to babble. 'That's lovely for you, Ted, you can all be together. I'd love to stay in a hotel myself sometime, but I'm staying with my *mother*.'

Mrs Ryan looked at her with narrowed eyes. 'I'm sure your mother wouldn't mind at all if you were to stay in a hotel,' she said pleasantly.

'No, no, no, I can't. And anyway, Mother has a lot of bats in the house,' she floundered wildly to Ted, 'so that's where I'll be staying.'

Ted might not even have heard her.

'So the odd thing was that when they thought they saw me, they asked at Reception was that me and Reception, of course, goddamn interfering nosy parkers that they are, said that Mr and Mrs Ted O'Connor were there.'

Rose said, 'What did you do?'

'I told them that suddenly at the last moment Susie couldn't come and then Reception said did I want to move to a single room because it would be cheaper, and I said yes, but that I'd rush up and pack my things and so I did and they're in the back of the car, if you know what I mean.'

Rose looked at him. His face was scarlet; he looked like a madman talking to other very mad people.

'If you get my drift,' he roared.

Rose felt a sudden maturity sweep over her. She knew now that she had had enough excitement to last her a long time. On the grounds that she was helping Ted to park his car, she left with him, retrieved her suitcase. They were both too shocked to speak.

She returned to the restaurant, where the diners looked up with interest, hoping for Round Two.

Ted had given the red rose to Mrs Ryan. 'I bought it for you,' he had said without explanation. Nora Ryan saw nothing odd in this. In her youth it had happened a lot, she said.

Rose spoke courteously to her mother, planned the night in the house that she had forgotten was bat free and worked out what train to get back to Dublin and how to retrieve her car from beyond Newlands Cross. To begin what she hoped would be a fairly even-tempered and unexciting period of her life.

A Villa
for Four

Molly had been saving up for a cookery course as her holiday. It was very expensive, but it was the last word they said. You stayed in this inn in France and the Great Man taught you to make sauces all morning, and pastries all afternoon. The secret of cooking was sauces and pastry apparently. Any fool could just put things into ovens or under grills or, heaven forbid, into a frying pan.

Molly worked in a big supermarket with a very lively crowd of girls. Every year four of them went on holiday together. They would rent a villa between them.

On their coffee breaks they talked of little else when it came to the time of booking the holiday.

Now a villa meant different things to different people, Sheila said, but wasn't that all part of the adventure?

In one part of Spain one year they had a terrific

villa with white walls and purple flowers all over the place, but it was a mile and a half from the town and the action. In another part of Spain they had a great place, but it was more a flat over a café, and was almost too near the action. And in the Canaries the villa was like part of a huge block of apartments, and in Italy the villa had been a huge house where they could have had a house party for twenty if they had only known.

So this year they were booking again, their fifth holiday together, 'and none of us has got a man out of it,' Sheila said, rolling her eyes up to heaven.

'We got plenty of men between us in our time, they just didn't stay around,' said Kitty.

'Or we didn't want them to,' said Brigid.

Mary said nothing. She had been very quiet recently.

Molly noticed this, but the others didn't seem to, because they were too excited, waving brochures and recalling tales of other people's adventures in Greece.

Greece had been chosen as the holiday destination this year. Further away than ever before. More exotic, more exciting, maybe.

Then Sheila started collecting the money. They all had to give thirty pounds each as a deposit before the New Year so that they could get their pick of the best places.

On two mornings, Mary had forgotten to bring in her three ten-pound notes.

'Listen, Mary, I have to book it today, but I'll put it in for you and you can give it to me at the end of the week,' Sheila said and Mary burst into tears. She wasn't able to go. She was going to get engaged to Frank and she had hardly dared tell them that she was going to break up the happy foursome.

They forgave her, because an engagement was good, and they began to plan her shower and then her hen party. But of course it did mean they needed a fourth.

'Are you sure you wouldn't like to come, Molly?' they asked again.

But Molly was very sure.

She would love to learn how to make magic sauces and talk to people who were interested in doing the same.

She would not like to lie on a beach covered in suntan oil and dance all night in a disco.

Maybe they were pleased that Molly said no. She wasn't as glamorous as the others, she didn't wear such short skirts and as much make-up. Molly thought she probably looked a bit puddingy, a bit like one of those big desserts she just adored to make.

And then it all happened at once. Molly got a letter saying that because enough people had not signed on for the course, the Great Man was now cancelling it, and money was refunded, apologies were offered, regrets were expressed.

Molly was bitterly disappointed, and all around her she heard the woe as Sheila, Kitty and Brigid heard the bad news from the travel agency. The holiday price was based on four people sharing. Without Mary it was going to cost them a small fortune.

'I can't give up my marriage and future to save you all a few quid,' cried Mary.

'If only there was someone who would come with us, someone we know,' they said over and over, and Molly heard herself saying that if they had nobody else, she could come as her holiday had fallen through.

They were wild with delight.

The holiday was on again, Mary could marry Frank, the world had settled down.

The villa in Greece was delightful, a little white house at the top of some wonderful steps with flower pots on them. It looked down over the harbour and out to sea. People said it was owned by a little old lady who went to live in a hut in the mountains herself for the summer. She was saving money so that her son could start a business.

The girls loved it all. Soon it had the familiar look of all their holiday homes, draped in clothes and suntan oils and drying swimming costumes.

They decided that Molly on holidays wasn't as much fun as they had thought she would be.

Not exactly prim and proper, but not topless either. Not temperance, but certainly not too free and easy with the bottles of retsina. Not prissy quite, but not as eager and delighted as she might have been to befriend all the handsome Greek men that were waiting in the village for their arrival.

Sheila, Kitty and Brigid were set in their own rather liberal ways. They hadn't quite expected that Molly wasn't going to be the same.

Now she was never disapproving, just said that she would prefer to go for walks or boat trips, and even excursions up into the mountains. Sometimes she would make them lunch on the terrace of the villa, beautiful salads, and fresh fish that she would buy at the harbour. She learned the few words of Greek needed for these transactions, and even the names of some of the local men.

'*Ti kanis*, Molly,' they might call.

'*Kala, poli Kala*,' Molly would cry back.

'*Orea*,' they would say.

239

'That's a real conversation you're having,' Sheila complained indignantly to Molly.

'No, it's not,' Molly laughed, 'it's only "howarya, fine, great". Honestly, that's all it is.'

It was more than the others knew, and they noticed she had learned to count in Greek and could add up the bill and work out the service, and say please and thank you.

Sheila said it would be great to do all that if you had the time but then who had the time if they had a busy social life?

Molly always joined them for the earlier part of the evening. They went to one of many tavernas around the harbour. Sometimes the Greek men stood up, formed a circle, and did their traditional dances.

But soon after this, Sheila, Kitty and Brigid would say it was time to go to the disco at the hotel.

'Come on, Molly, time for real dancing,' they'd say.

Molly preferred to be where she was, watching, admiring and praising as the men did great swoops and leaps. And she drank little cups of sweet coffee.

There was one restaurant that she particularly liked. It had no name over the door and it wasn't very smart. It had no big lights like some of the newer places had, no flashing signs or expensive awnings. But it was very friendly, people seemed glad to see you. She didn't feel plump and a little old-fashioned in her cardigan in this cheerful little place.

Fortunately, it was also very inexpensive so the others were happy to have supper there most evenings. Molly soon told them that she really preferred to sit on here than to go to the disco.

She didn't actually say that that was really being abroad, while the disco could have been anywhere. They worked so hard – the family that ran the place. They never stopped running in and out of the tiny kitchen, they remembered what everyone ordered, they had smiles that seemed very genuine.

There was an old woman, the mama, her son, Georgi, and a beautiful girl, Maria. Probably Georgi's wife, as he smiled a lot at her.

She didn't wear a ring but perhaps it was different here.

They seemed delighted that Molly stayed on. 'It's not dull for you here with just us people, no tourists?' Maria asked her.

No, I came to Greece to meet Greek people,' Molly said simply, and that pleased them all.

That evening the old lady came out and gave her a big cake full of honey and nuts.

'A present to you from us,' she said and vanished before she could hear the thanks.

'How do you speak such good English?' Molly asked Maria another evening.

'Georgi says we must learn it for all the tourists we would have, but as you see, alas, the tourists never come to us.'

Molly thought about it that night. The place was really very shabby, the food was not especially good. It had to be said that nobody there – Georgi, his wife or his mother – were real cooks. It was not totally surprising that the visitors went to other places to be entertained.

And yet what could be more entertaining than to see the people of the little fishing village enjoying themselves with their old songs and dances?

Molly looked at Maria enviously. Imagine having such a marvellous husband, a great dancer, with a huge smile, courteous to everyone. But then she was very beautiful.

And beautiful girls got the nice men, that was the rule.

Molly felt sad at the thought. It wasn't fairly divided, was it?

If a girl was beautiful, she had so much luck already, with people admiring her, knowing that she caused a sensation just walking by. And then on top of all that she would get a nice man as well. Too much, Molly thought, her face despondent.

Maria noticed her.

'You look sad tonight, Molly,' she said.

Molly looked up at the girl's face, a perfect oval shape, with huge dark eyes, olive skin and thick black curly hair. No wonder a man as marvellous as Georgi loved her and smiled so much at her.

'I wish I was beautiful,' Molly said suddenly.

'Oh but you are,' said Maria with her dazzling smile. 'You have a lovely face and you are a lovely person, everyone here loves you to come in.'

'No, I'm not. For one thing I would love to have beautiful curls like you.'

'Well, why don't you?' asked Maria. 'My cousin runs the hairdresser's shop, she gave me these curls.'

'A perm?' Molly couldn't believe it.

'I do not know the word perm.'

'Body wave? Someone to make the curls for you with hot things?'

'Yes, this is what she did.'

Maria laughed, and they laughed together like old friends.

Next morning Sheila, Kitty and Brigid had terrible hangovers.

'Are you making an omelette by any lovely chance?' Kitty croaked.

'No, I'm going to have a perm,' said Molly and ran off down the steps with all the flower pots on them.

The hairdresser was called Anna. She said she would make beautiful curls for Molly and she did. She also told her that Maria was Georgi's sister not his wife, and that it was Georgi's mother who owned the lovely villa where the girls were staying and how they hoped to open a restaurant there. But now it didn't look likely. They hadn't made any money in the little place and they couldn't afford a cook.

'I can cook,' Molly said suddenly.

'Then perhaps you are an answer to a prayer,' said Anna, offering her the mirror so that she could see how the curls looked at the back.

Georgi said her hair looked beautiful when she went to the little café that night.

'You have always look beautiful but now your hair looks beautiful too. *Orea* . . . beautiful,' he said again.

'Thank you, Georgi, *efkaristo*, but now we must think of something more important. You buy nice chickens here but they are a little dry. Would you let me try to make a nice chicken dish for you tomorrow, chicken with olives and sun-dried tomatoes and wine?'

Georgi seemed surprised. 'Well, yes . . .'

'Could you and Maria and I go to the market together, do you think?' Molly asked.

Georgi thought it was a terrific idea.

When the girls got up next day, there was no sign of Molly. She had left a note saying she had a lot of things to do, she might see them later in the usual place.

That evening Sheila, Kitty and Brigid came in and sat at the table. There was no sign of Molly, then they saw her in the kitchen, smiling at Georgi, with no cardigan, but lots of curls, and she actually seemed to be in charge of the food.

Steaming plates of chicken casserole came out of the kitchen and people ate them eagerly. And there were baskets of Greek bread so that they could wipe up all the juices.

'Hey, this is great,' Sheila said in amazement. 'Did you make it, Molly, and can I have some more?'

'Shush, no way,' Molly hissed. 'There isn't half enough, so it's family hold back time.'

'Where did you get the hair?' Kitty was equally amazed.

'I told you I was getting a perm. Listen, will you, have cheese or something, and when you're down at the disco can you tell the crowd you meet there to come here tomorrow night. We'll give them a special price.'

'We?' said Brigid.

'Georgi, his mother, Maria and me.'

There was a silence. The three friends looked with new eyes at the girl who had come with them at the last moment. Molly, the plump girl in the cardigan who preferred cooking to dancing, and who preferred talking about ingredients to romancing under the moon, seemed to have got the undivided attention of the most handsome man in the whole place. Not only was it unexpected, it was very galling.

Still, there was the wife to consider.

'Will Maria like you moving into her place in the kitchen?' Sheila said with a very thin smile.

'Well, like any sister, she'd be pleased to see the fortunes of the restaurant improve. If they do improve.' Molly was confident but not arrogant.

'Sister?' they all chorused.

'Yes, of course, aren't they the image of each other?' Mollie's eyes rested fondly on the family who were beginning to depend on her.

It was almost time for the fun crowd to move on to the disco. But they were loath to leave. So much had happened already in this place. But on the other hand, there might be magical things altogether up at the disco.

If Molly, who was coming from so far behind in her cardigan, had done so well in this little backwater, what might the rest of them not find where the thudding beat and the bright coloured lights of the disco beckoned?

They left Molly talking ingredients, and trying to find the Greek word for sauce, and planning tomorrow's menus with people who already saw her very much as part of their family.

Holiday
Weather

Robert said that after dinner they would curl up with the map of the South of France and plan the journey. Frankie was looking forward to it. This was always a great part of the holiday, when he would sit on the sofa with his arm around her, the fire crackling in the grate, glass of wine at hand, and together they would point out magical names to each other. It had been like this last year, when his conference had been in Spain and they had hunted for little Spanish idylls for their rambles afterwards. And the year before, when it had been in Italy, and their fingers had traced the names by the lakes.

Of course, Frankie knew that the evening would not organise itself. She would have to escape down to the shops at lunchtime to buy something she knew he would like, and this was getting more difficult since he had begun to worry about his waistline. Gone were the evenings of fillet steak, mushrooms, and garlic bread. Perhaps she might get some monkfish – very expensive, but it did seem special – and a small selection of vegetables. She could even top and tail them at work; there would be so little time when she got back to her flat. She would have to rush around it tidying, of course, getting rid of all the work things that littered the place. Well, Robert hadn't been around for over a week, so she had been doing her Open University course every evening.

Frankie thought happily about the evening ahead. She would wear her green dress, the one that he had once said matched her eyes. A long while ago. But of course he still loved her, and people didn't have to go on about eye colour for ever. It would have been unnatural, and possibly a bit repetitive.

The only good thing about working for a man like Dale was that it took up such a small amount of time and so little brain. All that the awful Dale wanted was someone to sit in his front office and look pleasant, ask them to wait a moment while they could thumb through some of the fairly horrible cuttings about Dale's success in the world of public relations, and then ask them to go straight on in. Frankie was far too intelligent for this job, and that knowledge alone gave her great satisfaction. But by being with Dale and his outfit, she had an excuse to see Robert almost every day. And as far as Frankie was concerned, she would work in a coal mine or as a steeplejack if it meant being close to Robert.

Robert needed excuses to meet Frankie. Robert was married to his boss's daughter – a marriage of convenience that he had entered into at a time before he knew what true love, real love, was like.

Robert and his wife had two children, who were eight and seven. They were at the age when they could not be upset by things that had nothing to do with them; it wasn't their fault that Robert had found true love too late. Robert was the rising star in the organisation; he must work harder than ever now that he intended to leave home and set up two establishments. He must make himself totally indispensable to his boss, his father-in-law, so that there would be no question of letting him go once the divorce was brought up. Frankie didn't ask when that was going to be but thought that it would be unreasonable to expect it before the children went to boarding school. Three years, perhaps?

She would wait. Naturally.

But in the meanwhile there were wonderful things like the great summer honeymoon. They always called it that: Our Italian, Our Spanish, and now Our Riviera Honeymoon.

Frankie made her shopping list and took out the map of France. Whenever Dale passed by she looked as if she were making notes or looking up a reference. Dale would not stop to question her.

Frankie looked fine for the job, with her long dark curly hair and her bright green eyes. And even more important, she was the friend of Robert the whiz-kid in Benson's. Dale would have employed any kind of person at that front desk if it kept him well in with Benson's. He regarded it as a bonus that Frankie was both bright and beautiful.

The only thing that bored Frankie was that she had to put in the actual hours at her horseshoe-shaped desk. If only she could have slipped away for the afternoon. She could have gone to the hairdresser and even had a manicure as a luxury; her hands would be greatly in view tonight as they traced the route south through the Côte d'Azur down from Cannes past St Raphael to Saint-Tropez. Or should they go the other way from Cannes, over past Antibes to Nice and Monte Carlo? It was heady stuff even saying the names. Perhaps Frankie would even buy a little guidebook at lunchtime so that she would appear knowledgeable tonight.

It was all a rush, as she knew it would be. But the dinner had gone well. Robert was relaxed; he had loosened his tie and kicked off his shoes. Frankie had been able to wash her hair, and she had bought green earrings at lunchtime.

'They're lovely,' he said. 'The colour of your eyes.'

She felt that the fuss and the bustle had all been worthwhile. She even felt glad that she had spent that money on a dishwasher. It had been very extravagant, but Robert adored it. His wife was playing Earth Mother, according to his reports, refusing modern gadgets, but for them it was all right – there was the help and the au pair. In Frankie's flat, however, he loved to see technology. Cuts out all the fuss, he had said. They arranged the china and glass and cutlery carefully and listened to it humming away in the kitchen as Frankie got out the map.

'Darling,' he said. 'Wrong map, I'm afraid.'

'It says Provence on top, but it's all Cannes and Nice and everywhere down on the coast,' Frankie said, surprised. Normally Robert knew where everywhere was; that was why she had studied it so much in advance all afternoon.

'We're not going, my love,' he said.

Her heart lurched with the kind of jump that almost reached her throat.

'I don't understand.'

'Neither do I, but it's true. Listen, don't think I'm pleased . . . Stop looking at me like that, hey?'

'Why can't I come? We've always been able to swing it before. I tell Dale I'm taking my vacation, you tell Mr Benson you need someone from Dale's to run over the implications of the conference with you. Why can't I come this time? Why?' Frankie knew she was sounding like a seven-year-old, but her disappointment was so huge she couldn't hide it.

She had bought her clothes, her terribly expensive shoes, the knockout beach gear. The operation was foolproof – why was he pulling out now? Was it possible that he had found someone new? If he had cheated on his wife once, then obviously he could do it again. But don't go down that road. And don't *cry*. Frankie forced her face to stop puckering.

Robert sounded weary and resigned.

'It's not you, sweetheart, it's me. It's a non-starter.'

'But you always go to the conference. You *are* Benson's.' She was aghast. And yet there was a seed of hope. Suppose he had been discovered, and maybe even demoted. Did that not mean that the day they could be together might be nearer than they had thought?

'This year being Benson's means going somewhere else and shoring up someone else's cock-up,' he said. 'A whole project is going down the Swanee, and apparently I'm the only one who can sweet-talk us back where we were. What a bloody crowd of fools he employs. I'd have got rid of three-quarters of them. I will – I tell you I will one day.'

This was an old refrain. Frankie didn't want to hear it all over again – Robert's plans for the day when he ran the place himself. This was an old set of lines they had said to each other; she wanted to know what was new.

What was new was Ireland. A new plant, a lot of bother, nobody had been there to straighten it out, to tell the people on the ground what was happening, what was expected of them, what they could expect.

'They're bound to be suspicious of us, think we're in it for what we can get out of it.'

Frankie said nothing; for once she didn't murmur her usual words of encouragement. In fact, she knew that Benson's was in it for what they could get out of it, that's what business was about.

'So you see what's happened. In the very week of the conference in Cannes, I have to be over in the middle of the boglands talking to the mutinous forces over there and promising them wealth beyond their wildest dreams.'

'Can't you go now? Before the conference?'

'Don't you think I asked that? But old man Benson is adamant. It has to be that bloody time, something to do with some European thing or other that's being held there. They're much more interested in Europe over there, for some reason that escapes me. God, I could kill them for not setting it up right at the start, allowing all these discontents to grow up. If we don't go in and fly the flag or show our face or whatever the expression is ... then the whole thing could collapse like a house of cards.' He looked so handsome when he was annoyed. She could understand why so many people were impressed with him.

'Will we have any honeymoon together this year, you and I?' she asked in a small voice, looking down at the ground lest he see all the pain in her green eyes.

'You could come to Ireland,' he said doubtfully. 'I can't be tied up with them all the time. We'd have some time together.'

'To do what?' She had no maps of Ireland, she had no magical names like Juan les Pins, like Saint-Tropez.

'I don't know, darling, I don't know, give me space. I only heard about this today, this afternoon. We'll do something. It could be a rest for you, getting away from it all, and then I'd escape when I could.'

A more courageous woman would have told him to forget it. A tougher woman would have told him in no uncertain terms what he could do with this half-hearted offer.

Frankie was neither brave nor tough. Which was why she found herself in the small hotel on the west coast of Ireland. A hotel called the Greener Grass standing on a low cliff over a long, empty beach. When you looked across that sea the next stop was America, they told you. Frankie could believe it – it looked endless. And on the first days it looked grey and lonely. The seagulls calling to each other and other seabirds coming in to perch on rocks. She saw a school of porpoises go by one day, and she became familiar with the habits of a cormorant and a kittiwake and a tern and a gannet.

'I could do another Open University course in the habits of seabirds,' she said ruefully to the proprietor as he set her lobster before her at a table, which, for the third time, had been set for one.

'There are worse ways to spend your time, you

know.' His voice was soft, but it was distant. He was Shane, he said, a returned Irish American. He had called his place the Greener Grass because of the grass always seeming greener when it was far away. He had saved up for seven years to buy his own small hotel.

He was different from the other local people, who wanted to know all about Frankie and Robert, and what was their business in the place, did they have any children, where had they been for holidays before. Did they love the Irish way of life? Shane asked none of these questions. He had the air of someone contented with his own way of life. She saw him choosing his own vegetables from the fields where he had tilled the land to grow them. She watched him sometimes writing the menus in slow, careful, calligraphic script.

Robert set out in the early mornings and was rarely back to the Greener Grass before dark.

'Not much of a honeymoon, is it, darling?' he said more than once. Frankie saw his face, white and tired.

'The honeymoon bit is at night, remember?' she said, laughing.

But at night the weary Robert slept suddenly and soundly as soon as he got into bed. Some nights Frankie sat at the bay window, where there was a lovely three-part window seat, and looked out at the night sky over the water. Sometimes she saw Shane and his dog Tracey walking.

So he couldn't sleep either, Frankie thought, even though he had saved seven years to build his dream and had it now in his hands.

She saw Shane bend to pick up shells by the moonlight. He looked peaceful, she thought, and somehow at ease. Even though he didn't really belong here, not like locals – he had been away too long, and he had a slight New York tinge to his voice.

Next morning at breakfast, she asked him about the shells.

'You sat at the window and looked out over the moonlit sea,' Shane said.

Robert seemed annoyed somehow. 'You didn't tell me you couldn't sleep.' She felt she had been disloyal.

Later Shane came and gave her some cowrie shells. 'You could do another Open University course on these and still know nothing about them,' he said with a smile.

Robert liked to think that it was somehow a rest for her, that sharing some fraction of his life was reward enough for the broken promise, the conference that never was . . . the ribbon of the French coast not visited.

'I bet this is doing you no end of good,' he said

each morning as they ate brown soda bread and fish just in from the sea.

For the first few days she had smiled bravely, and taken a book disconsolately to walk along the hilly cliff or down to the rock pool, and try to stop thinking that her life was as grey as the skies all around her.

But then one morning the sun came out, and everything was different. Even Robert seemed loath to go.

'It's very beautiful, this place, you know,' he said as he stood beside his hired car about to head off for the day with the mutinous men he was finding it harder to placate than he had thought possible.

Frankie looked down at the beach she had walked so often in the dull days. Today it sparkled, as if there were little particles of precious metal hidden behind the rocks instead of soft sand. She thought she could see the cowrie shells that Shane had been collecting. The sea was twenty different colours of green and blue, with little white flecks.

'I might have a swim,' she said.

'Yes, well, be sensible. It's the Atlantic Ocean, don't forget.'

'Next stop, America.' Frankie laughed.

Robert looked at her, puzzled.

'I hope I won't be too late,' he said, but doubtfully. 'This lot seem to need conversation and explanation way into the night, as well as all day.'

He drove away along the road, and as Frankie looked after him up at the purple mountains and over beyond the small green fields with their stone walls to a dark, velvety forest, she began to feel as if a film had just turned from black-and-white into Technicolor.

She ran lightly upstairs to fetch the red bathing suit that had cost her so much in the days she thought it would be seen on the Côte d'Azur. As she came down, carrying the pricey beach bag and her red and white fluffy towel, Shane's dog Tracey came up and looked at her hopefully.

'I'd be very grateful if you would,' Shane said. 'He needs a walk, and with today's weather I'll have the world and its wife for lunch, so I can't take him.'

'I don't know a lot about dogs,' Frankie began.

'Well, Tracey is half sheepdog and half setter, we think. A lovely nature, and he'll bark if you start to drown or if anyone comes and bothers you.'

'Who'd come and bother me?' Frankie laughed, looking at the empty beach.

'I haven't seen you in that swimsuit, but it

might attract a bit of local attention.' He laughed too; the good weather made him seem less remote.

'Would he run away or get into a fight or anything?' It had never been part of her life, walking with a big, bounding dog.

'Not a chance. And as a reward, I'll come and find you and take you a little late lunch and take Tracey off your hands.'

'Oh no.'

'Oh yes. It's the minimum fee for dog minding. There's a nice flat rock in the next bay. It makes a good table.'

She had never spent a day on a beach like it. Tracey ran for sticks with never-ending energy. She really thought she could see his foolish face smile at her as she threw them again and again.

Tracey barked at the waves, but swam in and paddled near her as if to look after her when she swam. She collected shells and laid them out on the flat table rock.

Soon, far sooner than she had expected, Shane arrived with a picnic basket.

'You abandoned your lunchers. How can you expect to earn a living!' she said sternly.

'You're not wearing a watch. It's after three o'clock – they've all been and gone. You must be starved.'

Imagine. She had been playing with this idiotic dog for hours on a shell-covered beach, no cloud had come across the sky, and no thought of Robert and their situation had come across her mind.

Companionably they shared the picnic, local prawns, homemade bread, cheese made by some nuns in a convent across the valley, red shiny apples from the small orchard behind the Greener Grass.

'It's like heaven.' She sighed as they drained the bottle of wine to the dregs.

'Thank God we don't get weather like this all the time,' said Shane.

'Why do you say that? Because you'd have to work too hard?' Frankie had been about to say the very opposite; she had been on the point of wishing that every day could be so sunny.

'Because we would be parched and dry, it would not be a green island, and we'd be so used to it we wouldn't be calling out our thanksgiving to the very heavens as we are today,' he said.

'Yes, I know, and that's a point, but what about your business? If it was much sunnier, there would be many more people here. This beach would be full.'

'And could you and I and Tracey have had such a picnic if the beach were full?' he asked.

'We had meant to go to the South of France,' she said suddenly.

'Yes, so your husband told me, when he called to book.' Shane had his distant face on again. 'He seemed very disappointed and told me in several different ways that this was not his first choice.'

Frankie was going to explain that Robert was not her husband, but she let it go. Instead she apologised for him.

'He's normally very charming and would never have given you that impression. He has work problems to see to here. We had thought we could have made a holiday out of a conference in Cannes.'

'But why did he take you here, and leave you all alone?'

'I'm glad he did,' Frankie said positively. 'Now, do you think it's an old wives' tale about not swimming after lunch, or should we risk it?'

'Just as long as we don't go out too far, any of us,' he said, and they raced to the edge where the foam was breaking and drawing out the sand with it as it gathered for another wave.

'Have you ever been to the South of France?' he asked.

'No.' Her voice sounded small.

'Neither have I, so let's pretend this is a

hundred thousand times better,' Shane cried, and threw himself into the waves.

'You caught the sun,' Robert said when he got back earlier than usual. He had phoned to ask if dinner could be kept for him, and had been surprised and not altogether pleased to hear Shane say that his wife had had a late lunch.

'Did you tell him we were married?' Robert asked as they sat at a window table and watched the sun set, leaving red and golden paths and crisscross lines across the bay.

'No, darling, I didn't, but in this country they are likely to assume it if we check in to the same room and you have booked us as "Mr and Mrs".'

Robert looked at her sharply but decided not to make it something to argue about.

'Is it better? You know, are you sorting it out up at the plant?' Frankie asked.

'Yes. I think they believe our heart is in the right place,' Robert said.

'And it is?' Frankie's face was innocent, bland.

'What are you trying to say?'

'Well, I mean that a lot of them came back from jobs overseas because they really believed that it was going to be a proper plant, not something that would pack up and fold its tent when things got a bit hairy.'

'Oh, come on, Frankie, what do you think Benson's is, part of Mother Teresa? Of course we have to be practical. If things get hairy, as you put it, we can't stay on here for ever, bleeding hearts keeping returned emigrants in beer money.'

'That's all right, as long as they know it.'

'That's all right whether they know it or not,' Robert flashed.

'You remind me more and more of Dale,' Frankie said. 'The same cynical way of looking at everything.'

'You are beginning to remind me more and more of my wife. The same way of picking a row and nagging over everything.'

Frankie had read somewhere that you know when something is over, you know that this is the moment, but you won't accept it. You try to say it was because one person had too many tiring days negotiating, and the other person had too much unexpected sun.

Robert probably knew, too, because when he was called to the phone he went with eagerness and came back to say that some of the men needed him for a further conference.

They parted pleasantly, almost with relief.

Frankie went walking on the beach in the last rays of the sun. She felt Tracey rushing up to her before she knew Shane was on the beach as well.

'I had a friend in New York, a great friend, she was going to come here and run the Greener Grass with me. You know, a joint enterprise. Then she said she'd join me later. Then she said she needed thinking time. Then she said she'd write.'

They walked in silence; there seemed no need to say anything. Frankie thought about all those years, and those two honeymoons where she had felt she needed to entertain Robert all the time, talk to him, be bright, show no hurt, no loneliness.

'He's not my husband,' she said after a long time.

'Oh, I know,' said Shane.

'How?'

'Labels on suitcases, his instructions about not ever calling him to the phone if the office rang but always taking a name and a time he should call at. If you were married, he would have asked you to take the messages.'

After another long time Frankie asked, 'Is it all right? You know, running the place as a single venture, not a joint one as you had thought?'

'Yes, it's all right. It mightn't always be single. You never know your luck.'

The sea was calm now. They skimmed flat stones and made them hop.

'He'll be going back soon, I imagine,' Shane said. 'The lads tell me it's all settled.'

'Yes, well, they wouldn't want to rely on that too much.'

'They're smarter than they sound,' Shane said with a laugh. 'All us fellows who worked over the water learned a bit about business.'

'We had planned to stay on a bit when it was settled, but I don't think so now.'

'No, he'll want to be off. He might even catch the tail end of the Cannes thing.'

'A place where the sun shines all the time and there's no sense of surprise?' Frankie smiled at him.

'The very spot,' Shane said.

'And what's the weather forecast like here?' she wondered.

'Optimistic but unknown,' said Shane.

'I'll stay,' said Frankie. 'I'll certainly stay on awhile until I know how it turns out.'

They walked back to the Greener Grass in a companionable silence, because they knew there was no need to say anything, or plan anything, or spell anything out, or indeed say anything at all.

Victor and
St Valentine

Victor was brought up in a home where they made a huge fuss of St Valentine's Day. His sisters spent weeks wondering if anyone would send them a card; his mother cooked a very special meal for her husband that evening and served it by candlelight. His father bought something romantic like a heart-shaped charm for her bracelet, a little pendant, a glass vase for a single rose.

No wonder he thought it was a special day.

In the real world, he discovered, things were different. At school, for example, fellows didn't send girls cards unless they were jokey ones, often with hurtful remarks on them.

Nobody made any mention of St Valentine's Day ceremonies in their homes, so Victor stayed quiet about his own household. No point in *inviting* mockery. It was quite enough that he was already the subject of a lot of ridicule because of gentleness, good manners, and a lack of interest in beating up his classmates in the playground.

Then, later, when he went to train as an electrician, they did make a bit of a fuss and celebration at Technical College for a St Valentine's Day dance but mainly the chat was about which girls would be likely and which would not.

Victor never wanted to talk about people being likely; he thought it was too personal a thing to be speculated over in the bars. So the others more or less gave up on him in this area.

His first boss was not a man with much time for St Valentine. A load of commercial claptrap, he said.

Around that time Victor sent a valentine card to a nice girl called Harriet who had gone to the pictures with him several times. Harriet telephoned him at once.

'Listen, Victor, I'm sorry, there has been some awful misunderstanding. I wasn't being serious or committed or wanting to marry you or anything.'

Victor was alarmed. 'No, heavens no, neither was I,' he said, panicking at the very thought.

'Then why did you send me this card with all the roses and violets and sign your name?' she asked.

'Because it's St Valentine's Day,' he said.

'But you signed your own name. Naturally I

thought you wanted commitment.' Harriet was outraged at the misunderstanding.

'I'm very sorry,' Victor said humbly. 'I'll never do it again.'

But of course he did do it again, when he met Muriel, and did fancy her greatly.

Muriel said he should have had the courage to come straight out and say it if he loved her rather than relying on a card and somebody else's verses and sentiments. She couldn't see a future for them. She was sorry.

Victor decided he was not good with women. He wasn't without dates, a social life, and indeed the odd little romance, but none of them led to anything.

He was, however, a very good electrician. He had a pleasant manner and a lot of skill, and soon he didn't have to have a boss at all – he had his own business. A mobile phone, a business card, and a lot of word-of-mouth recommendations, and Victor had more customers than he could deal with.

Sometimes they asked him about his private life. 'Never met the right woman for me,' he would say. 'And here I am a hopeless romantic. But the girls don't take me up on it at all.'

He was thirty-eight, tousled hair, a warm smile. People didn't really believe him. They thought that he might have a very colourful private life but just wasn't telling.

People liked Victor and told him things. And he liked listening to them, because in his own way he was a little lonely.

He would have liked a companion to go out with on weekends. Someone to go on holiday with.

Victor had saved money for a holiday, but it wasn't quite the same going alone. So he enjoyed talking to his clients. Like the couple who were going to adopt a baby, and were so excited when it arrived that they invited Victor to the welcome party.

'Are you a relation?' somebody asked him.

'No, but I rewired the nursery,' he said, and again nobody believed him.

And there was the man who dared not tell his wife that he had been made redundant; Victor had many a cup of tea with him on a day when he was merely meant to be putting in new sockets.

And mainly there was old Mrs Todd.

She was very fond of Victor. She told him all about her family, her son Frank who was so protective of her that he had set up this door-entry system where she could see on a little screen who was there before letting them in. Mrs Todd hadn't wanted it at all, but her son Frank had insisted; the world was full of bad, dangerous people, he said.

Frank didn't come much to visit his elderly mother, which Victor thought was a pity, but Frank laid down the law a lot from a distance. Mrs Todd said that Frank had given instructions she was not to invite any new people that she met to coffee. This was hard, but she was sure Frank must be right.

Victor thought Frank sounded like a bully but was too tactful to say so. Frank's daughter, Amy, had gone off to Australia as soon as she was old enough to leave.

Mrs Todd said that Amy wrote regularly; she lived in Sydney, she worked in a flower shop there, and she was very happy. She wished that her gran would come out and see her.

'Why don't you go?' Victor encouraged her.

He was in Mrs Todd's flat yet again over an allegedly loose connection. He knew and she knew that there was nothing wrong electrically speaking, but that she was very, very lonely. He would arrange to call on her at a time that suited him to, when he was in the area, and she paid him a token fee to keep the thing on some kind of professional basis.

'Oh, I couldn't go for lots of reasons,' she said.

'I'm not really able to travel on my own, and anyway it would be a bit awkward. You know Amy doesn't get on with her father, so even if I were strong enough to travel there alone, it would cause a family upset, and we don't want that.'

Victor sent her a Valentine's Day card, but after his earlier frights in such matters, he didn't sign it.

It was on her mantelpiece when he next called to check the mythical mystery of the immersion heater.

'Thank you so much for the valentine, Victor,' she said.

'What makes you think I sent it?'

'Apart from my late husband, you are the only really romantic person I know,' she said.

The months went on. Her son Frank appeared less and less and gave yet more and more directions.

The letters from Amy were more and more yearning. 'Please come out here, Gran, I want to show you my Australia. You are not old, because you have a young heart. I'm saving to send you the fare.'

Around Christmas, when it was cold and wet in London, Victor made a decision.

'Mrs Todd, why don't you and I go there early next year together? I'll deliver you to your granddaughter, then I'll go off and see a bit of the Outback. I might hire a car and drive to Broken Hill. I'd enjoy that. Then I'd come back and take you back home.'

Her eyes filled with tears.

'You are such a kind man, even to *think* of it. Believe me, that's enough to make me very happy.'

'No, Mrs Todd, you must believe me, this is for me as much as you. I've always wanted to go to Australia. I've had the money saved and waiting, I just couldn't find the excuse.'

'But Frank?'

'Frank will have to accept it.'

'No, Victor. That's easy for you to say, you're a young man. I'm an old woman. Frank is all I have. He wouldn't dream of letting me go out all that way with . . . with . . .'

'With the electrician,' Victor finished for her.

'Well, yes, in a word.'

'Then I'll have to be a friend of Amy's, that's what we'll say.'

They smiled at each other. The adventure had begun.

It didn't take long to become a friend of Amy's, much less time than anyone would have thought possible, and all because of email.

Every morning he got a message from her. It was night-time in Sydney, and Victor sent one back, before she went to sleep. Bit by bit they put together the subterfuge, they invented a way in which they had met and become friends. They rejoiced at each other's inventiveness.

She said nothing hostile about her father, but made it clear that they were people who, while minimal courtesies would be maintained, would never have a meeting of the minds.

Frank was told, as he had to be, about the upcoming trip. He had a dozen objections, all of them rehearsed, and answered by the three conspirators. But he was up against unequal odds.

And then they were on the plane. Mrs Todd and Victor. They laughed when the steward thought they were mother and son.

'No, we are partners in an enterprise,' Mrs Todd explained.

They drank Australian wine to get into the mindset of the New World. They slept and woke.

And slept. They got out for coffee in the Middle East and for Tiger Beer in Singapore. Neither of them thought it the slightest bit odd to travel together to a continent on the other side of the earth.

They watched movies, they read magazines, and they talked about their past. Mrs Todd told

Victor about Mr Todd, who had been a wonderful, kind man who brought flowers home every Friday night and had told her she looked like a flower herself.

Victor told Mrs Todd about the various ladies in his life and how he had been a little too romantic for them. Perhaps his luck would change. No he didn't, he didn't really think it would in Australia. They were very modern there, forward looking, they would think he was a silly old Pom.

Mrs Todd said there were romantic people everywhere in the world, and he must not make generalisations.

Then it was dawn, and they saw the Opera House and the Bridge and all the things they had dreamed of, and they landed.

Crowds waited in the sunshine.

Victor wheeled Mrs Todd out in her chair.

A girl with a wonderful smile was waving at them. She had on pink shorts and sunglasses. Long black curly hair, dimples in her cheeks.

He knew immediately it was Amy.

'We're here,' he shouted.

'It's about time,' she called back.

Mrs Todd and her granddaughter embraced each other. They hugged and cried, and looked at each other with amazement. Around them the same scene was being acted over and over again. Australians welcoming the relatives from Britain.

Victor the electrician stood a little apart. Then they remembered him.

'This is Amy,' said Mrs Todd with huge pride.

'Welcome to Australia,' said Amy. She had a warm smile.

Suddenly he wished he hadn't made such firm arrangements about leaving Sydney to drive to the Outback. Sure it would be exciting, and that was one of the reasons he had come all this way. But Sydney looked as if it had a lot to offer as well. And he had only given himself three days to see it.

Amy showed them the city in style. She drove them over the famous Harbour Bridge and got them on a ferry to sail under it. She rightly regarded nothing as being too tiring or adventurous for her elderly grandmother.

She brought them to small restaurants where she knew the Greeks and Italians who ran the place. She liked that, it was all so international, she said.

'London's getting like that, too,' Victor said.

'Oh, London.' Amy shrugged.

'They're not all like your father,' Victor said before he could stop himself.

But she only smiled.

'Just as well,' she said.

They had pretended to be old friends as a ruse to fool her father. Already they felt they *were* old friends.

He longed to give her a valentine's card before he drove off across the bush, down the ribbon road that would take him past scrubland and ostriches. Amy had told him to be very careful of the kangaroos at sunset, they could jump out in front of the car. But Victor reminded himself of the many times his greetings had been misunderstood.

Perhaps there was a chocolate koala bear with hearts on it. But then, there was no point in sending a jokey thing; he couldn't understand a whole industry based on that.

He wanted to say thank you for lighting up our lives. Why should it have to be dressed up as a joke?

He came to say goodbye, and Amy handed him a single red rose. There was a card on it: 'I'll miss you, Victor Valentine.'

When he could speak, he said, 'I was thinking I needn't stay away all that long.'

Amy said, 'And I was thinking maybe we might come with you.'

The September Letters

September 1984

James wondered why people thought it was more glamorous to work in a bar in an airport than in an ordinary bar. They told him he must meet more interesting people, get a sense of the excitement of foreign travel maybe, huge tips from generous tourists.

But it wasn't so at all.

He might have liked it more being in a place where there were regulars, a bar where people dropped in regularly and knew his name and he knew theirs. People who would say, 'Another bloody day in the hell-hole, James,' or, 'I've been looking forward to this pint since four o'clock.'

And James would say, 'Come on now, Harry, you love work, you'd have to have a surgical operation to separate you from your mobile telephone.'

And everyone would laugh.

They didn't talk like that much at the airport. An airport was a place of High Anxiety, and great unease. James wondered why some people went on holiday at all. Husbands and wives fighting with each other about who had the tickets, the passports, whether the dog was happy in kennels or the gas had been turned off.

Children wanted to go and play video games, husbands wanted to buy motorbike magazines, wives wanted to get waterproof mascara and no one seemed happy for anyone else to follow their wishes.

Oh, James could write a book about Life just from two years of seeing people under the worst of conditions. He often said as much to Paula, the quiet Scottish girl who worked as his assistant. Paula agreed with him, but then she always did.

James felt that in her mind she was a million miles away. She was efficient and pleasant to the customers. She never got the change wrong, and she was able to hold contradictory orders in her head.

'Two gins and tonics, one of them slimline, and a half of that lager over there, and a pint of best bitter. No, make that a half, and make one of the gins a large one. Come on, it's a holiday, make them both large ones.'

Paula took it as part of the series of blows that each day dealt you in exchange for giving you a wage. She wanted to be a full-time student, but she had got neither a place at a university nor a grant. But she knew that she would get both if she could just keep herself and keep studying.

James didn't know what had happened to her after school. She was twenty-two now: why had she wasted the years when she might have been expected to go for a university place? But when he had tried to ask Paula had managed politely not to answer. So there the matter stood. It was her own business. He would never know.

Paula didn't seem interested in weaving stories about the people whom they served. There was a businessman sweating and stammering and holding his briefcase tightly in front of him.

'Bet he's got hot money in there,' James said.

'Could be,' Paula agreed.

'Or he's off on his first naughty weekend, perhaps?' James puzzled.

'Left it a bit late,' Paula remarked.

The sweating man was only in his forties, but the young are very cruel, James thought. James himself was almost in his forties and had not been on nearly enough naughty weekends. That could be part of his problem. But James never considered his own life as interesting enough to ponder on, he preferred to think about other people's goings-on. That's why he would have liked to have been a Mine Host barman, involved in his customers' lives.

That's why his wife said he would never amount to anything. Too interested in passers-by and paying no attention to what was meant to be important. Like his own home life.

It was a quiet September day, not much business, so James noted the middle-aged American couple. Well, if *he* called them middle-aged, they must be getting old.

Quiet people in light raincoats, perfect for the mysteries of European weather. They had flat, sensible shoes and each read a book while sipping slowly at their white wines and sodas. They had a look of utter compatibility, as if they need only raise their eyes and smile and it would say a great deal.

And eventually they both raised their eyes because there seemed to be a disturbance at the next table. A much younger couple were having what looked like a serious argument. In fact, James realised with a sick feeling in his throat, it was much more than a serious argument: it was about to turn into violence. The woman, young, dark haired and tear stained, was shouting at the man and was totally out of control.

'I've told you get away from me ... Don't come near me ... Unless you leave at once I'll make you leave ...'

The man was aware of others listening even if the girl was not.

'Be reasonable,' he begged. 'Listen, I can't leave you here in this state. Let me stay until you get on the plane.'

'Leave me *alone*!' she shouted. 'That's what you are going to do anyway, so do it now.'

'Katy, darling, please.' He was beseeching her now.

Suddenly Katy picked up a glass on the table and banged it against the side of a metal ashtray. It broke, leaving a jagged edge. She leaned over the table, using it as a weapon.

'*Now* will you leave me alone?' she cried.

The man was shocked and drew backwards, but she went after him.

'Go away, go away from here, and from me, don't call me Katy or darling as long as you live ...'

James felt his whole chest constrict with fear. Here in front of his eyes a woman was going to stab a man, and it would be his responsibility.

'Is everything all right?' he said foolishly.

The girl didn't appear to notice him, she was still following the man, her eyes never leaving his.

The man was stumbling backwards, shouting at James, 'Can't you *see* everything's not all right? Get the police, quickly.'

It would take a time to summon them, time that James thought he might not have. When he played the scene over to himself afterwards as he often did, James wondered where his courage had come from.

'I don't think that's the right thing to do, sir, why don't you leave now as the lady asks and then everything will calm down.'

The girl with the dark hair and the tear-stained face looked at him gratefully. The man, white as snow, looked wildly from one to the other. At least the glass wasn't advancing on him now. He made a decision. He ran. James watched him. He was about thirty, good-looking, blond haired, like the kind of man you saw in advertisements or in films about rich young chaps.

The girl stood there as if she were frozen. She looked at the broken glass she held as if she had no idea how it had got there. In that moment the American man stood up and removed the glass from her hand.

'Come and sit at this table,' he said in a gentle voice as if it was some kind of social occasion. 'You sit here and let the barman take care of all that broken glass,' he said softly.

The girl followed him obediently. James moved into action, got a brush and swept up the fragments, and carried the girl's small leather suitcase over to her new table.

'I'll pay for the glass,' the girl said.

'Nonsense, these things happen.'

James was proud of himself. He was behaving as if there had been no drama, which there hadn't been, thanks to his own quick thinking. How inspired it had been to get the guy to leave. Now it was almost impossible to imagine what the scene had been like. He left and went back to the bar where Paula stood looking at him in admiration.

'You were great,' she said. Paula hardly ever offered an opinion, a view, even a greeting. James felt that he *must* have been great.

At their table, the two Americans talked as they might have talked to any other passenger in a foreign airport. They had had a simply wonderful visit to Britain, and this time they had given themselves enough time, well, three weeks, but that was a great deal of time for Americans to spend in one country. They told Katy about the inns they had stayed in, old, old places, some of them had been in existence before the United States was founded. They had gone to the theatre often, they came from a city in the States where there wasn't much theatre, so they wanted to stock up on memories. They had walked a lot and talked to people. It was surprising that people said the British were hard to talk to, as they found them just charming.

'I'm sorry for the upset just now,' Katy said.

They brushed it aside. They seemed to think it was just a broken glass, as if they hadn't heard her shouts of pain and anger, her threats, her accusations.

'I'm Maurice, and this is my wife Jean,' the man said. 'Can we get you another drink since yours got spilled?'

He was kind and concerned. He reminded Katy of one of those TV doctors in an American television series. Saintly, listening people, who would do anything to help a patient.

'Are you a doctor?' she asked him suddenly.

'No, alas, not that kind of doctor. I do have a PhD, but that's not what you mean.'

There was something hypnotic about the way he talked, Katy was beginning to breathe normally again.

'I'd like a brandy, please. It might steady me a bit.'

'Sure.' He got up and walked at a leisurely pace over to James. 'The lady will have a brandy,' he said.

'Has the lady calmed down?' James whispered.

'Oh yes, most definitely,' said the American. 'Congratulations on your quick thinking by the way.'

James felt as pleased as anything.

'It was nothing,' he said, reddening with pride.

Back at the table Jean was saying how sad it was that Richard Burton had died, a very fine actor, and also James Mason in the same year, another great. Katy appeared to be listening.

'It *has* been a bad year for people dying,' she said. 'Eric Morecambe died, he was one of the funniest men in the world.'

Jean said they should think of something cheerful, so wasn't it wonderful that Princess Diana was any day now expecting a new baby?

'That's nice,' said Katy, but her voice was suddenly flat.

Jean glanced at Maurice anxiously. He put the brandy into her hand.

'Drink it slowly, as you don't look like a serious brandy drinker to me,' he said, smiling at her.

'You're very kind, both of you,' she said, her eyes brimming with tears.

'No, no, it's nice to have somebody to talk to at an airport,' Maurice insisted.

Katy hadn't even sipped the brandy.

'My life is over,' she said. She looked from one to the other, expecting them to laugh and dismiss it. But they didn't. They both took her seriously. They said nothing at all, just sat looking at her and waiting for her to say more.

'You see, he said he loved me, he said he was going to leave her.' Katy shook her head as if she were trying to clear water from her ears. 'I mean, you don't know me or anything about me, so you wouldn't know the kind of person I was before I met him. I was normal then. Before it all happened, before Colin.'

They still looked interested, not agog with curiosity but as if they had all the time in the world.

'So you changed?' Maurice said.

'I changed totally. I gave up everything for him. I loved him so much it's ridiculous, but you can't say things are ridiculous if they happened, can you?' She looked from one to the other.

'If they happen they are part of you and therefore important, I guess,' Jean said, sympathetically.

'Yes, well, war is ridiculous and yet that happened and will happen again, and people starving, that's ridiculous, when there's so much food on the earth . . . But falling for someone like Colin, that's sort of the same, you know it's going to end badly for everyone, for every single person, but you go on and do it regardless.'

'And will everyone get hurt, do you think?' Maurice sounded caring rather than curious, it was an odd distinction.

'Yes, almost everyone I know. My parents are hurt because I left their home and called them backward and old-fashioned and killjoys, and my friends ... Do I have any friends any more? I walked out on them. They're hurt, I suppose. And Colin, he's hurt because I told his wife, I told her I was sorry. And his wife's hurt because she didn't know. Imagine that, she didn't know anything about me at all.' Katy's eyes were wide with disbelief. 'Three years and she didn't know I existed. So much for all this business of her trying to work out what to do, and how we owed it to her to wait until she sorted herself out.'

Katy pushed the brandy to one side and laid her head down on the table and sobbed. They waited and soon it was over. Katy had a packet of tissues in her pocket.

'At least I provided myself with these,' she said with a watery smile.

'That's good forward planning,' Jean said admiringly.

'And where are you off to anyway?' Maurice spoke as one would speak to any traveller rather than to a girl who had brandished a broken glass, declared that her life was over and then cried like a baby.

'To Greece,' she said simply.

'Oh, really, one of the islands?'

'Yes, Crete. We go every year, Colin and I. Well, this is the third year. Except that he's not going now.'

'No, no, that's true.'

'It might be a bad place to go without him,' Maurice said. 'You know, every place you see reminding you of other days, different days.'

'But I tell you I am going,' she said defensively. 'I paid for my ticket. I took my two weeks' holiday from the office. I'm not going to be denied my holiday.' Her lip started to tremble again.

Maurice laughed at the very thought of anyone being denied a holiday.

'Why not go somewhere else?' he suggested.

'Because the plane leaves in an hour, and I won't get my money back,' Katy said.

'It's no reason to commit yourself to two weeks of feeling miserable,' he replied.

'I'll feel miserable anywhere,' Katy said, stating a fact.

'All that Greek music, it will only remind you,' Maurice said.

'He's right, Katy,' Jean agreed.

Katy shook her head.

Music anywhere reminds me . . . How do you think I feel when I hear Stevie Wonder sing "I Just Called to Say I Love You"?'

It was unanswerable.

'You've been very kind,' Katy said, getting up to go.

'Do me a favour, just one?'

'I *am* going to Crete,' she said.

'No, no, of course you must if you want to. Just write to us this day next year, will you? Here's my card.'

'What will I say?'

'Say you survived. Tell us something about the year.'

'I don't think I could. I'd be embarrassed, I cried all over you . . .' Katy looked around her. James was coming to clear the tables.

'Please, Katy, it would mean a lot to us. Just a note. It's not much to ask.'

James joined in. 'Go on, they bought you a brandy,' he urged her. 'And anyway I'd like to know you're OK too.'

'How would you know if I was all right?' Katy asked.

'They'd tell me,' James said.

'Sure we would.' Maurice gave his card to the

barman. 'Now you've all got this? Next year's a big year for me. On September 17 1985 I'll be fifty, so call it a birthday card. Give your addresses to me then, we won't plague you, just once a year. Hey, that's not much?'

His smile was warm.

'I'll write next year,' Katy promised.

Colin went straight home from the airport. He had told Monica that the firm wanted him to go for two weeks to Greece, and that he would be travelling around, he would call her from time to time. Sounded like paradise but in fact it wasn't. It was all a consultancy job for hotels, with hard graft, sweating in rooms with lots of people who didn't want to spend money. How much he'd prefer to be at home. He had told Katy that this time he really would sort it out with Monica and that this trip to Crete, their third trip, would be a real honeymoon. No more hiding, they would be able to live together openly from now on.

When he arrived at the airport, with suitcase packed and looking forward to the trip, all hell had broken loose. Katy had just called Monica to say she was glad it was all in the open and to assure Monica that there would be no trouble about money and alimony and everything. Monica was to have the house, as Katy had a job and could finance a flat for both of them. She had actually picked up the phone and said all this to Monica, because she thought Monica knew.

Now Colin was going home to face the music. Unpleasant music. He would have to say that Katy was mad, quite disturbed, in fact. Which, judging from the last glance he had seen of her brandishing a broken glass at him, did not seem too far from the total truth.

James went home to Miriam and told her all about it.

'Real hero,' she said sarcastically.

'Don't you like me at all, Miriam?' he asked her mildly.

She paused to think.

'I don't know, James, to be honest, I've forgotten.'

'How could you forget when you live with me?' he asked.

There was a silence.

'It's odd all right,' Miriam agreed. 'It's just that we live such separate lives. I have my sisters and all their comings and goings, and you have this life through the people that pass through your bar. I suppose we're just interested in different things. I don't dislike you though.'

'No. No indeed.' He was quiet.

'Why do you ask?'

'It's just I was looking at this couple today, the ones I was telling you about, who looked after the girl. I mean, they're only ten years older than I am, but they had something you and I will never have. They're sort of friends, you know.'

'I know,' Miriam agreed sadly. Then to cheer him up she said, 'Of course, you and I, we're not enemies or anything.'

'No, no. And then this girl, she had something we'll never have, a sort of passion.'

'We're too old for that, James.' But her voice was softer. She didn't go out to her sister's that evening, and they watched television instead. It was companionable. James was glad he hadn't told Miriam that they had always been too old for passion, even when they were young.

Paula couldn't concentrate on her studies. It was a warm night, but that wasn't the distraction. She kept seeing the face of that girl in the bar today. The girl who was prepared to kill the man who had wronged her. Maybe that's what Paula should have done when she was seventeen, killed the schoolteacher who told her he loved her, then denied that he had ever said it and insisted she have an abortion. Paula had no counselling, no guidance, no friends to talk it over with. Her parents would never have understood.

She had been unable to get the A levels that were hers by right. She couldn't study for them the following year. The teacher was still in the school, smiling at everyone but especially at another sixth-former that year. Paula knew what it was to feel like that, but she had never shown it. She would have died rather than make a scene in a public place, and yet the skies had not fallen on the girl, Katy, everyone had rallied to her.

Perhaps Paula should have been less secretive and reached out for help, there might have been a lot more of it available. Suddenly she made a resolution. That is what she was going to do this year, be more open to people. Like those two nice Americans. She wished they had asked *her* to write to them the following year too. But of course she always hung in the background. Nobody would approach her because she looked like a person who could not be approached.

Katy went to Crete. She knew the moment she stepped from the plane that it had been the wrong thing to do. The familiar heat, the taxi drivers calling, the little glasses of ouzo at the small tables, the bread and cheese and olives on the coloured plates. At night, the lights reflecting in the harbour. The swimming alone on the beach that used to be their beach. She got into the habit of taking a long bus journey to another beach and coming home late and tired. She counted the days until the holiday ended.

One night, she looked at the moon and asked herself if it were possible that she had been here only six days, it felt more like two years. And for no reason next morning she bought five postcards and sent them to her parents, her sister and three friends. She thought of sending one to the American couple, Maurice and Jean, but no, they said they wouldn't plague her, so she wouldn't plague them either. Next year they said, next year it would be.

Tuesday, 10 September 1985
Dear Maurice and Jean,
I don't know whether you will remember me or not. I was a very distraught, mad woman at London airport who got upset because my boyfriend had lied to me. You were very kind and supportive to me, and I have never forgotten you.
I would love to be able to write and tell you that it all turned out wonderfully and then when I was in Crete I met a new man and we loved so happily that the patter of tiny feet is

now a definite sound. But no, life doesn't work out like that.

I came back from Crete and I made friends with my mother and father and sister again and that was great. And other friends, and that was great too.

But truthfully it wasn't enough, I yearned for Colin with such a pain you wouldn't believe it. And when he wrote a letter saying how bad he felt, I took him back. He said he realised how much I loved him when I was prepared to kill him that day. He had no idea how strongly I felt.

Men are so strange. What else did he expect me to feel?

He hasn't left Monica, as she is being very difficult and could cause trouble for him at work so it's better not to rock that boat.

I have less foolish dreams than I used to, I know it won't all be plain sailing. We won't have that holiday in Greece, but we have had a couple of nice weekends away together, and of course he comes round to me on Wednesday afternoons.

You are both very kind people. I wish you knew how often I think of your kind faces and how helpful and concerned you were for me. I feel sure you didn't forget me.

Warm wishes and great gratitude,
Katy

Dear Dr and Mrs Hunt,

I am James Green, barman in one of the departure lounges in London airport. We agreed that I would write to you and find out whether the young lady, Katy, recovered from all her worries on that day. If you think this is an intrusion and you did not mean to write, please forgive me.

It's hard to write news of things to strangers, hard to know what you would be interested in. There was a wonderful concert this year called Live Aid, where all the famous stars appeared free and it made a huge amount of money for famine in Africa.

My wife, Miriam, and I went to it and we were both very moved by it all. I believe there were similar concerts in the United States. I hope everything turned out well for the young woman who was so distressed.

Yours sincerely,
James Green

When Katy picked up the letter from the Hunts, she knew it would be warm and kind and she wanted to read it properly, but it arrived in the second post on a Wednesday, the only free time that Colin could get these days.

She had organised her own schedule around

this quite easily. Katy worked in a solicitor's office. There was a great deal of routine work to be done. She had managed to convince her boss that if she were to have Wednesday afternoons free, she would be happy to work on Saturday mornings. They had agreed readily when no overtime pay seemed to be demanded, hence her Wednesday afternoons were her own.

She tried to hide the letter but she wasn't quick enough. Colin reached for it.

'Hey, have you a lover in America?' he asked playfully.

'No, no, just friends.'

'Why don't you want me to see it then?'

'We don't live each other's lives, Colin, there are lots of things I don't ask you.'

'Like what?' He looked impossibly over-confident.

'Like whether you still sleep with Monica or not,' Katy said.

There was a silence. He seemed to look at her with more respect.

'I'll never take you for granted,' Colin promised her.

'I hope not,' Katy said, kissing him on the nose.

'I heard from those nice Americans.' James Green was pleased.

'Tell me, what did they say?' Paula was interested.

She had changed a lot, James thought, she was much more outgoing these days. He showed her the letter, and she read it with interest.

'Pity she's gone back to the fellow.'

'Well, she loved him, you see, people like you and me don't know about passion.'

'Speak for yourself, James Green,' Paula said in her clipped Scots accent.

'Well, pardon me, I shouldn't have spoken.'

'Speak on your own behalf. I know what passion is, or I knew once.'

'You're lucky,' James said simply.

'No, not really. It ruined my life, but I'm putting it back together again.'

James Green felt weak at the knees. They say you get used to everything when you work behind a bar but James thought this was one of the most unexpected things he had ever heard in his life.

In September 1986, Katy wrote to tell the Hunts that her father had been very ill and she had gone to spend her holiday with him. And she had been there when he died. She said it was so good that she had made her peace with him, and never again would she cut herself off from family or friends. It wasn't a real kind of love that made you do that, it was desperation. And Colin and she *did* have a real kind of love.

Katy understood love better now, it could be compartmentalised, one part of Colin was for Monica, one part of him was for her. That was the way to look at it, and not to keep demanding more time, or attention, as a child would do. They had never been happier.

Katy wrote that she sounded so self-centred, and she knew nothing about the Hunts' life. What did they do with their time, and were they coming back to Britain again?

The Hunts wrote about how good it was that Katy was happy, how sad it was that her father had died, and also that James Cagney had died that year too, but how wonderful that there was to be another royal romance, Prince Andrew and Fergie. How marvellous. And they had no plans for a further vacation at the moment. They said Katy should call in to see that nice barman in the airport who enquired about her.

James Green wrote and told the Hunts that he and Miriam had gone to South America for a reason that he might tell them next year. But at the moment it was enough to say that the Argentines were stark staring mad about football, and if you thought the British were bad, please have a look at the boys that followed Maradona.

*

September 1987

Dear Jean and Maurice,

 Wasn't it sad that Danny Kaye and Fred Astaire died this year? What great entertainers they were. Colin and I are fine, just great these days. Most Wednesdays we meet, when he can make it. Monica got involved with someone, had an affair, I mean. The man was apparently a total loser, he disappeared, of course, took no responsibility for anything, and now she's pregnant.

 Colin says it's not the child's fault so he's going to give the baby his name. Which is very good of him but then I'd expect that of him.

 I went to see James Green, the barman, he is very nice, you were right. I expect he told you his wonderful news, he has pictures of it stuck all over his bar.

 Thank you for your continued interest.

 Love,

 Katy

Dear Dr and Mrs Hunt,

 Here is a picture of our pride and joy, Marco, isn't he wonderful? That's what Miriam

*and I were doing in Argentina, but we had to
keep very quiet until it was all organised and
legal. Well, as near to legal as makes no
difference. He's a wonderful child, and when
we think what his life would have been like if
we had left him where he was, we both
shudder.*

*We are saving very hard, we want to have a
small place in the countryside where Marco can
grow up with green fields and fresh air.*

We are all very happy.

*Wasn't it wonderful that Mrs Thatcher got
in for a third term? Miriam isn't so happy
about it and neither is Paula who works with
me. Paula is only part-time as she has a place
at university now, but women are inclined to
be jealous of each other.*

Yours ever,
James Green

In September 1988, Katy wrote to say that Colin
was worn out pacing the floor at night with a
baby girl that was not his, and weren't some men
wonderful.

James Green wrote to say he had a change of
address. Miriam and Marco and he were moving
to the West Country, to a lovely place in Somerset

where his brother-in-law had helped them to get a start.

In September 1989, Katy wrote to say that she had very nearly fought with her mother and sister again because they said Colin's wife, Monica, was pregnant once more, and once *might* have been due to this somebody unreliable whom she had turned to because of Katy, but twice could not be.

James and Miriam sent another picture of Marco, this time playing outside their pub. They did bed and breakfast too, if ever the Hunts were coming this way again.

In September 1990, Katy wrote to say she was sure they must have been laughing at her all this time, they were adult people, mature and secure in their love, they must have realised that Colin had never loved her. Not one little bit. This time she was not suicidal, she was just waiting to stop needing him and aching, she was sure it wouldn't be long now.

She also said that that nice man, James Green, owned a pub that had been written up in all the magazines, and that his assistant, Paula, back in the airport-pub days, had got a first-class honours degree and was going on to do a Master's and a PhD.

In September 1991, Katy's letter said that on the tenth anniversary of the day she had met Colin, she stopped loving him. It was as straightforward as that, and as lengthy. Imagine a decade of her life, more than a third of the time she had lived, spent in a dream. It had ended very simply. She had told him not to come and see her one Wednesday, and then the next. And the third time she said it, he said it was just as well because he had to look after the children while Monica went to a Women's Group meeting.

She felt old now, Katy wrote. Old and wise. Twenty-nine.

She would regard Colin as if he had been some illness and now she was cured.

James and Miriam sent some press clippings about the pub to show it was a really good place to stay if they wanted to visit, and they must, believe it or not, book in good time, they even had reservations six months in advance.

In September 1992, Katy wrote to say she had spent a wonderful weekend at James and Miriam's pub and met a marvellous man.

'So, it's all due to you dear, dear Jean and Maurice,' she wrote. 'And when are you two going to come back this way? Otherwise I'm going to have to come and find you in America. Turn up at your door even.'

My dear Katy,

I'm so happy you have found happiness. So very, very happy. I have told you lies for many years for a reason that I will never fathom.

That day when we met you in the airport was a big day in my life. An hour earlier Maurice had told me that he was going to leave me for another woman. A much younger woman, I need hardly say. He said that he was approaching fifty and he felt that he had never lived life properly. The affair had been going on for some years, I was the only person in our circle who didn't know about it.

I thought that I would die. I couldn't even speak to him about it. He begged me to talk, to rail against him even, but I said no, I wanted to read my book. I didn't see a word on the page, all the time I was thinking, what do I do with the rest of my life? Then I saw you, with so much fire and love and despair in your face. Perhaps this girl felt about Maurice like that. I certainly did not.

It was helpful to us as well as to you to talk you out of doing anything foolish. We spoke on about our holiday and the plays we had seen, it dulled the pain of the news I had heard in the last hour.

And *there was something in your face that gave me a resolve. I knew that not only could I live without him, but I should. I saw his hypocrisy, pretending to be the wise, all-knowing psychologist, asking you to get in touch, knowing that he would be long gone from that address by the time you wrote.*

I never saw Maurice after that day. I asked him to take his things away as soon as possible, and I remained in the house.

The letters came from you and from James. I kept up the correspondence and the fiction.

It has been deeply satisfying, watching your lives go from strength to strength. Don't stop the September letters, please, Katy, and always remember I needed them as much as you ever did and I learned more from your face that day than you ever learned from mine. Yours was honest, mine was an act.

And now that we know so much, maybe they could come more often than once a year.

You might think of inviting your young man to come and see me and I will surely think of

making a long-distance booking for James's
and Miriam's splendid pub.
  Love and happiness,
  From your fond and accidental friend,
  Jean Hunt

Cross
Lines

Martin tapped his fingers in irritation on the phone. He was unsure of himself in this new and unfamiliar world of the arts where he was heading. There were already too many stresses involved in this whole business without having to part from Angie in such an unsatisfactory way. Beautiful Angie, why hadn't she got up and pulled on a track suit? Why hadn't she said she'd drive him to the airport, they'd have coffee and a croissant together; it would have been so good. It would have calmed him down, to have sat with Angie, looking into her big dark eyes watching the passers-by envy him with this girl with the great mane of streaked hair and the big slow smile. He would have felt a million times more confident about the venture ahead. Instead of edgy and jumpy.

In the next booth he saw one of those kind of career women he disliked on sight. Short practical hairdo, mannish suit, enormous briefcase, immaculate make-up, gold watch pinned to a severe lapel. She was making a heavy statement about being equal and coping in a man's world. She was having a heated discussion with somebody on her telephone. Probably entirely unnecessary, shouting at someone for the sake of it. He would give Angie another three minutes and dial again. She had never been known to talk this long to anyone. And at nine-thirty a.m.

Kay wished the man in the next phone box would stop staring at her; she had enough to cope with with one of Henry's tantrums. She had explained to Henry over and over how important it was for her to be at the trade fair a day in advance; that way she could supervise the setting up of the stand, make sure they had the right position, the one they had booked near the entrance, see that the lighting was adequate, decorate the booth, get to know the neighbours on her right and left so that she could rely on them and call on their support once the doors opened and the day's business began.

Henry had said he understood, but that was yesterday; today he was in one of his moods.

Kay would be gone for five days; she *hated* leaving him like this, it was so uncalled for, he had nothing to fear from her trip to another town. She would be far too weary and exhausted to consider going out partying at the end of a long day; all she would want was a warm little telephone conversation every night, reassuring her that he loved her, that he was managing fine but not so fine as he managed when she was around and how he greatly looked forward to Friday. She had called him at the office to try to dispel his mood before it got a grip of him.

It had been a mistake. Henry's black disapproval came across the phone line loud and clear.

She had made her choice. She had decided for an extra day on this junket, and against going with him to his staff party. It was quite simple; she could take the consequences.

'What consequences?' Kay shouted, turning her back on the arty pseudo-bohemian in the next phone box.

He was handsome, she supposed, in that vain peacock way that a lot of actors or showbiz people adopt, mannered and self-aware, stroking his cravat. The kind of man she most disliked. But it was increasingly hard to talk to Henry, the kind of man she most admired. He was showing none of those qualities that had marked him out when she met him first.

He pointed out that if Kay, his constant companion, was not going to bother to turn up at an important corporate gathering, then he would regard himself as a single and unattached person with no commitments.

'That's blackmail of the worst kind.' Kay was appalled at herself for reacting like a teenager.

'The solution is in your hands,' Henry said coldly. 'Come back from the airport now and we will forget the whole incident.' She hung up immediately, not trusting herself to speak to him.

Martin told himself that Angie's deep sleep was always important to her. She was a model; her face had to be unlined, untired at all times. She must have taken the telephone off the hook. His brow cleared when he remembered this, only to darken again when he remembered that as he kissed her goodbye he had said he would call from the airport and she had said that would be super. Why, then, had she cut off his way of getting through to her?

Lost in their thoughts, neither Martin nor Kay realised that they had in fact been seated beside each other on the plane . . . They looked at each other without pleasure. Martin took out the long, complicated report on arts funding that he was going to have to explain to various theatrical and artistic organisations, all of which were going to brand him as a cultural philistine. Kay read a report on last year's trade fair, and noted all the opportunities missed, contacts lost, and areas of dissatisfaction. Their elbows touched lightly.

But they were unaware of each other. From time to time they lifted their eyes from the small print in their folders and Martin thought of all the times *he* had driven Angie to her modelling assignments and Kay remembered all the corporate functions in *her* firm that Henry had refused to attend without even the flimsiest excuse.

Above the clouds it was a lovely day, bright and clear. Kay felt her shoulders relaxing, and some of the tension leaving her. They were far above the complications and bustle of everything they had left behind: buildings, traffic, rush, corporate functions. She breathed deeply. She wished they could stay up here for ever.

At that moment Martin sighed too, and with the first sign of a pleasant expression that he had shown, he said that it was a pity they couldn't stay up here for ever.

'I was just thinking that. At exactly this moment,' Kay said, startled.

They talked easily, he of the problems ahead trying to convince earnest idealistic artists that he was not the voice of authority spelling out doom for their projects. He had been trying to dress like arty people, as he knew that otherwise he would be dismissed as a Man in a Suit, which was apparently marginally better than being a child molester.

She told him of the poor results the company had achieved at last year's promotion, and how this was her first year in charge. There were many in the organisation who hoped she would fail, and she feared they would be proved right. She knew that people thought she had got the post through some kind of feminine charm; she was dressing as severely as she could to show them that she wasn't flighty.

They were sympathetic and understanding. Martin told her what Henry never had, that perhaps she was overcompensating, making herself look too stern and forbidding, killing off the good vibes she might otherwise have given.

Kay told Martin something that Angie had never thought of – that possibly the cravat might be over the top. There was the possibility that the disaffected artistic folk might think he was playing a role.

They fell into companionable silence in the clear, empty blue sky. And Martin thought that Angie probably didn't care about him at all, she cared only about her face, the magazine covers she appeared on, and what bookings her agent might have for her next week. He would call her when they landed, a cheerful call, no accusations about taking the phone off the hook, she would wish him well, and he would take the whole thing much more lightly from now on.

Kay wondered if Henry would seriously take up with someone else, as he had threatened. And would she mind very much if he did. She decided she would ring Henry's secretary and say how sorry she was to miss this evening's function, she would wish it well and say that sadly work had taken precedence. She would ask that Henry not be disturbed but insist that her message of goodwill was passed to those in the right places. This was a professional, businesslike approach, not a very loving one. But Kay didn't feel very loving any more.

Then, just at the same moment, she and Martin left their private thoughts and turned to each other to talk again. Angie wasn't mentioned, nor was Henry, but strategy was, and optimism was exchanged.

Kay encouraged Martin to be straight with the groups, to tell them the worst news about funding first and try to work back into a position they felt was marginally more cheerful. Martin advised Kay to let her colleagues in on her hopes for their joint success, let them think they were creating it too. By the time they left the plane they were friends in everything but name. Martin considered asking her name but thought it might sound patronising. Kay wondered about giving him her card but feared it would look stereotype female executive.

There was a bank of telephones facing them in Arrivals. They both headed towards them.

Kay paused with her hand on the receiver. In the next box she saw Martin's fingers, not drumming this time but hesitating. Through the transparent walls they smiled at each other.

He looks less affected, she thought, the velvet jacket's fine really.

She is quite elegant in spite of all that power dressing, he realised.

Neither of them made the phone call.

But it was too soon for any sudden decisions. There was work to be done. If they met each other somewhere again, well and good.

They wished each other luck and got into separate taxis.

As they settled back into their separate seats they each gave their taxi driver the name of the same hotel.

A Holiday with
Your Father

Rose looked at the woman with the two cardboard cups of coffee. She had one of those good-natured faces that you always associate with good works. Rose had seen smiles like that selling jam at fêtes or bending over beds in hospitals or holding out collection boxes hopefully.

And indeed the woman and the coffee headed for an old man wrapped up well in a thick overcoat even though the weather was warm, and the crowded coffee bar in Victoria Station was even warmer.

'I think we should drink it fairly quickly, Dad,' said the woman in a half-laughing way. 'I read somewhere that if you leave it for any length at all, the cardboard melts into the coffee and that's why it tastes so terrible.'

He drank it up obediently and he said it wasn't at all bad. He had a nice smile. Suddenly and for no reason he reminded Rose of her own father.

The good-natured woman gave the old man a paper and his magnifying glass and told him not to worry about the time, she'd keep an eye on the clock and have them on the platform miles ahead of the departure time. Secure and happy, he read the paper and the good-natured woman read her own. Rose thought they looked very nice and contented and smiled, cheered to see a good scene in a café instead of all those depressing gloom scenes you can see like middle-aged couples staring into space and having nothing to say to each other.

She looked at the labels on their suitcases. They were heading for Amsterdam. The name of the hotel had been neatly typed. The suitcases had little wheels under them. Rose felt this woman was one of the world's good and wise organisers. Nothing was left to chance; it would be a very well-planned little holiday.

The woman had a plain wedding ring on. She might be a widow. Her husband might have left her for someone outrageous and bad-natured. Her husband and four children might all be at home and this woman was just taking her father to Amsterdam because he had seemed in poor spirits. Rose made up a lot of explanations and finally decided that the woman's husband had been killed in an appalling accident that she had borne very bravely and she now worked for a local charity, and that she and her father went on a holiday to a different European capital every year.

Had the snack bar been more comfortable, she might have talked to them. They were not the kind of people to brush away a pleasant conversational opening. But it would have meant moving all her luggage nearer to them, which seemed a lot of fuss. Leave them alone. Let them read their papers, let the woman glance at the clock occasionally, and eventually let them leave. Quietly, without rushing, without fuss. Everything neatly stowed in the two bags on wheels. Slowly, sedately . . . they moved towards a train for the south coast. Rose was sorry to see them go. Four German students took their place. Young, strong, and blond, spreading coins German and English out on the table and working out how much they could buy between them. They didn't seem so real.

There was something *reassuring*, she thought, about being able to go on a holiday with your father. It was like saying thank you, it was like stating that it had all been worthwhile . . . all that business of his getting married years ago and begetting you and saving for your future and having hopes for you. It seemed a nice way of rounding things off to be able to take your father to see foreign cities ... because things had changed so much from his day. Nowadays young people could manage these things as a matter of course; in your father's day it was still an adventure and a risk to go abroad.

She wondered what her father would say if she set up a trip for him. She wondered only briefly, because really she knew. He'd say:

'No, Rose my dear, you're very thoughtful, but you can't teach an old dog new tricks.'

And she would say that it wasn't a question of that. He wasn't an old dog. He was only sixty, and they weren't new tricks since he used to go to Paris every year when he was a young man, and he and Mummy had spent their honeymoon there.

Then he would say that he had such a lot of work to catch up on, so it would be impossible to get away, and if she pointed out that he didn't really have to catch up on anything, that he couldn't have to catch up on anything, because he stayed so late at the bank each evening catching up anyway ... Well, then he would say that he had seen Europe at its best ... when it was glorious, and perhaps he shouldn't go back now.

But he'd love to go back, he would love it. Rose knew that. He still had all the scrapbooks and pictures of Paris just before the war. She had grown up with those brown books, and sepia pictures, and memos and advertisements, and maps carefully plotted out . . . lines of dots and arrows to show which way they had walked to Montmartre and which way they had walked back. He couldn't speak French well, her father, but he knew a few phrases, and he liked the whole style of things French, and used to say they were a very civilised race.

The good-natured woman and her father were probably pulling out of the station by now. Perhaps they were pointing out things to each other as the train gathered speed. A wave of jealousy came over Rose. Why was this woman – an ordinary woman perhaps ten years older than Rose, maybe not even that – why was she able to talk to her father and tell him things and go places with him and type out labels and order meals and take pictures? Why could she do all that and Rose's father wouldn't move from his deck chair in the sun lounge when his three-week holiday period came up? And in his one week in the winter, he caught up on his reading.

Why had a nice good warm man like her father got nothing to do, and nowhere to go after all he had done for Rose and for everyone? Tears of rage on his behalf pricked Rose's eyes.

Rose remembered the first time she had been to Paris, and how Daddy had been so interested, and fascinated, and dragging out the names of hotels in case she was stuck, and giving her hints on how to get to them. She had been so impatient at twenty, so intolerant, so embarrassed that he thought that things were all like they had been in his day. She had barely listened, she was anxious for his trip down the scrapbooks and up the maps to be over. She had been furious to have had to carry all his carefully transcribed notes. She had never looked at them while there. But that was twenty, and perhaps everyone knows how restless everyone else is at twenty and hopefully forgives them a bit. Now at thirty she had been to Paris several times, and because she was much less restless she had found time to visit some of her father's old haunts . . . dull, merging into their own backgrounds . . . those that still existed . . . she was generous enough these days to have photographed them, and he spent happy hours examining the new prints and comparing them with the old with clucks of amazement and shakings of the head that the old bakery had gone, or the tree-lined street was now an underpass with six lanes of traffic.

And when Mum was alive she too had looked at the cuttings and exclaimed a bit and shown interest that was not a real interest. It was only the interest that came from wanting to make Daddy happy.

And after Mum died people had often brought up the subject to Daddy of his going away. Not too soon after the funeral, of course, but months later when one of his old friends from other branches of the bank might call . . .

'You might think of taking a trip abroad again sometime,' they would say. 'Remember all those places you saw in France, no harm to have a look at them again. Nice little trip.' And Daddy would always smile a bit wistfully. He was so goddamn gentle and non-pushing, thought Rose, with another prickle of tears. He didn't push at the bank, which was why he wasn't a manager. He hadn't pushed at the neighbours when they built all around and almost over his nice garden . . . his pride and joy, which was why he was overlooked by dozens of bed-sitters now. He hadn't pushed Rose when Rose said she was going to marry Gus. If only Daddy had been more pushing then . . . it might have worked. Suppose Daddy had been strong and firm and said that Gus was what they called a bounder in his time and possibly a playboy in present times . . . just suppose Daddy had said that. Might she have listened at all or would it have strengthened her resolve to marry the Bad Egg? Maybe those words from Daddy's lips might have brought her up short for a moment . . . enough to think. Enough to spare her the two years of sadness in marriage and the two more years organising the divorce.

But Daddy had said nothing. He had said that whatever she thought must be right. He had wished her well, and given them a wedding present for which he must have had to cash in an insurance policy. Gus had been barely appreciative. Gus had been bored with Daddy. Daddy had been unfailingly polite and gentle with Gus. With Gus long gone, Rose had gone back to live in Daddy's house. It was peaceful despite the blocks of bed-sitters. It was undemanding. Daddy kept his little study where he caught up on things, and he always washed saucepans after himself if he had made his own supper. They didn't often eat together . . . Rose had irregular hours as a traveller and Daddy was so used to reading at his supper . . . and he ate so early in the evening. If she stayed out at night there were no explanations and no questions. If she told him some of her adventures there was always his pleased interest.

Rose was going to Paris this morning. She had been asked to collect some samples of catalogues. It was a job that might take a week if she were to do it properly or a day if she took a taxi and the first fifty catalogues that caught her eye. She had told Daddy about it this morning. He was interested, and he took out his books to see again what direction the new airport was in . . . and what areas Rose's bus would pass as she came in to the city centre. He spent a happy half an hour on this, and Rose had looked with both affection and interest. It was ridiculous that he didn't go again. Why didn't he?

Suddenly she thought she knew. She realised it was all because he had nobody to go with. He was in fact a timid man. He was a man who said sorry when other people stepped on him, which is what the nicer half of the world does . . . but it's also sometimes an indication that people might be wary and uneasy about setting up a lonely journey, a strange pilgrimage of return. Rose thought of the good-natured woman and the man who must be ten or fifteen years older than Daddy; tonight they would be eating a meal in a Dutch restaurant. Tonight Daddy would be having his scrambled egg and deadheading a few roses, while his daughter, Rose, would be yawning at a French restaurant trying not to look as if she were returning the smiles of an ageing lecher. *Why* wasn't Daddy going with her? It was her own stupid fault. All those years, seven of them since Mummy had died, seven years, perhaps thirty trips abroad for her, not a mention of inviting Daddy. The woman with the good-natured countenance didn't live in ivory towers of selfishness like that.

Almost knocking over the table, she stumbled out and got a taxi home. He was actually in a cardigan in the garden scratching his head and sucking on his pipe and looking like a stage image of someone's gentle, amiable father. He was alarmed to see her. He had to be reassured. But why had she changed her mind? Why did it not matter whether she went today or tomorrow? He was worried. Rose didn't do sudden things. Rose did measured things, like he did. Was she positive she was telling him the truth and that she hadn't felt sick or faint or worried?

They were not a father and daughter who hugged and kissed. Pats were more the style of their touching. Rose would pat him on the shoulder and say: 'I'm off now, Daddy' or he would welcome her home clasping her hand and patting the other arm enthusiastically. His concern as he stood worried among his garden things was almost too much to bear.

'Come in and we'll have a cup of tea, Daddy,' she said, wanting a few moments bent over kettle, sink, tea caddy to right her eyes.

He was a shuffle behind her, anxiety and care

in every step. Not wishing to be too inquisitive, not wanting, but plans changed meant bad news. He hated it.

'You're not *doing* anything really, Daddy, on your holidays, are you?' she said eventually once she could fuss over tea things no longer. He was even more alarmed.

'Rose, my dear, do you have to go to hospital or anything? Rose, my dear, is something wrong? I'd much prefer if you told me.' Gentle eyes, his lower lip fastened in by his teeth in worry. Oh, what a strange father. Who else had never had a row with a father? Was there any other father in the world so willing to praise the good, rejoice in the cheerful, and to forget the bad and the painful?

'Nothing, Daddy, nothing. But I was thinking, it's silly my going to Paris on my own. Staying in a hotel and reading a book and you staying here reading a book or the paper. I was thinking wouldn't it be nice if I left it until tomorrow and we *both* went. The same way . . . the way I go by train to Gatwick . . . or we could get the train to the coast and go by ferry.'

He looked at her, cup halfway to his mouth. He held it there. 'But why, Rose dear? Why do you suggest this?' His face had rarely seemed more troubled. It was as if she had asked him to leave the planet.

'Daddy, you often talk about Paris, you tell *me* about it, I tell *you* about it. Why don't we go together and tell each other about it when we come back.' She looked at him . . . he was so bewildered she wanted to shout at him, she wanted to finish her sentences through a loud-speaker.

Why did he look so unwilling to join? He was being asked to play. Now, don't let him hang back, slow to accept like a shy schoolboy who can't believe he has been picked for the team.

'Daddy, it would be nice. We could go out and have a meal and we could go up and walk to Montmartre by the same routes as you took in the good old days. We could do the things you did when you were a wild teenager . . .'

He looked at her, frightened, trapped. He was so desperately kind, he saw the need in her. He didn't know how he was going to fight her off. She knew that if she were to get him to come, she must stress that she really wanted it for her, more than for him.

'Daddy, I'm often very lonely when I go to Paris. Often at night particularly I remember that you used to tell me how all of you . . .'

She stopped. He looked like a hunted animal.

'Wouldn't you like to come?' she said in a much calmer voice.

'My dear Rose. *Sometime*. I'd love to go to Paris, my dear, there's nothing in the world I'd like to do more than to come to Paris ... but I can't go just like that. I can't drop everything and rush off to Paris, my dear. You know that.'

'Why not, Daddy?' she begged. She knew she was doing something dangerous, she was spelling out her own flightiness, her own action of whim of doubling back from the station ... she was defining herself as less than level-headed.

She was challenging him, too. She was asking him to say why he couldn't come to a few days of shared foreign things. If he had no explanation, then he was telling her that he was just someone who said he wanted something but didn't reach for it. She could be changing the nature of his little dreams. How would he ever take out his pathetically detailed maps and scrapbooks to pore once more with her over routes and happenings if he had thrown away a chance to see them in three dimensions?

'You have nothing planned, Daddy. It's ideal. We can pack for you. I'll ask them next door to keep an eye on the house. We'll stop the milk and the newspaper, and, Daddy, that's it. Tomorrow evening in Paris, tomorrow afternoon we'll be taking that route in together, the one we talked about for me this morning . . .'

'But, Rose . . . all the things here . . . my dear, I can't just drop everything . . . you do see that.'

Twice now he had talked about all the things here that he had to drop. There was *nothing* to drop. What he would drop was pottering about scratching his head about leaf curl. Oh, Daddy, don't you see that's all you'll drop. But if you don't see and I tell you . . . it means I'm telling you that your life is meaningless and futile and pottering. I will not tell *you*, who walked around the house cradling me when I was a crying baby, you who paid for elocution lessons so that I could speak well, you, Daddy, who paid for that wedding lunch that Gus thought was shabby, you, Daddy, who smiled and raised your champagne glass to me and said: 'Your mother would have loved this day. A daughter's wedding is a milestone.' I won't tell you that your life is nothing.

The good-natured woman and her father were probably at Folkestone or Dover or Newhaven when Rose said to her father that of course he was right, and it had just been a mad idea, but naturally they would plan it for later. Yes, they really must, and when she came back this time they would talk about it seriously . . . and possibly next summer.

'Or even when I retire,' said Rose's father, the colour coming back into his cheeks. 'When I retire I'll have lots of time to think about these things and plan them.'

'That's a good idea, Daddy,' said Rose. 'I think that's a very good idea. We should think of it for when you retire.'

He began to smile. Reprieve. Rescue. Hope.

'We won't make any definite plans, but we'll always have it there, as something we must talk about doing. Yes, much more sensible,' she said.

'Do you really mean that, Rose? I certainly think it's a good idea,' he said, anxiously raking her face for approval.

'Oh, honestly, Daddy, I think it makes *much* more sense,' she said, wondering why so many loving things had to be lies.

Bran's
Horizons

Bran hated his name, and he hated even more the explanations of it. His father used to say it was the name of a Celtic god reduced to human stature; his mother said that it was all very well to sit in ivory towers calling children after Celtic – which meant pagan – gods, but it was a different story when you sent the same children to the Brothers. Say it's a pet name, she suggested, called after the faithful hound of Fionn MacCumhaill. Neither of these definitions appealed to Bran. Everyone thought he was called Brian and was just trying to say the name in a posh accent.

Bran wished that he could be like some of the other fellows with grand, reasonable names like Seán and Jarlath and Carthage. Fellows who didn't start several rungs down. They were able to laugh at the awful things that kept happening because they didn't have the daily indignity of apologising for their names. Nobody made jokes about high fibre to them. There were no awful books of F-Plan diets based on their names. Nobody ever said that you should have a spoonful of their name with each meal.

Brother Simon, who was very nice, said Bran should rise above his name and not be going on with this nonsense of changing it by deed poll. Brother Simon told him a secret and said that, for years at school, people used to call him Simple Simon, but he had risen far, far above it, ignored them completely. He *knew* he wasn't simple, that was the important thing, and the louts who had been jeering at him were on the Labour, or getting their bones rotted in wet weather in farms they would never own, while Brother Simon lived a great life, educating boys in the school on the hill.

It was hard to rise above it. In Brother Simon's day it was probably easier, the jeering wasn't so sophisticated, so hard to think of an answer to. Hardly a week passed by without one of them bringing in a cutting about 'The Need for Bran', and even an article from a newspaper asking 'Are We Going Overboard on Bran?' Brother Simon said he had risen above it by putting his mind to his books, but Bran wasn't sure about the total honesty of that statement. It might be just a ploy to get Bran to work harder. If there was any rising above it, and this term there seemed to be a greater need than ever, then it would have to be by some other avenue.

He was only average at everything and all he wanted was to be left alone. It didn't seem much to ask. His mother was nice, she left him alone mainly because he wasn't a bird with a broken wing or a small, wounded deer. If he had been a badger with a bleeding paw, she would have lavished attention on him. The kitchen was full of overfed sparrows with splints made from match-sticks, and in the outhouse was a litany of things that needed warm milk at one time and tins of catfood at others.

His mother had a kind face and was often very tearful over animals. Animals had no voice, she told Bran, over and over; she was trying to be their voice for them. He agreed with her basically, even though some of them, like the dog with three legs, had very loud voices indeed. But Bran knew this wasn't the point; the point was that they couldn't get up a protest about the unfairness of their being used in laboratories to experiment on, and the meanness of their being starved or beaten.

Sometimes he wished that his mother would concentrate a little bit on looking more ordinary, combing her hair and wearing a real skirt and coat rather than a poncho and waders, but his mother was so kind it seemed ungracious and bad to have such thoughts about her, and when they occurred, Bran tried to banish them.

And his father was very kind to him too, and left him alone most of the time, which was what Bran wanted. His father left most people alone. He was in the bank, and, according to himself, he had been greatly over-educated, a fact that made him entirely unsuitable for any appointment in banking. He had made a resolution that the same fate would never befall his only son. No, indeed, an ordinary education at the Brothers would fit a boy for life in this banana republic.

Bran wished his father wouldn't feel he had to deliver himself of this opinion so forcefully on every occasion he met the Brothers; they didn't seem to share his belief that they were being regarded as an under-education, nor were they sure about the compliments he heaped on them about how well they were creating citizens for the new Ireland. But then again, compared to a lot of people's fathers, his was really the berries. Jarlath's father got drunk and belted him. Carthage's father took off his shoes and put his feet up on the coffee table and drank beer out of a can, and Seán's father was a religious maniac hung down with scapulars.

Bran's sister left him alone, too. Strictly alone. She lived in London, and she sent him a fiver and a rude card for his birthday. She sent him marvellous things from a joke shop every Christmas; apart from that, she never communicated with him at all. She had a cockney accent, like the people in *EastEnders*, and on the rare occasions she got him on the phone, she'd say, 'You're all right, our Bran.' She worked as a telephonist, so she could make free calls home. Sometimes she had to put up with their mother asking her to contact some animal lovers' organisation or to send her posters about banning hunting, other times she had their father telling her that the plug had been pulled out on Ireland and that she was a wise young rossie to have emigrated while it was still possible, before the whole country thundered over to Holyhead looking for a job.

Bran's sister was called Morrigan, apparently a war-and-slaughter divinity who helped the Tuatha de Danaan at Moytura. She had risen above this name with great ease, and had worn her hair in spikes before anyone else in Ireland. She was living with a bloke, as she called him, but Bran's mother said not to dwell on it, in fact not even to mention it, since it wasn't the accepted thing.

It was the end of the Christmas term and it seemed to Bran as if everyone else in the world was going to have a great Christmas. There was snow forecast and everyone else was busy making

351

toboggans out of old pallets. Brother Simon said that it had all changed now since the bad old days and they would have a great feast. People in the town had given them plum puddings, cakes, bowls of brandy butter and tins of biscuits. The butcher nearly had a special room for the Brothers, so many geese and turkeys had been given to them. Many of these they redistributed to needy people, but they kept a feast for themselves as well. There would be cards and songs and television.

Morrigan was going on a sunshine holiday with her bloke. You just turned up at the airport with your bag packed and took the cancellations, to anywhere; it cost half nothing. It was going to be 'brill'. Bran's mother was organising a fast for funds to combat the use of live animals in experiments, and all the dogs and cats, the stoat, the plovers and assorted birds, howled their approval and gratitude at her being a voice for them.

Bran's father had been asked to deliver a lecture on 'Whither Ireland?' and he had been preparing it since September. It was the biggest and best forum he had ever been given. He deliberated nightly over whether he should buy a new jacket or whether that was giving in to the ethic and ambition of the gombeen man.

Bran knew that boys of fourteen were meant to feel odd and lonely and left out. It was just the time of life, it would pass, all the books and the magazine articles said so. And his position was made much worse by not having any brothers or sisters at home or a normal mother and father, not to mention a normal name.

If he were to rise above things, he felt he must broaden his horizons. Brother Simon had often told them in class about people who broadened their horizons. It seemed a sound step. Bran decided to interest himself in something new. That was the advice that Frankie Byrne and Angela MacNamara and all the kind, wise folk who answered tortured people always suggested. Find some new interest.

There was a private bus company in the town, a very successful organisation altogether. They had a big shop window full of all the glittering places you could go on their buses.

Not just Dublin, but you could go to Galway or up to Newry for the shopping, or to anywhere there was a match or even as far as London. They put the bus on the boat.

It was run by a fellow with a lovely, ordinary name. He was called Seán Ryan. Bran envied him his name and his bus company. Bran's father said Seán Ryan symbolised every single thing that was wrong with Ireland, from his big belly swollen with foreign lagers to his permed head of hair. Seán Ryan was King of the Gombeens, according to Bran's father, nay more, he was Emperor Gombeen man.

Bran liked looking in the window of the bus shop, your horizons were broadened just by looking, way, way beyond the town. Pictures of warm seas and sunny beaches took you far away from the cold and damp . . . If he were able to go to these places, perhaps he would be able to rise above his name, like his sister Morrigan had, like Brother Simon had. Bran suspected it had a lot to do with travelling.

In the window were details of an Exciting Christmas Competition. Seán Ryan wanted to find a new name for his bus company, he wanted his local townspeople to be involved, he was offering a prize of a trip of the winner's choice, plus ten pounds for the name and slogan chosen. It should be a name with dignity, and have an Irish dimension, as well as somehow explaining the magnificent scope of Seán Ryan's bus services.

Bran had often read that opportunities come to everyone but that the trick is to see them. Millions of people are passing opportunities by every day of the week. If he were ever to rise above anything, this was the moment.

'What is it, young lad?' Seán Ryan didn't see much of a potential customer in the thin young boy at the counter.

'Is there any law that you have to be old to win the competition?'

Seán Ryan sighed. 'No law at all, but there's no point in calling it Superbus, or Shamrock Bus. You'd need to be more a man of the world, if you know what I mean.'

'If I were to give you a name now, how would I know you wouldn't cheat me, we've no witnesses.'

Seán Ryan had had a long day.

'Hold on a minute. Miss O'Connor, please can you come and witness the entry that our young friend is writing for us. He's a man of sound business sense, he doesn't want to be conned.'

Miss O'Connor, with an enormous bust and a tight green skirt, came over to watch what was being written. Together with Seán Ryan, she read it out. The letters went downwards.

Best
Regionally
And
Nationally
BRAN Bus Company

Seán Ryan had adopted his most gombeen-man look. He put his arm around Bran's shoulder.

'Not bad at all, young fellow, not bad. I doubt if we'll get much better than that. And if we don't, then you're on your way to . . . well, where you would like to go. Dublin maybe.'

'It's not far enough,' Bran said. 'The horizon is too near. I'd like to go to the Continent of Europe, please.'

'Wait now, it doesn't say anything . . .' Seán Ryan began to bluster.

'Go on, Seán. Bran Buses, it's terrific,' said the busty Miss O'Connor.

'You do make a point of advertising Continental connections,' said Bran, who knew all the advertisements by heart.

'You're too young to go off on your own to Europe, they'd eat you for breakfast,' said Seán Ryan.

'I won't want to go immediately,' Bran said. 'I might wait a bit until there's no danger of them eating me for breakfast. By winning it, I'll know that the horizons have been pushed back and that I have risen above it all.'

Seán Ryan began to wonder was the young fellow unhinged. That's all he needed, to award the prize to the local madman.

'Where does your father work?' he asked.

'Not that it's at all important, but he works in the bank,' said Bran.

As always, this seemed to make things more cordial. Bran wondered why. His father didn't have power and influence, he wasn't the man who would lend Seán Ryan the money to buy a further fleet of buses, but people always treated a bank person's son with respect.

'And we're a travelling family,' he said proudly. 'My sister Morrigan has planned to go on a standby holiday from Gatwick Airport with her bloke. To anywhere. Anywhere in the world.'

'I'll give you the tenner now. It's a good name, it's a name with power to it. Bran Buses. Best Regionally and Nationally. God almighty, that's a good name all right.'

Seán Ryan peeled a ten-pound note off a pile of pink notes with pictures of Dean Swift on them. Bran nodded graciously and thanked Miss O'Connor for her participation in the whole business.

Once he had risen above it, his name didn't seem a bad one. He almost relished the thought of new wholefood recipes. There would be no ammunition for the fellows at school now, not when the bus company was called Bran, not when Mr Ryan the gombeen man had said it was a name with power to it and paid a tenner for it, plus a trip to the Continent of Europe when he was ready.

Golden
Willow

The children were dying for the school bell of course, but Amy Moran was happy to stay in the warm, safe classroom. The sound of the bell only meant that the fearsome Friday rush began.

She would have to race out and get into her 4x4 parked in the school yard; it was already packed with food in refrigerated bags and boxes full of extra duvet covers, pillow cases and towels, and table napkins. They were having a barbecue lunch party this weekend and of course there was the possibility that some people would get drunk and be unable to drive home.

'Don't fuss,' Dan would say to her. 'They can all stay here, surely?'

Amy knew the other teachers envied her the huge car, the farmhouse in the country, her successful husband and her two little girls at an expensive school. But she envied them not having to rush and shop and make lists and remember everything on a Friday. How much she would have preferred to sit down for a family meal and when the children had gone to bed, to be able to talk to Dan by the fire. But this didn't happen any more.

Knockglass had been her home town, but the beautiful farmhouse, Golden Willow, was Dan's find, Dan's project. It was a bit like his new toy. He loved showing it off to people, and now of course, there was the new billiards room. This weekend there would be an opening ceremony, a tournament and a special cup engraved with the words 'First Golden Willow Billiards Tournament'. He had laughed over it so often during the week like a little boy laughing at the toys from Santa Claus. But then Dan Moran wasn't a little boy – he was a well-known financial advisor who, they all said, had a Midas touch. He loved the description. He felt that they had got him right. He had faith when all around were losing theirs, he held his nerve in a stock exchange crisis and always he had come up smiling.

The bell rang. It was time to leap into the car, pick up the laundry, the dry-cleaning and be outside the big private school when the girls were coming out.

'Mummy, I got an A for my essay.' Sophie was delighted with herself.

'Well done, sweetheart. What was it on?'

'The title was "simple things are best" so I wrote all about our weekends in Golden Willow.'

'Good girl. And what did Miss Bailey say?'

'She said that I had caught the true heart of the countryside. Will I read it to you now?' Sophie was afraid the moment would pass and the praise might stop.

'No darling, wait until we are back at Golden Willow, just now I have to concentrate on the traffic, full of mad people trying to get out of town.'

'Like us,' Sasha said.

'How did *you* get on, Sasha?'

'She had a detention at lunchtime,' Sophie revealed.

'Darling, why? What on earth for?'

'It was last night's homework.' Sasha was glaring at her older sister, while trying to change the subject.' Are you looking forward to the weekend, Mummy?' she asked.

'Yes, of course I am. Back to Golden Willow. Marvellous. And once we clear this traffic and get on to the open road we'll be fine.' She looked into the mirror to see did she look as tired as she sounded. She saw the girls exchanging venomous glances. Sophie obviously thought that the younger girl was getting away with murder, as usual. Amy knew that she must say something to Dan about their giving conflicting signals to the girls. It couldn't go on. They were old enough now to be able to play one off against the other.

She would sort it out. But not this weekend. This weekend there was far too much to do.

The first thing was to stop in Knockglass and visit her Aunt Nora in the retirement home.

'Do we have to, Mummy?' The girls weren't delighted with this. It meant that they would be asked to do their homework.

'You're in no position to argue, Sasha Moran, you are in bad trouble. Get half an hour's homework done – that will be less to do when we get back to Golden Willow.'

They grumbled but there was nothing for it. It was an iron rule. Homework had to be finished and examined every Friday before Dad came home on the train. Dad hated seeing them with their heads bent over work when they should be relaxing and enjoying the second home he had built for them all.

They drew into the courtyard of the home where Amy's Aunt Nora lived. Nora had more or less brought her up – Amy's father had been away a lot and her mother had drunk a lot of vodka. She realised now of course that the two facts were related. But Nora had always been there for Amy and her brother Brian. Nora, who was single, had been better than a mother to them.

It was sad now when she could no longer manage on her own that neither Brian nor Amy could take her in. Nora was practical and cheerful: it made more sense for her to be here in Knockglass where she had so many friends. And didn't Amy come to see her every weekend, and bring her books and magazines? Brian and his family came mid-week; Nora said she hadn't a care in the world.

Sophie and Sasha came in to say hallo and to hand over the little box of fudge and the packet of greetings cards that Amy had bought them to give to her aunt. Then they went unwillingly and grudgingly to begin their homework.

Amy sat and talked easily to her aunt for half an hour. She would like to have spent longer there on a Friday to unwind from the journey down and to gear up for the weekend ahead, but they both knew that half an hour was the limit. Then Amy would have to be back in Golden Willow getting everything ready.

Dan's homecoming was a big event – it had to be orchestrated properly. There must be no occasion when he would ask her not to fuss. That meant serious time making the preparations. As the girls would do their school essays, their history questions and algebra, Amy would fly around the house pulling on clean duvet covers and pillow cases and laying out towels. She would light the log fire. By the time she had put a supper dish in the oven, prepared the salad, checked the girls' homework, combed her hair and put on some make-up and perfume, it was ten to nine. His train got into Knockglass at nine. She would be standing on the platform to welcome him home for the weekend.

He would be flushed with too many after-work drinks, maybe a fitful sleep on the train but through it all there would be his overpowering energy and a list of further plans for the already crammed schedule they had until Sunday evening.

Tonight he was more excited than ever and seemed to have had more after-work cocktails than usual. But Amy made no comment: she lived in a different world from him in many ways, a world of staffrooms and pupils and timetables, and old aunts in residential homes and getting meals ready and changing bed linen. She wasn't going to criticise his world, the one that provided them with such luxury.

She reversed expertly from the station and headed for home. It was always wonderful when you left Knockglass and drove along by the river.

It was only a kilometre and a half, but you were moving into a different world. She had played here as a little girl, she had gone to the riverbank to these very wooded places where she now had a home. She would make up stories to take her away from the lonely life where her father cared only about his travels and her mother only about her vodka.

Amy had learned to emphasise the good side of life and not the problems. She wouldn't tell Dan about Sasha's detention at her school. Nor Amy's own fears that she might never find time to mark thirty essays from her own school. Nor that she felt guilty every time she had to leave Nora in that home. Instead she told him that there was a lovely chicken filo pie in the Aga, waiting for him. The girls would have some soup with him and then go off to bed.

The journey down had been fine, and yes, she had done all the shopping for the lunch on Sunday.

'It's important, this lunch,' Dan had said.

'Of course it is, they're our friends,' Amy said.

'Not just that,' Dan snapped.

She wondered where to go now in the conversation. As she had done so often recently, she said nothing, waiting for him to develop the theme.

'I want them to see how well we're doing, there

must be no doubt about that. No complaining about the price of things.'

'I'd never do that if anyone else was there.' Amy was stung. 'It's only to you that I sometimes say . . .'

'Oh, darling, you fuss on and on, day and night. But this weekend there must be no hint.'

She felt a cold alarm rising from under her breastbone to her throat. 'Sure. I get you. Anything in particular?' She hoped she sounded light.

'Nothing, nothing, only I had to take out another mortgage, this time on Golden Willow. You know, to pay for all the renovations and everything . . .'

'We can meet it all right?'

'Of course we can, darling, that's what I do, I make money, to give you and the girls a good life.'

A blur of tears came suddenly across her eyes as Amy looked at Dan. He was doing it all to prove something. To show these people who were coming to lunch on Sunday that he was a huge success. That's what it was all about. It wasn't any longer about a good life for her and the girls.

He had been delighted to see their daughters all pink and clean from their baths, waiting in their pyjamas; he had funny stories for them about work. They loved this, and went off to bed like little lambs. Amy had no stories from her school that held their attention.

Dan ate his chicken pie and patted his stomach, fearing that he might be putting on weight.

'I told Joan and Martin to come on Saturday and spend the night,' he said.

'Great,' Amy said automatically. In her mind she was wondering about the logistics. She had enough bed linen, all that was fine, but as for meals . . . She hadn't planned to cook a meal on Saturday evening, in fact she had been hoping that Dan would take the girls into Knockglass to the new Thai restaurant and give her a little space and time to get her marking done. Now it looked as if she would have neither.

'Would they like a Thai take-away do you think?' Amy asked. She knew that Joan and Martin were easy company: they would be happy with anything. But no.

'I don't think so, darling. I mean they are travelling miles to see us, it's a bit inhospitable just to offer them a few noodles.'

'I could go into Knockglass and get some chicken I suppose. They'd like a chicken tarragon, wouldn't they?'

Dan had lost interest. 'Yes, sweetheart, whatever. Just don't *fuss* about it. Remember that Golden Willow is a fuss-free zone.'

She smiled at him weakly. Would the time ever be right to tell him how wearying and exhausting she found these weekends with the constant running to keep up. It was only ten-thirty and she could barely keep her eyes open.

Dan looked at her affectionately. 'You're thinking of your bed, aren't you?' he said.

'Well . . . I was a bit.'

'And so was I. Maybe tonight is the night we make our son and heir?' he suggested.

Amy had been down this road so often. She didn't want another child, her family was reared. But it was the one area where Dan Moran had not been successful. He had not yet produced a son. It was almost a matter of pride now.

Amy left him to douse the fire and turn off the lights. She went to the bathroom and very deliberately unzipped her sponge bag; from an inner pocket, wrapped carefully, Amy took her contraceptive pills. Looking in the mirror at the reflection of her tired face with the dark lines below her eyes, Amy took the tablet from the day marked Friday and swallowed it with a glass of water.

She was into the day before she had woken up properly. Sophie brought the phone into the bedroom. 'It's Joan, she wants to know what to bring.'

'Thanks, Sophie. Where's Dad?'

'He's out chopping wood.' Sophie skipped off to join him.

'Joan, you're so good to ring. There *is* something I'd love – fresh tarragon.'

'Sure, no problem. I don't envy you this lunch party, but at least we'll be there to hold your hands if it goes pear-shaped.'

'Why should it go pear-shaped? It's only a barbecue – with potatoes and salads and starters and desserts. Dan has his brand new apron with "Super Chef" written on it.'

'I didn't mean the food,' Joan said.

'What do you mean then?' Amy was totally awake now.

'Nothing at all,' Joan said. 'You'll do it beautifully. You always do.'

Amy got up, troubled, and had her shower. What did she mean, pear-shaped? What could go wrong? Apart from Joan and Martin, there would be Kevin, their best man, and his wife Geraldine; and Dan's new bank manager, who was called Declan and according to Dan was a little pussy cat who kept flinging more money at them. Mr Hayes who was the senior partner in their firm of solicitors; someone called Sally Anne who was an old friend of Dan, Martin and Kevin. She had gone to America but was now back and looking up all old contacts. And Amy's cousin Tom, who was a journalist. Okay it might be an effort but no more heavy than any Sunday lunch at Golden Willow.

'There you are!' Dan cried when Amy joined them at the wood-chopping.

He made it sound as if she had slept in until lunchtime. Amy noticed that he had brought out the chocolate shortbread she had bought for the after Sunday lunch coffee.

'Anyone for breakfast?' she said brightly.

'No, darling, don't fuss about breakfast. The girls are going to help me tidy up the place and make Golden Willow look respectable for our guests. Then I thought we'd have a picnic on the river bank.'

'A picnic!' Sophie and Sasha were delighted.

'Yes, that's a great idea. I have to go into Knockglass to do a few things so I'll leave you all to it.'

'Oh.' Sophie showed her disappointment.

'You're always rushing round doing things,' Sasha said, disapprovingly.

Amy put aside some pâté and ripe, scented tomatoes with some fresh bread and salty butter. She put a label on them *'for Martin and Joan when they arrive'* then she got the car keys and drove off. She felt a great sense of anxiety. Why was this lunch tomorrow something they needed their hands held over? She sighed and realised it would all become apparent soon enough. But now she had time to go and see her aunt again and to shop properly.

Nora was doing a Sudoku puzzle when Amy came in. She was seated in her wheelchair at a table and was completely absorbed.

'I think you're marvellous to do those. Were you good at maths at school?'

'It's got nothing to do with maths. Let me show you – it's a great thing to take your mind off other things.' Nora was about to get out a fresh puzzle.

'God, Nora, I can't. I don't have time to do anything as it is – I'd better not learn anything new from now on,' Amy laughed.

'That would be a sad way to be.'

'Sometimes it is a sad way to be.' Amy very rarely let this side of her show.

'Tell me about it.'

'No, I won't, I should be shot for whinging. I have it all, Nora, the man, the children, the clothes, the travel, two houses no less, a huge car but . . .'

'But what?'

'But I don't know. That's the problem. I'd tell you if I did. Truly I would.'

'You're tired, that's all, you do too much.'

'It only seems the other day you were telling me I didn't do enough.'

'That's because you were in a dream world then. No mother, no father to speak of, I was afraid you'd end up having no future as well. That's why I kept you at your books.'

'I must have got it from you, then, I'm the demon at home, constantly dragging the girls away from whatever they're doing and sitting them down with their homework.'

'Oh, the world will be totally different for them.'

'I'm not sure. I think they'll have worse problems. Growing up with everything and having to get used to less . . .'

'But there's no question of that surely?'

'There has to be a question of it, Nora, this whole thing can't last for ever, they're not going to be little Rich Girls with credit cards, they'll have to be able to earn a living.'

'Well of course, but that won't be for ages . . .'

'No, I know that. But I wish things were different.'

'Then make them different.' To Nora it was simple.

'How? In the name of God, how? The only time we could have to talk about it is down here and then he fills the house up with people to make sure we don't get a chance to talk.'

'I didn't say talk about change, just change things,' Nora said.

'How do I do that?'

'You are over-tired,' Nora said.

'So why ask me to do something? Ask me to change things? If I'm so tired maybe I should just go to sleep for a few weeks and hope it will have got better when I wake up.'

'There's a teaching job going here in Knock-glass. They'd love you – local girl comes home.'

'I can't, Nora. Our life has to be in town.'

'You don't sound as if you enjoy it, each week it's complaints about the traffic, the shopping, driving the girls to this place and that, and having to dress up and go to receptions and dinners and the lot . . .'

'God, I sound a complete pain in the arse!' Amy was penitent.

'Think about the school here, Amy, it's very good, and it might be just what Sophie and Sasha need. And then Dan could get a smaller place in the city and come down here at weekends.'

Amy laughed. 'You have no idea, Nora, if I got to the first sentence of such an idea he would have laughed and changed the subject.'

'That's not much of a partnership then.'

'You've said it!'

In the new organic foods shop, Amy bought new potatoes, asparagus, and some very healthy-looking bread, full of nuts and seeds.

'That will have you chirruping like a canary,' said the shopkeeper. He said that there was a great demand for this kind of produce now that there were so many people down for weekends from the city these days.

'Are you one of the second-homers?' he asked.

'I'm from here originally,' Amy said, avoiding the answer.

'Oh well, that's all right then,' he laughed.

She didn't like the exchange but she couldn't fault him. Still, it wasn't the way she saw herself. Being forgiven for having a second home.

Back at Golden Willow she could hear the screams of pleasure before she had parked the car. Dan had given the girls a new fishing rod each and was showing them how to cast. He was also urging them to be quiet so as not to alert the fish to their presence but he might as well have asked the river to reverse its direction.

Amy leaned against the big, old tree and wondered how much the fishing gear had cost. When she was young they had gone to the river bank with little fishing nets or sometimes a bent safety pin on a string. It had seemed a fairer struggle against the fish in a way. But that was silly and she must not blame Dan for being a good, loving father. She heaved all her bags of vegetables and bread into the kitchen where she discovered that Dan had brought out her expensive runny cheese and jar of black olives for the picnic on the river bank.

That had all been intended for tomorrow's lunch too. If she mentioned it, he would say she was fussing; if she didn't, he would say tomorrow that she had nothing to do except put a meal on the table and she was skimping on things. She watched them enviously from the kitchen window. Best put all this stuff away now and start dinner. She looked over at the corner where children's essays poked out of her big canvas school bag. No hope of any time to mark them now, of course. Like every weekend.

Joan and Martin arrived just as she had the kitchen clear. The children had seen the car arrive and they came running; Dan was delighted to see them too. They sat and talked easily. Martin had not done as well in life as Kevin and Dan but that never mattered. He and Joan had no children but that never seemed to matter either. They were both marvellous with Amy and Dan's children and Kevin and Geraldine's. This time, Joan had brought the girls a book about identifying birds, and a small nesting box each. They were delighted and went off to find suitable places to fix them on the trees; then they dragged Martin out to show him the fish they had caught.

Dan took Martin on a tour of the new billiards room while Joan and Amy sat companionably at the kitchen table, sighing over the eaten cheese and olives and finding alternatives. It had been like this for ever. Amy making light of their wealth and possessions, Joan showing no envy but genuine delight in all the new appliances that had begun to line the kitchen. The huge American-style fridge-freezer, the espresso machine and the big juicer for smoothies. Joan stroked them admiringly, and then sat down to peel potatoes for tomorrow's potato salad. She was a comforting, easy person. And she had a huge admiration for her hard-working husband Martin, who, with his nephew, had two gleaming Mercedes cars. They wore chauffeurs' uniforms and spent most of their time delivering or collecting executives from Dublin airport. Martin wore a chauffeur's hat and gloves. He said that if the punters liked those kinds of trimmings why not provide them? And Joan thought he was quite right. Anyway it saved his real clothes for leisure time, she would say cheerfully.

Amy wished that she had such an easy companionship with Dan. She shivered slightly, and of course Joan noticed.

'Have you a touch of flu?' she asked sympathetically.

'A touch of fatigue, more like it. We don't need these people tomorrow, Joan, why couldn't it just be the four of us? Maybe Kevin and Geraldine too – then we could really relax, like the old days.'

Joan looked startled. 'Well, it will hardly be Geraldine,' she said.

'Why not, she's coming to lunch tomorrow, isn't she?'

'I don't think so.' Joan was firm. 'Kevin is coming all right. But not with Geraldine.'

'You mean he's not *with* Geraldine any more?'

'I gather not,' Joan said.

'God Almighty! What happened?'

'Ask Dan, he sees Kevin all the time.'

'Ask Dan? *Ask Dan*? I'd have a better chance of asking the Pope or the Queen of England. Dan just says, "Don't fuss!" He won't talk, he's spending money like water. We don't *have* the kind of money he's spending.'

'His clients do, and he gets a percentage of what they make. And they're all mad about him. Don't be such a puritan. If we had it, we'd spend it, believe me. Right, are we going to make that knock-out Moroccan salad for tomorrow?'

'Yes but it's better made on the day. I have all the stuff, oranges, carrots, sultanas, cinnamon.'

'Too good for them, I say. Tell me again who's coming . . .'

So Amy ran through the list again. 'Let me see . . . There's Kevin and Geraldine, sorry, Kevin on his own, then there's Declan, his new bank manager, only a youngster but according to Dan very supportive. And this Sally Anne that they all lusted over when they were young, she's back in Ireland apparently. Mr Hayes from the solicitors, fussy little man, never says anything straight out, my cousin Tom, who's a journalist, you and Martin. That will be ten altogether or nine without Geraldine.'

'Unless he brings someone of course . . .'

'He wouldn't, we'd run her out of here.'

'No we wouldn't, we'd accept the inevitable and offer her a drink.'

'Okay, that's what we'd do, but we wouldn't mean it.'

Joan laughed at her. 'You never change, Amy. Let's have a glass of wine and relax.'

'I wish you lived here all the time, Joan.'

'No you don't – you'd want to murder me if I were here for a week!' Joan said, and between them they had finished the preparations and taken the chicken from the Aga just as Martin and Dan came back from the new billiards room.

'You should see the new room, Joan!' Martin was beaming with admiration and pleasure. 'It's a full-size table, I mean the real thing. And beautiful, heavy brass fittings. It's really top of the range.'

Dan glowed in the praise.

As they sat down to eat, Amy wondered was she the one out of step? Joan and Martin were enjoying it all and talking to the girls about birds and how to identify a goldfinch from a bullfinch. Nobody was in the least uneasy except herself. She made a conscious effort to relax and be part of things. She joined in the speculation about whether it would keep fine tomorrow for the barbecue.

As they reached their bedroom that night, Dan whispered in Amy's ear, 'Let's make a little boy tonight.'

'Why not?' she said, going into the bathroom to brush her teeth. She took her pill but was so tired she didn't wrap up the package and return it to its zipped compartment. He was never going to hunt through her sponge bag looking for something. That way madness lay.

Next morning there was the wonderful smell of toast and because Joan was in the house Amy knew that Dan and the girls hadn't used all the expensive organic bread.

'This place is paradise,' Joan said as Amy came to the table.

Dan was pleased. 'It's simple but it's home,' he said unconvincingly.

Outside in the garden the girls had the bird book and were squabbling happily over whether they had identified a reed bunting or a coot.

'Which is it?' Amy asked Martin.

'It's neither, it's what Joan would call a Common Bird,' he said.

'He mocks me but there are birds that you should not spend any time identifying because as soon as you have found out what they are, they're gone and there are another hundred which look almost the same around the place. You'd lose your sanity.'

'Never you, Joan.' He patted her hand and Amy felt a surge of envy. They were true friends those two.

Dan was like the captain of a ship drawing up plans and duties and rosters. They would need deckchairs out under the apple tree; and the folding dining chairs as well, these were all kept in the boathouse, let's get the girls to pick some flowers ... And would Martin ask Tom just casually if there was any news on that new hotel project down the river. Because if it was going ahead they really had to buy up some land around it, it would go through the skies when the hotel was announced. Journalists often got a sniff of things before other people but Dan didn't like to be seen to ask.

He didn't know what Declan's interests were. Amy was to draw him out a little, get the feeling for what he was interested in. If it was operas she might suggest that he join them for one of their evenings. It was better, he said, if the invitation came from her.

'What will we do to please Sally Anne?' Amy asked. 'Joan and I are dying to meet her, part of your wicked past.'

'In our dreams,' Martin said ruefully. 'Sally Anne had barely time to say hallo to the likes of us.'

'Even Kevin? He was the real Romeo?' Amy probed.

'Not even Kevin,' Dan said. 'Though God

knows it wasn't for the want of trying. Kevin never gives up.'

'Maybe he'll finally score with her today,' Amy said. She caught Joan's eye but nothing more was said.

The girls returned with glorious flowers in jam jars.

'Something a bit more classy than that, I think.' Their father was frowning. They found four little vases and arranged them on the table. 'Perfect.'

Amy was taking the table napkins out to the garden.

'How many again – ten? Nine?' she asked Dan.

'You know there are ten, darling, try to focus.'

'I am focused, sweetheart, it's just you said that Geraldine might not be coming.'

'I did?'

'Last night,' she lied.

'Ah well, I don't know what I said last night.' He tickled her neck in remembrance.

The girls watched disgusted.

'Ugh – Daddy's about to sing "Amy Wonderful Amy", I know he is,' Sophie said.

Sasha was even more disapproving. 'You look silly when you do things like that, Daddy, you know, yucky stuff.'

'I see someone coming!' Sophie shouted. A small red sports car was coming up the lane.

'Hardly Mr Hayes,' Amy said.

'Not Kevin,' Martin said.

'Hardly the new bank manager – a bit pacey.' Dan squinted.

'Not Tom either,' Amy said, then they all realised.

'It must be Sally Anne!' they all said at once.

She must have been the same age as the boys if she had been at school at the same time. That meant she was early forties, but there was no way Sally Anne looked it. She looked at least fifteen years younger. She wore a crisp white shirt and some very well-cut black pants. Her sunglasses were holding her very carefully streaked hair back and she had a really expensive designer silk scarf with the label showing. She was the goods.

As she got out of her car she carried a decorated gift bag with a bottle of wine and a tub of very up-market ice cream.

'Just fling it into the freezer someone,' she said with a big smile from face to face. 'It's probably turned into a chocolate milkshake by now.'

Every cubic inch of the freezer was in use but you would never know that from Amy's reaction.

'What a *thoughtful* present, Sally Anne. I'm Amy by the way, and these are Sasha and Sophie, our children.'

Sally Anne looked at the girls without huge pleasure. 'Lovely,' she said vaguely.

Dan's mouth was open. 'Come here to me, Sally Anne, let me give you a hug,' he said and then he lifted her off her feet and swung her around. 'Lord, don't you look wonderful, no cares and woes, no signs of ageing . . .'

'Hard work, believe me, Dan. And haven't you done well for yourself! This is a gorgeous place. How on earth did you find it?'

If Dan was disappointed that she didn't stress how young he was looking, he gave no sign; instead he was about to hold forth on his wisdom in picking the old farmhouse up for a song before the real demand hit. Suddenly Amy knew that he must not be allowed to start. It would set the mood for the whole day. So she interrupted.

'I'm actually *from* this part of the world, Sally Anne, I was able to tell Dan every stick and stone of the place . . .'

Sally Anne had lost interest already.

'Martin, I would have known you anywhere. Aren't you marvellous?'

'Sally Anne, this is Joan, my wife.'

'How are you?' Her interest was slight. 'And where's lovely Kevin, the most likely lad of you all?'

386

'There's his car!' Sophie called; and indeed the low-slung Citroën came up the lane.

'That's not Geraldine!' Sasha said in a voice clear as a bell.

Out of the car stepped a girl who looked like a teenager. She had long, curly red hair and a very short emerald-green skirt. She wore high white boots, more suitable for a skating rink in winter than for early summer in a country farmhouse. She couldn't have been more than a couple of years older than Kevin and Geraldine's eldest daughter.

This was so gross. So humiliating to Geraldine who had been part of their circle for sixteen, even *seventeen* years. Amy longed for the kind of courage or possibly sheer rudeness and bad behaviour that would allow her to say that the girl's presence here was totally inappropriate. But at that very moment she saw her cousin Tom's motorbike come up the lane, closely followed by Mr Hayes in his sedate Volkswagen and Declan, the new bank manager, in a very new Volvo which looked as if it had come straight from a car wash.

So it was show time.

Introductions and drinks for everyone and gasps of admiration at the house, the view, the river, the wonderful insight Dan Moran had shown in getting a place like this well ahead of the posse. So it was a good fifteen minutes, including five minutes serious arm-wrestling with the freezer to make room for Sally Anne's bloody ice cream, before she was properly introduced to the child that was now Kevin's travelling companion.

Her name was Silver. Yes. Silver Sullivan.

Silver smiled at everyone except Sally Anne – she knew there was no point in smiling in that direction. She may have been young and not very bright but there were some things she understood instinctively. She followed Amy and Joan into the kitchen and picked at the canapés. She told them she was terribly interested in business and she hoped to get a degree in business studies. Meantime, she was studying the Art of Make-up. Make-up was so important – didn't they think? She looked from Joan to Amy and back to Joan again. It made such a statement. That's what make-up did.

Joan said that as a bookseller, there were very few statements she wanted to make. Amy said that as a teacher there were even fewer, but Silver shook her head sadly.

'I don't think you have faced the facts to be honest. You see, of course, that without a proper beauty routine, the poor face is left ragged and beyond all repair,' Silver explained patiently looking from what must to her have seemed one ragged face to another.

Joan recovered the power of speech before Amy. 'You are so right and maybe this is what might be called a wake-up call. If you have any time to advise Amy and myself we would be just delighted,' she said.

Amy looked at her open-mouthed.

'Well, of course, if there's time I'd love to,' Silver said graciously. 'I'm not sure what the plans are – Kev was a bit cagey, he said it could all go one way or the other.'

'As indeed it could,' Amy said grimly.

But Joan was in control. 'There'll be plenty of time. This is a wonderfully relaxed home, you'll be delighted with your lunch here today.'

'Oh good, thank you so much, I was sort of afraid I mightn't be totally welcome, you know what with Geraldine and all that. And Kev is such a poppet. I don't think he ever had much fun before. It's great to see him having a good time now.'

'Isn't it,' said Joan and eased the girl out of the kitchen. She came back and wiped her brow.

'I think you are mad,' Amy said.

'Yes I could be, but at least this way we have something to tell Geraldine when we meet her –

we'll be able to tell her what a clown she is. Geraldine will like that. If we went your way half those cars would be down the lane by now. What would Dan think of that?'

'You're right, Joan, the show must go on. Will you take a plate of those asparagus boats and come outside and help me pass them round . . .' Amy said and headed for the solicitor.

'Mr Hayes, we never see you these days, delighted you could make it.'

'Well of course I see your husband a lot, Mrs Moran.' He must be the only person left in the western world who would call a much younger woman Mrs. Dan hadn't mentioned that he met him a lot. He had only said it was good to keep old fuddy-duddy Hayes on board. On board what? Amy wondered. The lawyer was giving nothing away. He coughed over the little canapés and sipped his white wine slowly and nervously as if it were going to bring on a fit of binge drinking. There had never been any mention of a Mrs Hayes and Amy wasn't even going to start to find out.

'Do you like the countryside, Mr Hayes?' she asked brightly.

'Oh yes, of course, I mean, most admirable,' he said afraid to cause offence.

'I love it too, in fact I wouldn't mind if we

never went back to the city. But it's a bit too dull for Dan here.'

Mr Hayes looked around at the ten adults and two children. Drink and food were being passed round, the top-of-the-range barbecue was leaping into life. There was a roar of conversation. Dull was what it did not look.

'You don't like city life, Mrs Moran?' Mr Hayes reminded her of the dormouse at the Mad Hatter's Tea Party, once he had woken up. She tried not to giggle.

'Oh I like it all right, Mr Hayes, it's just that it's exhausting. There's no time to curl up and be grateful for all we have.'

'Well of course the world would come to a standstill if we were all to curl up and do nothing.' Mr Hayes sounded almost disapproving. Amy had read him wrong; she thought he would be all for caution where he actually sounded even more gung-ho than Dan did.

'You've met Sally Anne, I think?' Amy drew the two most unlikely people in the gathering together.

'Yes indeed,' he said surprisingly. 'I have handled some business for Miss Harris.'

Amy hadn't even known Sally Anne's second name. 'Oh, good and this is . . . um . . . Kevin's friend. Silver.'

'Ah, I know Silver's father well. I have also had business dealings with Mr Sullivan,' Mr Hayes said.

Amy noted grimly that Silver was young enough for Mr Hayes not to call her Miss or Mrs. But how odd that he should know so many of their guests today. She moved away and left them all to it.

Tom was looking at Sally Anne with unconcealed interest. 'Well who does she belong to?' he asked.

'Nobody . . . they all fancied her from afar when they were young, at school, I gather.'

'Don't tell me she's the same age as Dan and Kevin and Martin?'

'Yeah – triumph of the Art of Make-up, as that spoon-face Silver would say. Or maybe even the cosmetic surgeon's knife. What do you think?'

'I think you've got a very odd assortment gathered around you today. What is Silver Sullivan doing here?' Tom asked.

'She's Kevin's new interest. Do you know her?'

'I know old man Mouth Sullivan, everyone does.'

'I don't. Who is he?'

'A gangster, not to put too fine a point on it.'

'God, this day is going from bad to worse,' Amy said.

392

'Are you okay, Amy? You sound a bit edgy. Aunt Nora thinks you should come and work here, in Knockglass.'

'Yes, and she thinks that if you're good you'll be happy and if you eat your crusts you get curly hair . . .'

'It must all be a bit stressful.'

'What must?'

'All the things that Dan's into.'

'He says he hasn't a worry in the world.'

'Well maybe he should have,' Tom said.

Amy felt a cold pool of water in her stomach. 'What do you mean?'

'Ah, nothing, you know me, I'm Knockglass born and bred, terrified of all these whiz kids, wide boys, speculators . . .'

Amy was troubled. 'Dan's not a wide boy is he?'

'No, no, of course not but he does dance with wolves . . .'

'Will you stop that, you have me weak at the thought of it all. Sally Anne – did they introduce you to my cousin Tom?'

'Not properly,' Sally Anne said with a marvellous throaty growl Amy knew that she would never be able to achieve. She left them and moved further amongst the guests.

Kevin had been avoiding her eye but he

couldn't do that any more as she was standing in front of him.

'Bad business, all this,' he muttered.

'No, it's a lovely day, we're just delighted to have so many old and indeed new friends here . . .' She looked pointedly at Silver.

'It's not what you think, Amy,' Kevin began.

'What do I think?' Amy smiled a very insincere smile.

'Oh, you know, a mid-life crisis, a girl same age as my daughters, that sort of thing, but it's not that.'

'No, of course.'

'And when you get to know Silver as I hope you will . . . you'll find that she's just as, I don't know, *mature* as the rest of us.'

'Maybe even more mature?' Amy offered.

'Maybe.' Kevin looked foolish and uneasy. He scowled at her.

Standing beside Sally Anne, Dan and Martin were competing for her attention. Dan was telling her about the plans his office had to sponsor a big horse race in the New Year. Sally Anne was giggling and saying that if there was anything she liked it was to be in an enclosure, while telling Martin that she 'always loved a man in uniform. Does it for me every time!' And on the fringes

Tom was hovering, hoping to say something that would attract Sally Anne's attention.

Kevin looked most put out. His beautiful nymphette Silver hadn't caused a quarter of the stir that Sally Anne was creating. He was not being admired at all. He scowled again.

Also on the fringes was Declan, the young bank manager. He was eyeing Sally Anne appreciatively too. Could any one woman deserve the interest that she was getting from all quarters? Suppose Dan had succeeded in his early attempts to woo Sally Anne – what kind of a wife would she have made?

Sally Anne would have oohed and aahed over every new sign of wealth rather than looking anxious as Amy did. She would have had paid help to serve today's lunch and floated around amongst the guests. She would have found a wonderful caterer and two local girls from Knockglass to tidy up afterwards.

And would Dan have liked it better? Probably.

Dan saw Amy standing there and came over to her.

'How's my beautiful wife?' he said a little too loudly.

Amy did not feel beautiful, not in a garden that contained the languid Sally Anne, the sexy Silver and even crisp, elegant Joan. She felt washed-out and tired. No amount of under-eye concealer could take away the dark circles. She would like Dan to have said she was his beautiful wife when they were alone. But that didn't happen. It was always 'Amy, don't fuss' or 'Let's make a baby boy.'

But here in front of people, he stood, arm draped around her neck, picking delicately at the tray of quails eggs. He stayed until he was certain everyone had seen him marking his territory then he announced that the event of the weekend was about to begin and they must all tell him how they liked their steaks. He put on his chef's hat and went to the barbecue.

Event of the weekend! He had done no shopping, preparation, no cooking. Those steaks and the sausages for the girls would have looked a poor lunch without all the trimmings that she had ordered, collected and assembled.

It was Sunday lunchtime. Tonight they would begin the journey back to town. Those essays in her tote bag were still unmarked. Beds had to be stripped, laundry bags packed. There would be no help from anyone. Dan would take the children for an evening stroll to say goodbye to the riverbank. Joan and Martin would help with the clearing up but would themselves have gone back to town.

Kevin would have managed to get through the whole afternoon without mentioning his wife Geraldine, while Silver cooed at him and called him a poppet. The men would regret their missed chances with Sally Anne. Tom would probably wish that he had the self-assurance of these guys, but he wouldn't dare to ask her out. Mr Hayes would eat a lot and drink little. He would see everything and see nothing. Declan, the bank manager, would make jokes and keep his opinions to himself.

If only Amy knew what she was meant to be looking for among the guests. Why had Dan asked her to suss out the situation and made such a thing about *this* lunch? She couldn't think.

She noticed that Silver couldn't hold her drink. Amy knew that she must focus, concentrate. She forced herself to talk to Mr Hayes.

'Are you very positive about the way the country is going?' she asked.

'Do you mean the countryside or the nation?' he asked. He had ordered his steak well done.

'Oh, the nation I think – are we heading over the cliff do you think?'

'Your husband certainly doesn't think so.' Mr Hayes looked around appreciatively.

'Yes, but sometimes I worry in case . . . in case

he is too enthusiastic, you know. I'm glad that you are there to keep an eye on him, as it were.'

'Oh no, I don't do that at all. That's not my role. I mean, if he and those young tigers want to go into something, in they go.'

'But as their lawyer?'

'Not every investment needs a legal contract, Mrs Moran.'

'No, no of course not.' Amy could hear Silver's laugh very loud from under the trees.

'How exactly do you know Silver's father, Mr Hayes?' she asked.

'Oh, well, you know, I've met him through this and that. You know the way it is in business.'

Amy didn't know the way it was but she had little time to speculate. Kevin was helping Silver towards the house. Please may she not be sick before he got her to the bathroom.

Declan had collected his steak and was busy filling up his plate with salads. 'This is really superb, Amy,' he said. 'Dan's a lucky man. I'm trying to get a word with him, in fact. We have a couple of things to sort out and I thought we might start sorting it out today. I understood he had invited me here on my own to discuss it all and to talk about the overdue repayments.'

'Sorry for repeating everything you say but

there are overdue repayments?' Amy's voice was a whisper now.

'Well there are huge debts as I'm sure you know. You know, in the current situation . . . Head Office are a bit concerned about it all. I was actually getting edgy myself. He made a lodgement the other day, but it wasn't nearly enough.'

'Yes, he said he took out a mortgage on this place here. That must have been it.'

'No, that can't be right, he told me that this place is absolutely in the clear.'

'I thought he did it through you, yesterday, that's what he said,' Amy said, anxious now.

'No way.' Declan was even more anxious.

'Listen, take no notice of me, I get everything wrong,' she begged. 'Don't say a thing to him. Please. It will be sorted out next week. Please.'

He looked at her for a moment and nodded distantly.

Dan came over to them, all orders now completed.

'Well, that's the main work of the day over. I'll just get myself a sticky plaster. I burned my thumb.' He headed for the bathroom. Amy let him go. He could deal with Kevin and Silver. Damn that child to the pit of hell for taking Geraldine's husband and then vomiting all over their bathroom. Dan could help them clear up but she'd better see if they needed more towels.

But to her surprise, as she followed him into the house, she just heard laughter from the direction of the bathroom and Dan's voice urging discretion. They couldn't have! He couldn't have taken that brassy girl to the bathroom to have sex with her there? Amy crept closer. No, it didn't sound as if Dan had walked in on anything sexual.

'Give me a break, Kevin, not in the house, not in Golden Willow. My girls are here. We can't have any of this stuff in the house, not in front of the girls . . .'

And instantly Amy knew it was cocaine.

A great anger welled up in her. Dan was obviously well acquainted with drugs and his only concern was that it should happen here, in this house. She went back to the garden, sat under the apple tree and tried to hide her shaking hands.

'Where's Dad?' Sasha asked. There was a question of flying a kite.

'No idea, darling, he'll be back.' Amy's voice sounded far away in her own head.

'Are you all right?' Joan noticed everything.

'Not really. Tell you later . . .'

'At least your husband isn't here pawing bloody Sally Anne like mine is,' Joan said. She sounded more amused than bitter.

'Oh, she's harmless that one, all talk, no action,' Amy said.

'Lots of eyelashes though and pouting. I think your cousin is smitten too, not to mention the bank manager, and even old Hayes – except that he'd be too stuffy to get involved with her.'

'He's not as stuffy as you think. He surprised me earlier on. He knows Silver's father. It was him told me who he was. I don't know how he knows him, but it sounded a bit as though they'd had dealings. Lord, listen to me – I'm turning into Miss Marple!'

'At least you're smiling. You looked a bit shaken there.' Joan was relieved. 'For a moment I thought something awful had happened.'

'What time is it? Will they ever go home, do you think? Not you and Martin, but the rest of them.'

'Hayes told me that he is going to America on business tomorrow morning, for some property deal – did you know he has a house in Florida? And he was telling the girls about mosquitoes in the Cayman Islands a while ago. Anyway, maybe he might want an early start.'

'Hayes really is full of surprises, isn't he?' Amy saw out of the corner of her eye Kevin and Silver slink back to join the group. They looked a lot more subdued. Dan had obviously been much sterner than they had expected.

There was no sign of Dan. Making heavy weather of the blister on his thumb or searching the bathroom for traces of white powder? She didn't know which and suddenly she knew she didn't care.

Silver seemed to have recovered her senses. She approached Amy and Joan.

'You know, I realise I may have been a little insensitive suggesting that you both need a huge makeover,' she began.

'I didn't think you said *huge* makeover,' Joan said.

'More a little fine-tuning here and there,' Amy agreed.

'Well, just as long as I didn't say anything to offend.' Silver looked from one to the other.

'Not at all.' Amy's voice was tinny. Just then she heard her name being called from inside the house. 'Sorry, there seems to be a crisis in the bathroom, man in hunt of a sticking plaster,' she said and escaped.

Dan was sitting on the edge of the bath. Amy's sponge bag was in one hand – and in the other was her packet of contraceptive pills. He was almost beyond speech.

'That's *my* bag,' Amy said defensively. Foolishly.

'Indeed it is, Amy, your bag, your pills, your decision.'

'You never listen . . .' she began.

'I'm listening now,' he said coldly. She had never seen him like this.

'You were dead set on it, another baby, a boy this time, I don't *want* another baby, Dan. I want to get on with my career.'

'Career!' he sneered.

'Yes it *is* a career. It's a good career. And I'm doing well at it and I like it, I have a post of special responsibility this year and I'm well on the way to be Assistant Principal in a couple of years.'

Dan had put the red and white sponge bag on the floor. He clapped his hands slowly. 'Well now, Assistant Principal, no less. Now we are *really* talking. That wouldn't even pay the bills for this place, let alone anything else. Oh we'll be in the big time when you make Assistant Principal all right.'

'Don't mock me, Dan. A lot of families are glad to live on that salary.'

'But not *us*, Amy, you fool. We've made it, you have never understood that. We've got there, we have it all, the dream we talked about . . .'

'No we haven't.'

'Well, certainly I thought we had, until a few minutes ago. But now it seems I can't trust you any more – ever again about anything.'

'And I can't trust you either.'

'What did I do? Tell me that. What did I do except run myself ragged for you and the girls?'

'You lied about the mortgage on this house for a start. I was talking to Declan and he said . . .'

'You spoke to Declan about my business?'

'Your business? Your business, your house your mortgage, your loans, your repayments, your *overdue* repayments . . .'

'Stop this now, Amy.'

'Why did we get married?'

'Oh Jesus, Amy, I have far too much on my mind to be answering idiotic questions like this.'

'Idiotic?'

'Yes. Idiotic. I have a hundred things on my mind, and half a dozen people outside who are meant to be helping me in sorting them. What happens? You start blabbering about things you know nothing about to Declan and alarming him.'

'He's already alarmed.'

'And you freeze Kevin out just as I had him ready to invest in my business . . .'

'Oh, sorry. I should have said that I was glad to hear he had dumped our friend Geraldine and tell him that of course he must come into the bathroom and do a line of cocaine with that bird brain, should I?'

Dan was momentarily startled. 'That was out of order, I told him, totally out of order.'

'It was, and so are many things about today's gathering. You invited nobody here out of friendship. What's Old Man Hayes doing here for example?'

'To give it an air of respectability, I suppose. To let Kevin, Declan and even Sally Anne see how well I'm doing. If there's an old-style lawyer part of it all then they're not at risk.'

'What makes you think Mr Hayes is respectable?'

'Ah, come on, Amy, don't babble at me now . . .'

'Well, he's best friends with Silver's father and *he* is some sort of a crime lord, I gather. Hayes has more than one house in Florida, he was telling the girls that the Cayman Islands were full of mosquitoes. He's going to the States tomorrow for some property deal. What on earth is the matter?'

Dan was pale now. 'Hayes knows Mouth Sullivan? I don't believe you.'

'Well don't then. I don't care any more.'

'God, I have to talk to him . . .'

'He may be going soon – he might have left already, Joan thought he might have an early start in the morning.' Amy sounded as if she was a million miles away from all these people, and their comings and goings. It was as if she had untangled herself from it all.

Dan looked anxious. 'Nobody else has gone have they? I mean I need to talk to Sally Anne . . .'

'I'm sure you do.' Amy didn't sound as if she cared.

'No, not that way, you fool. I want her as a client.'

'Is that what they call it?'

'Sally Anne is rolling in money. She is in a few dodgy businesses and she needs to bury money for a while. I wanted to take it on for her. But she was wittering on about not mixing business and pleasure. As if Sally Anne knew the meaning of the word pleasure . . .'

'Whatever you say.' Amy couldn't bring herself to argue. She couldn't find it in her to argue any more.

'It's just the way she goes on, she's not interested in sex or affairs or fellows or anything. She never was, she was interested in money. And through her line of business she got plenty of it.'

'And her line of business was what exactly?'

'She runs a string of . . . sort of clubs, you know, clubs with floor shows and . . . sort of opportunities to meet people.'

'Brothels?' Amy suggested.

'No. Well, not really. But she does need to put her profits away somewhere carefully for a few years. She's been taking legal advice.'

'Oh that's how Hayes knows her . . .'

'Don't be idiotic, Amy, as if old Hayes would get involved in Sally Anne's business – or as if she'd listen to an old fusspot like him. She'll have a sharp American lawyer.'

'Whatever you say,' Amy shrugged.

'So that's what a lot of this is about. Getting Sally Anne's money to invest for her – and it couldn't have come at a better time for me. If you see what I mean.'

'Not really. Wouldn't it be a client account?'

'Yes, but you know there's always a little flexibility and there are fees and such . . .'

'Yes I see.'

'You don't see.'

'I see, but I don't understand.'

'That's the way I feel about all this.' He indicated her red and white sponge bag.

'I'm sorry. Yes, I am sorry truly.'

'For what, Amy? For taking these pills?'

'No, for lying to you. For giving you false hope.'

'It's monstrous, Amy, it's the greatest deception I ever had.'

'Would you not have liked making love if you had known there was no chance we could conceive?' She was very calm, as if it were something she was researching for her class at school.

'No, yes, anyway that's not the point.' He shook his head.

Amy stood up from the white stool where she had been sitting.

'I'd better go back,' she said in a dull voice.

'Amy, this is not over.'

'Oh, this bit of it is well over,' she said.

'You'll leave me now because the money's running thin? You were very happy to stay for the good times.' He was very angry.

'I haven't been very happy for a long time,' she said and went out.

Mr Hayes had indeed left his apologies and gone; Joan had got Silver to gather the plates and glasses from the grass and bring them to the kitchen. Martin, Kevin and Tom were still in a little circle around Sally Anne. The girls were sitting under the tree making a daisy chain.

'Sophie and Sasha, would you like to walk into Knockglass with me?'

'What for?' Sasha was always suspicious in case homework would be mentioned.

'Aren't we having a party, Mummy?' Sophie asked.

'Daddy's having the party, darling, come on we'll go and see Nora. No, there'll be no homework, Sasha, and I'll send you out for ice creams for us all. I want to talk to Nora about something.'

'Will we say goodbye?' Sophie was always polite.

'No need, I'll tell Joan. And Tom. Then we'll head off – we'll not be long. Okay?' The girls thought it was okay. Mummy didn't usually come up with ideas like this.

There was a carnival in Knockglass and a fairground. There were some very old dodgems and a ghost train and a roller coaster. Amy gave the girls some money to have rides.

'Do you want a go yourself, Mam?' asked the man in the coconut shy.

'Later, maybe, I'll be around for a while,' she said. And she headed off to see Nora.

It was as if Nora understood without an explanation. She told her aunt that she would indeed like to apply for the local teaching post if it wasn't too late. The shadows from the trees in the square grew longer, as they talked and planned. And soon the cries from the merry-go-round died down and the children came back carrying four ice creams.

Nora, without being asked to, told them all about the lovely school by the river and how the children went on nature walks. She sowed the seeds and made it seem like a fairyland. Then they walked back to Golden Willow.

The guests had all gone. Joan and Silver had obviously cleared up everything. The kitchen table was covered in parcels wrapped in foil. These would go back to the city. The hum of the dishwasher was comforting in the corner. Dan was sitting in the billiards room. The girls rushed to tell him about their adventures on the dodgems, and the ice creams. He put an arm around each of them.

'We did this bit right anyway, didn't we, Amy?' he said.

'We did indeed.'

'I just wanted more of it – was that a crime?'

'No. No, of course not.'

'You want another billiards room, Daddy?' Sophie was bemused.

'I did, but your mother was right, of course. As she always is.'

He looked sad, almost as if he were about to cry.

'Imagine!' he said. 'Imagine – we never played the First Golden Willow Billiards Tournament.'

'We can do it another weekend, Dad,' Sophie consoled him.

'I wish we didn't have to go back,' Sasha said as she always said.

'Maybe you won't always have to?' Dan suggested. 'Is that right, Amy?'

'Maybe so. But we have a lot of talking to do first.'

'When will you do that?' Sophie was interested. 'Dad comes home so late.'

'It will be done,' Amy said.

She told them they didn't need to bring all the sheets and duvets home, she would be coming down again during the week and she could see to it then. Could the girls find the thermal bag and fill it with the left-over food? Great. And pack their toys, schoolbags and books and anything else. They scurried off to do it and Amy sat with Dan in the billiards room.

'I see Tom left his motorbike behind.'

'Yes. Sally Anne gave him a lift in her car. I didn't tell him. About her line of work, I mean. But she may have told him herself, she's looking for someone to ghost her autobiography. She wasn't really interested in looking for anywhere to hide her earnings. And she was indeed a client of old Hayes. I got that one wrong too.'

'And Kevin?'

'Is too much of a coke head to make any decisions.'

'And Declan?'

'Is running away from me like mad, probably phoning Head Office emergency line as we speak.'

'Oh God, Dan, that's terrible.'

'James Hayes, here to lend respectability – laughing all the way from here to offshore. Little shit.'

'I'm sorry, Dan, really I am. What will happen now? Is there anything left? Will there be an investigation?' Her voice was flat.

'Maybe not. Not if I tell everything. And sell everything.'

'You are not going to have to sell this place here, are you? This is all you have ever wanted, Dan. You could send back the billiards table – but will you have to sell the house?'

'Well, I'll get over it.'

'What will we tell the girls?' she asked.

'The truth. That business is bad, we have to cut down.'

'About us, I mean.'

'Oh, the minimum. Children hate too much information.'

And they stood up like strangers who had only just recently met.

They headed out of the house that wouldn't be theirs for much longer, towards the big car that would be sold very soon. As they drove down the lane the girls seemed to think everyone was being too quiet.

'Are you and Daddy fighting?' Sasha asked.

'No, darling, of course not,' Amy said.

'So why isn't he singing "Amy Wonderful Amy" and tickling your neck?' Sasha asked.

'Because Daddy's old and tired and not as good at everything as he used to be,' Dan said.

And they found this a totally satisfactory answer.